Jade Sky

A Matt Rowley Novel

By

Patrick Freivald

JournalStone

San Francisco

JOURNALSTONE
YOUR LINK TO ARTISTIC TALENT

JournalStone books may be ordered through booksellers or by contacting:

JournalStone
www.journalstone.com

ISBN: 978-1-940161-43-3   (sc)
ISBN: 978-1-940161-44-0   (ebook)

Library of Congress Control Number: 2014932374

Printed in the United States of America
JournalStone rev. date: May 16, 2014

Cover Design: Rob Grom
Cover Photograph © Shutterstock.com

Edited by: Dr. Michael R. Collings

To The Redhead™. You're why I write.

Patrick Freivald

Endorsements

"*Jade Sky* is an ass-kicking action-fantasy that takes no prisoners. Lightning fast, brutal and way too much fun. Highly recommended!" – **Jonathan Maberry**, New York Times Bestselling author of *Code Zero* and *Fall of Night*

Patrick Freivald's latest novel, *Jade Sky*, is one of those all too rare reading experiences that just consumes you. I live for those moments when a book practically swallows me whole. I felt that way about Mieville's *Perdido Street Station* and Bacigulupi's *The Windup Girl*, and I felt it about *Jade Sky* too. Some authors just have that special touch when it comes to creating worlds, and for *Jade Sky*, Freivald made a future so rich in detail and so full of life and energy that I couldn't help but lose myself in it. This is a book full of wild invention and even wilder action, yet grounded by a genuinely sympathetic love for the people who live there. Freivald has truly reached a new high water mark here, which is pretty scary considering that he was already so damn good. – **Joe McKinney**, Bram Stoker Award-winning author of *Plague of the Undead*

"With *Jade Sky*, Patrick Freivald takes science fiction, the supernatural and action adventure, seamlessly combining the genres in a unique and page-turning thriller. He brings his world, characters, dialogue and narrative to life with skill and assurance that keep the reader turning the pages. Loved this book!" – **Dana Fredsti**, author of *Plague World*

Jade Sky rips like a bullet… or an entire armory of same. Cinch up your body armor and enjoy Patrick Freivald's blitzkrieg through dark trenches and the corridors of the human heart–I sure did. – **Norman Partridge,** Author of *Dark Harvest*

Jade Sky

Chapter 1

Blood rained from the ceiling. Matt Rowley gasped cordite-stained air into his lungs as crimson drizzle spattered his face. *I hope that's not mine.* His shoulder, knee, and gut itched, the tell-tale sign of muscle and bone knitting together. Whispered, alien gibberish clawed through his mind, warning him. He rolled to his left and squeezed his eyes shut against the coming shrapnel. Bullets raked the floor where he'd been lying, peppering his face with chips of concrete. An unaugmented man would have died twice in the past five seconds.

He slithered backward under the steel loading-dock platform, opened his eyes, and swore. His helmet lay across the factory floor, next to the face-down Sergeant Karle. Tendrils of smoke rose from Karle's ruined body, his entrails smeared across the shelving unit above him. *So much for radio.* He couldn't see the others, but heard the unmistakable chatter of their REC7 assault rifles outside. The throatier return fire probably belonged to German-made HK's.

A quick inventory wasn't promising: one flash-bang grenade, a bandolier of shotgun rounds, and a Beretta M9A1 with three bullets. He unholstered the pistol and took two shots. The room went black as the remains of the fluorescent lights tinkled to the floor. He cringed as bullets pinged off of the platform. He risked a look when they stopped. The heat rendered his infrared vision useless, but his brain processed the ultraviolet spectrum into a black-and-white picture.

The claustrophobic room, narrow with thick walls and not enough cover, could have been tailor-made for an ambush. The explosion had converted the door they'd just retreated through into a pile of smoking cinder blocks and twisted metal. The stock of his AA-12 combat shotgun stuck out from the rubble, too far out of reach, and he didn't see Karle's REC7 anywhere. The two men near the back door lowered goggles onto their faces. *Perfect.* Matt shot the one on the left. The man screamed, blood spurting from his neck, and stumbled back through the door as his partner returned fire.

Matt hissed when a ricochet hit his bicep. His carbon fiber sleeve spared him the worst, but it still hurt like hell. The man reached for his belt, and the whispers filled Matt's mind with future possibilities. He picked the one he liked best then reacted to what hadn't yet happened. He rolled from under the platform and kicked as the object skittered toward him. The man stumbled back in surprise, and the grenade followed him out the door. Matt accompanied the dull explosion with a prayer of thanksgiving for late-second precognitive therapy.

He pulled the combat shotgun out of the rubble and put on his helmet. "Room's clear, Karle's dead," he said into the mic. His heads-up display showed his own elevated heart rate and adrenaline levels, but no moving targets. "Status?" he asked no one in particular.

Lieutenant Kifer responded through the radio, an edge of panic to his voice. "Ryan's dead, and I'm pinned down behind these barrels. Can you give me some covering fire?" Small arms fire peppered the doorway. Matt ducked back.

A REC7 fired from the left, full-auto, then Conor Flynn's voice broke over the radio. "Brilliant, mates. I leave you guys alone for two minutes and you get in this kind of trouble?" He fired again. "Rowley, I got your shooters shitting themselves. Get Kifer." Two more bursts came from his direction.

Matt peered around the corner for a quick look, then jerked his head back. The recalled image flashed onto his visor, crisp and clean. Seven hostiles, armed to the teeth, covered each other as they closed in on Kifer's position from three directions. Little more than a stack of 55-gallon drums and a small shack, Kifer's poor defilade left him exposed. Matt looked out again.

"Kifer, the guys at eight o'clock are about to break cover. Take them, and I'll get the two at three. Ready? Go!" Matt's AA-12 roared four times, the finned projectiles adjusting to the information fed through his helmet. They hit their targets and exploded, spraying gore and organs across the ground. Kifer's first target grabbed his shattered leg and wailed. His companion dragged him back behind a burning, upended delivery truck.

"I'm out," Conor said. "Give me a minute."

Matt ducked behind the wall as Conor reloaded. Bullets chipped the brick from the right. "Rastogi," Conor said, "I'm going to pin those assholes on Rowley again. Go get 'em."

"Got it," Akash Rastogi said. Matt waited while the gunfire intensified, then silenced, and bolted out the door toward Kifer.

"Echo company ETA two minutes," a professional, male voice said in his headset.

"Might be late for that," Kifer said between wheezy breaths. "Rowley, how good are these things at lungs?"

Matt dove behind a pile of pallets as Akash and Conor kept the rest of the hostiles pinned with short, controlled bursts. He couldn't see Kifer, or any movement, but took comfort that regenerates could repair anything short of death. He fired his last three shots over the burning car, and they exploded downward as programmed.

Someone screamed, and everything went silent. Matt breathed a sigh of relief. "Are we clear?"

"Hope so," Kifer said. A grenade lobbed over the barrels toward Kifer's position. "Shit. Never mind."

The barrels erupted in a spray of blue fire. The shockwave knocked Matt back twenty feet. His head rang as he hit the wall, the tang of blood filling his mouth. The stink of petrochemicals overwhelmed everything else, and flame bathed the stockyard in flickering light. His foot hurt with a casual dullness. He looked down at the fire licking up past his boot onto his pant leg. Shaking off the concussion, he slashed through the boot laces with his knife and kicked it free, then scrambled deeper into the rubble. Rolling to his stomach, he crawled into the ambush room and took aim at the door.

A short silhouette stepped into view, face hidden by a reflective visor, and Matt breathed a sigh of relief. Conor's Friend or Foe transponder would have shown up green on Matt's helmet, were he wearing it. Still, he'd recognize the build and gait anywhere. Conor held out his hand. Matt took it, and Conor hauled him to his feet. "Brilliant, you're alive."

The sound of helicopters had never been more welcome.

* * *

Matt watched the third squad disgorge from their helicopter, then walked barefoot to greet his boss, whose black flat-top stood immune to the prop wash. Bean-pole tall, Jeff Hannes wore a $300 suit that matched his gray eyes, a windbreaker bearing the International Council on Augmented Phenomena eye-and-thunderbolt logo, and a constipated grimace. Matt shook his hand, and let Jeff lead him far enough from the chopper that they could hear each other.

"Well, that was a clusterfuck," Jeff said. His eyes hovered over the grunts dragging corpses into a line. They'd covered the ICAP casualties with white sheets; Dawkins's goons had been left in the rising dawn.

Matt ran his tongue over his teeth. "They knew we were coming. We'd all be dead if it weren't for the spidey-sense."

Jeff shook his head. "If they knew you were coming, they wouldn't have been here."

Matt turned his head and spat, but didn't raise his voice. "I'm not saying you're wrong, Jeff, but twelve dead agents, man. Three from the bonk, and the rest from these pricks." He gestured to the dead bodies behind him. "Since when can seventeen normals take out four augs, if they didn't know beforehand?"

The bonk lay on the ground next to the other bodies, a headless, eleven-foot-tall humanoid mass of muscle, bone, and bad attitude. Its head lay twenty feet away. Conor sat on it, katana on his knees, polishing the blade with meticulous care. The basketball-sized hole in the bonk's torso showed ribs fused to form a solid plate and a heart the size of a human head. The bonk was half-again bigger than even Russian military augs; Matt couldn't understand why anyone would augment themselves to the level of inevitable insanity.

Jeff said nothing for a moment, then nodded his head. "Okay. Say you're right, and they knew you were coming. Anybody sane would have run. Why didn't they?"

"Don't know." Matt looked at the bodies of his squad-mates, then at the two prisoners, one barbequed beyond recognition and strapped to a gurney, the other unconscious with a bandaged leg. His brain felt glad they'd lived to be questioned and prosecuted, but his heart wanted to tear them limb from limb. "Why don't we ask them?"

"We'll get them healed up and schedule an interrogation for oh-nine-hundred." Jeff put a hand on Matt's shoulder. "Meantime, why don't we find out what this butcher's bill bought us?" Matt closed his eyes against an onslaught of whispers, the mindless, unintelligible side effect to Gerstner Augmentation. "Matt? They died soldiers."

Matt opened his eyes. He felt numb, just as he had in the Siege of Baghdad. These men were older than those kids had been, but they were fathers, brothers, husbands, snuffed out in an orgy of violence. He exhaled, and realized he'd been holding his breath. The shakes, the crying, the hopeless rage, they would all come later. Meantime, he had work to do. "Yeah."

Akash sauntered up, REC7 slung from his back, helmet under his arm. "What are we talking about, eh?" Though he was a soft-spoken, first-generation Canadian, his north-of-the-border accent clashed with his chocolate skin, short black hair, and dark brown eyes.

Jeff nodded toward the bodies and wandered away, giving the soldiers space.

They stood in silence for a moment. Akash licked his lips, then said, "They died heroes."

Matt grunted. "That's what Jeff said. It won't bring them back." He turned to walk away, and Akash grabbed his arm.

"It's not your fault it was an ambush, Matt."

"I know." And part of him even understood it. But a deeper, softer part would howl in terror and sadness, drowned under the need for men like him to do their jobs.

Akash opened his mouth to reply, but Matt cut him off.

"Just don't, Rastogi." He forced his tone softer than he wanted to. "I know what you're going to say, and I appreciate it. But I'd rather not hear it."

"Sure," Akash said, and turned with him to watch the growing, well-ordered bedlam.

A legion of technicians, forensics staff, and scientists joined the squads of soldiers, and they got to work. It didn't take long to find what intel told them they would: algae vats, centrifuges, distillation equipment, dehydration tanks, and countless glassware, all the components of a world-class chemistry and biology lab. The third building they opened had four tractor trailers parked inside, each with a different logo: Joe's Meats, Lynne's Dairy, C.E.L. Trucking, and Midwest Cargo, Inc.

Conor ran a hand over his shaved head. "Bet you a pint what's inside."

"Jade?" Akash asked.

"Nothing."

They cut the lock and opened the first truck. Shrink-wrapped pallets packed two high and two across stretched as far as he could see.

Matt hopped up and tore the wrapping off the front-most pallet. He lifted off a wire crate and pulled out a plastic bag. He admired the emerald green crystalline powder. He tossed it to Conor, who handed it to Jeff.

"I owe you a pint, Rastogi," Conor said.

Matt ignored them. "Call it two kilos per bag, ten bags per crate, eighty crates per pallet, and," he peered into the back of the truck, "looks like twenty-four pallets. So, forty thousand kilos? That's a lot of Jade."

One of the soldiers let out a low whistle. "What's the value on this stuff, sir?"

Jeff snapped out of a slack-jawed stupor. "Uncut? Twenty bucks a gram wholesale, more or less. That's . . . Jesus, that's . . . ."

"An eight with a lot of zeroes," the soldier said, holding out the calculator on his phone's screen for them to see.

Akash let out a low whistle. "You owe me eight hundred million pints, Conor."

"Open the other trucks," Jeff said. The soldiers jumped to work. As the doors slid up, their incredulity grew. The first three were full, the last nearly so.

Matt snorted, then walked outside. The red sky heralded impending dawn, and the Atlantic looked like a sea of blood. It fit his mood.

Shoes crunched on gravel. A lighter flared next to him.

Jeff took a deep draw of his cigarette, held it, then blew the smoke downwind. "What's on your mind, soldier?"

"Puzzles. If they knew we were coming, two full squads of augged agents and a platoon of regulars, with choppers and planes and the wrath of God behind us, why leave behind three billion dollars of Jade?"

"Fifteen billion, once it's cut."

"Okay, then, fifteen. But the question remains—why leave behind that much?"

Jeff took another draw on his smoke. "Maybe they didn't have time to take it?"

"Okay, why protect it with so few guys? This place is set up for a garrison of what, two hundred? They could have met us in real force, turned it into a battle."

"If they knew they didn't stand a chance—"

"—then why protect it at all? Cut your losses and run. They've got boats, a plane, trucks . . . Dawkins had to know that nobody was getting off this island once we showed up." He gestured toward the legion of soldiers outside. "Seventeen guys against an army. It's just all wrong."

Jeff sighed, and they sat in silence as the sun freed itself from the horizon. An osprey danced through the light, hovered for a split second, then dove feet-first into the water, rising again with a fish in its talons.

Jeff opened his mouth, and Matt slammed his fist into the wall. The cinder block caved in a puff of dust, and Matt let the pain fuel his anger. "But they did know, dammit!" He locked eyes with his boss and realized that Jeff hadn't spoken. *The only explanation is that they didn't know you were coming.* Matt hadn't read his mind—he'd seen the future and reacted to it before it happened.

Jeff's face held the slightest of smirks. "That stuff really works." He dropped the smirk and put his arm on Matt's shoulder. "Anyway, I think you guys should have some leave time, after you talk to the shrinks." Matt didn't bother to complain, but Jeff kept on anyway. "No use whining about it, even if it is a pain in the ass. I'll keep you posted."

Matt looked down at his knuckles. The skin had already healed over little specks of cinderblock—he'd have to clean it out later. "Yeah."

Chapter 2

Two days later, Matt stepped out of the car into a cool August morning. The pine forest shadowed his two-story log cabin. Squirrels rustled in the low thickets, and a blue jay squawked its displeasure as he closed the door. He walked up the porch to the front door of his seventeen-hundred square feet of heaven. The third step creaked, and he added it to the mental list of things to repair.

Monica flashed a groggy smile as she opened the door. Her curly chestnut hair matched his but fell to her shoulders, and her soft blue eyes were glazed with sleep. His Blake Shelton shirt enveloped her, a tent that almost concealed the baby bump as she leaned against the doorframe. Her well-muscled, tan legs didn't show the slightest hint of pregnancy.

"Hey, sugar. You weren't getting back until next week." She must have seen something in his expression, because her eyes widened in concern. "You okay?"

He stepped inside and kissed her, ignoring morning breath the coffee didn't quite mask. He pulled back and kissed her forehead, breathing in her scent. She kept herself in great shape—they'd met as pre-teens in a children's kung fu class, and she hadn't let up with her training—but in the past two years he'd grown strong enough to crush a person with his bare hands and had to mind his strength. He squeezed her just hard enough, and the cross between her breasts jabbed him in the sternum. "No, I'm not," he whispered into her hair. "But I can't talk about it. Not yet."

She snuggled into him. "Is it . . . Baghdad bad?"

It wasn't, but the immediacy of the loss made it worse. Not trusting his voice, he nodded and looked at the plain wooden cross on the living room wall. She squeezed him tighter, and they stood in the foyer like that, frozen in time, until a whine interrupted them. Matt smiled, let her go, and dropped to one knee. He grabbed the Basset hound by the ears and kissed his nose. "How's my boy?" Ted's tail thumped against the floor as he licked Matt's nose. His breath stank worse than Monica's.

"Coffee?" she asked.

"Yeah."

She stepped into the kitchen, sniffed the dregs in the bottom of the pot, and poured it into the sink. "I'll make a fresh one." She puttered in the kitchen, and he couldn't help but try to catch a peek under the T-shirt when she reached up for the can of Folgers. Granny-panties, white cotton, fraying elastic. *Every husband's dream.*

They talked about nothing over breakfast—Deputy Drake had arrested Kevin Bartell for screaming drunken poetry at his ex-girlfriend's house again, Jen and Bill found out they're having twins, and PanTex laid off twenty more people. Nothing changed in White Spruce; it just got older, more tired. As Monica cleared the dishes she paused at the sink. "Are you home long?"

He nodded. "I reckon a week or two at least. I'll have paperwork, but I can do it from here, or if needs be, down at the local." ICAP didn't have an office in White Spruce, or anywhere else outside Washington, D.C., but the Clifford Davis Federal Building in Memphis wasn't too awful a commute once or twice a week.

"Good. Pastor Joe's been asking about you, and you can take me to my appointment on Thursday."

Matt polished off the last of his coffee. "I'd love to." A strong, proud, intelligent, willful woman, Monica remained . . . brittle. She'd lost their first baby just out of high school, ten months after their honeymoon, while he fought half a world away with the Third Infantry. They'd been "trying again" for eight years, and in that time his beautiful, loving wife had lurched in and out of depression and dependency. Now pregnant again, she lived in constant terror of losing their boy. "Hmph."

"What?" She put the dishes in the sink and turned on the water.

He opened his mouth and wasn't sure what to say. At that moment he knew that she carried their son as sure as he knew his own name. "Do we find out the sex this week?"

She nodded, defensive. "If we want to, and the bean cooperates on the ultrasound."

He smiled at her. "Whatever you want to do, babe."

She put a fingertip to her lips and rolled her eyes up to the ceiling. "Um . . . I'll think about it." Her dazzling smile emerged from the uncertainty. "It'll be fun to bounce around some names."

* * *

The conference call leached away two monotonous hours of Matt's life before anyone said anything interesting. He sat in his living room, staring aghast at his laptop, as Jeff defended the intelligence and their actions despite countless, repetitive questions that made it clear in no uncertain terms that the powers that be considered losing two squads of ICAP agents politically unacceptable.

Matt's mind leapt to dozens of choice comments about civilians in general and bureaucrats in particular, but he would never say them. It wasn't that he'd lose his job—the Six Million Dollar Man had nothing on your average aug—he just knew that it wouldn't help.

"Can't some of your men read minds, Agent Hannes?" the jowly pencil-pusher from Belgium asked.

Conor, onscreen next to Jeff, rolled his eyes. Jeff scowled for the millionth time. "No. Late-second precognitive therapy has enabled a few select agents to utilize short-term prediction, so they can predict what someone is about to say or do, but only the barest moment beforehand. Think of it like ultra-fast reflexes. Nobody can read anybody's mind."

Though the chances of anyone even looking at him were remote, Matt schooled his face into a blank mask. So-called "late-second" precognition, no more than a second or two out, happened all the time. Sometimes, beyond his control, his ability to predict future events would extend out two minutes or more. Or maybe months, if Monica carried a boy in her womb.

Mr. Jowly-guy continued. "What about this interrogation, then?" *Finally.*

Jeff folded his hands on the tabletop. "The prisoners were recalcitrant. We were able to ascertain that they are a part of Dawkins's cartel and that they knew we were coming."

The gray-haired Dutchman leaned toward his screen. "How did they know this?"

"They claim to have been tipped off an hour before we touched down."

"Tipped off by whom? Do we have a leak?"

"We have no idea. Dawkins told them, and gave them a choice: evacuate, or stay behind and earn a bonus. Most of them left."

"What was this bonus for, Mr. Hannes?"

"Killing us," Conor said.

Jeff cleared his throat and leaned forward, blocking Conor from the screen. "The survivors would split a bonus of one million euros for every ICAP agent killed." Blood gushed down the walls, and Jeff's face melted off his skull. Whispers gibbered and clawed at the empty sockets. Matt blinked, and the hallucination disappeared. *What the hell?* "—send a message that further incursions into his business will not be tolerated."

Jowls flushed with rage. "This drug dealer seeks to threaten us? Is he stupid?"

"Dumb as dumb," Conor muttered. Jeff shushed him.

The Frenchman rolled his eyes. "By all indications he is not. One does not run a multibillion-dollar criminal enterprise if one is stupid."

His phone buzzed. Akash's message read, *Is Flynn trying to get fired?*

Matt replied, *Dunno.*

Brian Frahm, Jeff's immediate supervisor, a baby-faced American in his forties who didn't look a day over twenty, lifted a hand from his thigh. They stopped and looked at him. "Debating Dawkins's mental acuity won't do us any good. The question now is what to do about him."

Brian dropped his hand, and the room erupted in raised voices. Matt tuned out their squabbling and looked out the window, where a few leaves on the deciduous trees showed signs of color. He jerked back to the conversation when Jeff said his name. "Sergeant Rowley has the combat experience, the investigative experience, the training, and the—well, the augs necessary to bring the entire enterprise down. He's the perfect man for the job."

"What do you say, Sergeant?" Brian asked. Everyone waited for his response.

"Yeah. That is, I'll think about it."

Jeff smiled. Akash texted, *Grats.*

Matt grunted. *Did I just get promoted, or fed to the wolves?*

* * *

A week later, Jeff sat on Matt's couch and cradled a cup of coffee in his hands. Conor sprawled over the recliner, and Akash perched on the loveseat. Monica puttered in the kitchen making sticky buns, a transparent pretext to eavesdrop, and the house smelled of gooey brown sugar and sweet bread. Matt leaned against the mantle, running his hand over the hearth. He'd hand-selected every stone and built it with his dad. Hard to believe they'd laid the last stone only five years ago, harder still that he'd been only twenty-two at the time.

"It's downright cold up here," Jeff said.

"It's the West Highlands in August," Matt said. "Nights get chilly sometimes."

"I wasn't expecting frost."

Conor chuckled. "Not a Boy Scout, then?"

Jeff ran his tongue over his teeth and looked out the window at the towering pines. "Not too prepared, I guess. So why's the town called White Spruce when there aren't any White Spruce?"

Matt shrugged. "I guess they planted a ring of them way back in eighteen twenty-something, right on the village green, but none of them survived the climate. Every couple of years the high and mighties talk about planting another, then cost and maintenance comes up and they drop the whole thing." He plopped down next to Akash, tired of small talk. "So I'm getting a command, an operations suite, and an 'as-needed' budget? That's a hell of a reward for just surviving. I don't know that I'm qualified."

Jeff grimaced. "It's not a reward."

Conor grinned. "I'll take it if he won't."

Akash snorted.

"You don't think I'm the leadership type?"

Akash shook his head so fast his lips jiggled. "Nuh-uh. Not even a little. Your idea of a plan is 'kill it until it's dead.'"

Conor laughed. "No, you're right." He turned to Jeff. "Let Matt do the paperwork."

Jeff kept his eyes on Matt. "You're the most experienced ICAP agent we have that's not already assigned to a high-priority mission"—Conor opened his mouth, and Jeff held up a hand to forestall the comment—"and you're the only aug stateside with investigative experience."

Matt took a sip of coffee. "My tenure with the Troopers wasn't exactly Sherlock Holmes."

Akash's wry grin contrasted with his flat tone. "Conor's got law enforcement experience. He spent most of his youth evading the cops."

Conor gave him a two-fingered "up yours."

Jeff ignored them both. "No," he agreed. "But it was solid. You did good, steady work, and you got results. Either way, Frahm's backing you, and so are these two clowns, so the job's yours."

All sounds from the kitchen stopped.

"I have a condition."

Jeff raised an eyebrow. "Oh?"

"I run operations out of Nashville. It's closer than Memphis, and a whole heap closer than D.C."

"D.C.—"

"—won't work for us. You're lucky I didn't ask for White Spruce." Rolling his eyes, Jeff opened his mouth to speak, but Matt talked right over him. "Monica's pregnant. I promised her I'd spend more time at home." In the kitchen, the dish-clanking continued. "I intend to do just that."

Jeff set his coffee on the side table and looked pensively at Conor and Akash. They shrugged. He ran his tongue over his teeth.

"C'mon, boss," Matt said. "We just hit the biggest drug bust in the history of everything. Working closer to home ain't much to ask."

Jeff slapped his hands on his knees. "Alright, buddy, done. The transportation piece should be easy enough. You can utilize an AH-14 when we need you in D.C., which shouldn't be that often."

Matt thought for a moment, then nodded. Not everybody got to commute aboard an attack helicopter. "Alright. What about our team? I'd like to get two more agents to round us out."

Jeff pushed a stack of dossiers across the coffee table. "You've got your pick of those seven. All combat veterans, all augs."

Matt flipped through the files with particular attention to their Gerstner Augmentations. Adrenal boosters, regenerates, muscle and nervous system enhancements, eidetic memory stimulators . . . . Nothing out of the ordinary. He looked at Jeff. "No precogs?"

"Nope. None of them cleared for it."

Conor looked out the window. Akash shuffled his feet and looked anywhere but at Jeff. Jeff's eyes didn't leave Matt's.

Matt cleared his throat. "Are they . . . stable?"

Jeff pressed his fingertips together. "Of course, they're stable. They're monitored weekly, same as everybody. Incidents within ICAP are down ninety-five percent in the past three years. We've got a great handle on the psychological issues of—"

Matt rolled his eyes. "Spare us the PR talk."

"Sure, okay. So that's why they didn't clear for precog. Two years ago they would have, now they didn't. We're being careful."

Public 'incidents' were the reason ICAP existed. Countries had founded the International Council on Augmented Phenomena as a joint UN-NATO venture to combat the spread of Gerstner technologies, but before long it became obvious that Pandora's Box wasn't going to close. Super-human abilities weren't just available, they were cheap. The Russians had learned the hard way that too many augs spiraled into uncontrolled mutation and murderous rage, officially called Gerstner-Induced Psychosis—their military wouldn't be a threat again for at least a generation. Many street gangs and drug cartels still hadn't taken GIP to heart, and between intentional augmentation and Jade's long-term side effects, bonks suffered psychotic breaks far too often for anyone's comfort. It wasn't something that civilians should have access to.

With bonks that could throw cars, shrug off bullets, and dodge tank shells, civilian and military law enforcement couldn't cut it. Selected from military units and law enforcement around the world, screened for suitability and augmented well below levels considered safe, ICAP agents walked the line between Captain America and Bane and were the only law enforcement capable of hunting down other augs.

Screening criteria ranged from training to education but most of all included the ability to resist the whispers. Incidents still happened, but with proper psychological screening, judicial levels of augmentation, and careful monitoring there were fewer ICAP bonks every year. Good thing, too. Once an aug bonked, nothing short of death would stop it from killing everything it could.

Despite the danger of rogue augs, Jade remained ICAP's primary focus. Euphoria with no immediate side effects, Gerstner technology made it the cleanest high of any drug ever produced. Once someone tried Jade, the risk of uncontrolled mutation and madness couldn't compete with the lust to get just one more hit. No one recovered from Jade addiction, with recidivism well over ninety-nine percent. Taking a hit of Jade meant playing Russian roulette with full chambers, but junkies didn't think long-term. That dealers laced Jade into other drugs didn't help matters.

Matt didn't look up from the files. "I want six weeks training time, with at least two bag-a-bonks before we go for Dawkins."

Jeff smirked. "As his majesty commands."

Chapter 3

Time to roll. In his mind, Matt went through their mission parameters one last time. Nineteen homes had been abandoned in the New Mexico mountains in the past three months. In that same time, cattle poaching had skyrocketed, and four young girls had been abducted from their beds. The criminality centered around the decrepit remains of a mining town abandoned in the 1870s, once called Gruta Plata. Satellite surveillance indicated activity surrounding the old mine, still ringed by a crumbling stockade. One infrared image suggested a large man carrying a dead cow — by himself.

The air smelled of the coming thunderstorm, and Matt's breath frosted his visor. *Odd weather.* His HUD blinked once at 3:30 am. He gave a tiny nod.

Tsuji "Blossom" Sakura looked like a stocky man in her full uniform and helmet. A veteran of Tokyo Metropolitan Police's anti-Yakuza division, on their first mission she'd revealed herself to be blunt, taciturn, and a consummate professional. She also moved faster than anyone he'd ever seen. She crossed the courtyard and climbed over the compound wall before Matt finished standing.

She opened the gate for the rest of the team. Conor covered the gate with Matt to let in Garrett and Akash. Corporal Garrett Johnson, late of the US Marine Corps 3rd Battalion, had stood almost seven feet tall before augmentation and now loomed closer to eight. Forty-three years old, he had four years on Blossom, the next oldest member of the team. Matt had let him plan both ops—when it came to using the resources at hand, rank meant little and age meant less. Garrett's dyed-blond, severe flat-top popped against his dark brown skin.

Akash slipped through the gate, his weapon up, with Garrett taking aim over his head.

Once through, they held position as Matt and Garrett moved up. Akash used American Sign Language, which they had all been required to learn. *Anyone else hear that?*

Matt shook his head, as did Garrett and Blossom. Conor replied, eyebrows raised to indicate a question. *Chanting?*

Akash nodded.

Matt crept toward the entrance, a timber-framed rectangle of blackness, and heard it—Latin-influenced gibberish, with touches of Hebrew and maybe Spanish. *Crazies*, he signed. *Perfect!* He meant no irony: some weird cult minimized the chances that ICAP agents should even be involved or that they'd face any real danger. In a best case scenario, recon would reveal no threatening augs, and his team would pull out to let the local police handle it. Then again, there was the guy with the cow.

Blossom peered through the doorway, then turned back, frowning. *I can't see anything.* Far more fluent in ASL than Matt, she hadn't said 'clear' in the military sense. He asked for clarification. *It's like nothing. The space between the stars before augmentation. No IR. No UV.*

He told her to hold position and moved up. At the doorway, his vision stopped, in all wavelengths. He triggered his radio and spoke a bare whisper. "Are you getting this?"

Jeff's voice blasted too loud in his ear-bud. "Five by five." After a pregnant pause, Jeff said, "Proceed." Matt signaled his team to hold position and stepped through the door.

The world went black. Countless unintelligible whispers urged him to give them . . . something. Life? Death? Devotion? Control? He never quite knew, but he could taste their hate in the back of his throat. He blinked, and they disappeared.

The dark hallway stretched twenty feet, lined with white columns. The block marble masonry belonged in a church, not a mine. Acrid smoke tickled his nostrils. Beyond the silhouette of a man carrying a hunting rifle, the mineshaft opened up into a large chamber flickering with a deep green light. The breeze outside didn't penetrate at all, and the chanting filled his ears, much louder than before.

Matt ducked around a column and whispered into the microphone. "I'm in, copy?" He looked behind him at the entrance. Nothing but impenetrable black.

Blossom appeared next to him and signed in the flickering darkness. *No radio contact. Ready?*

Take them, he signed.

The silhouette ahead became two, then fell to the ground. Blossom whispered in his ear. "Hallway clear. Two more guards on the other balconies." He blinked, and they disappeared from sight. A second later Blossom stood next to him. "Neutralized." Matt noted that the helmet didn't transfer the signal.

Over the chanting, Conor's bare murmur wouldn't have been caught by unaugmented ears. "Brilliant. Let's do this."

Matt looked back. Conor tapped his helmet, then signed, *No communication.* He drew his katana in one fluid motion—why an Irish guy used any sword, much less a Japanese sword, Matt would never understand. Next to Conor, Garrett appeared out of the darkness of the doorway. The huge man frowned, then gave a thumbs up as he made eye contact. Blossom disappeared through the arch in front of them, then reappeared.

She stood in the archway for a moment, a stocky black silhouette limned with green, before approaching. "I think radio's not working."

Matt nodded. "Satlink is out."

"You come up," she replied. "See what I see." They followed her forward into a white marble amphitheater.

Twin staircases circled the room, descending twenty feet. Eight marble columns held up the stone ceiling, the white stone veined with pink and gold. At the base of each squatted a huge obsidian brazier filled with glowing red coals. Hooded acolytes sprinkled powder onto them; they flared green with each pass.

The almost-transparent bowls caught the light and darkened it, accentuating the shadows more than bringing light.

They're burning Jade, Matt thought. He turned his eyes to the rest of the room.

Perhaps sixty people crowded around a central dais, every one hooded and chanting, their eyes a faint, luminescent green. Two massive forms, at least eight feet tall, stood on either side of an altar, muscled arms crossed over bulging chests. On the white stone slab a figure writhed, twice as tall as a man and hidden in shadow, its tortured gyrations in time with the persistent chant. The whispers gibbered in pleasure and an image formed in Matt's mind, not quite seen.

In the midst of the crowd a naked teen knelt at the altar, his body defiled by primitive tattoos still wet with blood. A dripping, crimson symbol pulsed on his forehead, a circle cut with a line, each half-filled with a snake-like, sinuous squiggle. He called out to The Servant in every tongue and none, and begged for a taste of Her glory. He sighed in pleasure as his skin sloughed to the floor, blood writhing from his skeleton into the cracks between the marble blocks. With a cry of delight, he collapsed in a puddle of wet, red pain.

Matt shook off the vision, or hallucination, or whatever, and glanced at his team. Blossom furrowed her brow, a look of ultimate confusion. Conor grinned, the green-tinged fire sparkling in his eyes. He turned back to the masses just as eleven people stepped forward from the first row.

They slipped out of their robes, revealing filthy, naked bodies, men and women, old and young, with shaved heads and crowns of thorns. They knelt. The chanting reached a crescendo, and the air around the altar shimmered. A breeze became a whirlwind, and the supplicants faded to a dusty white, then crumbled to black soot in the growing wind. Their remains darkened and writhed as the wind picked them up and swirled them above the dais.

On the altar, the ashy shadows gyrated. They took form; a massive man with wings of feathered silver, alabaster skin, a chiseled human face with the curled horns of a ram. Matt's soul burned in crushing awe, and he took an involuntary step forward.

He closed his eyes to the terrible beauty and struggled not to open them.

A burning need for his own slavery pulsed in his mind, entwined with the whispers, and urged him to join the maelstrom at the altar. Instead, Matt choked up the AA-12. He struggled to pull the trigger, but his finger wouldn't obey. He stepped forward. Someone grabbed him from behind. He stumbled, backpedaling, and the whispers shrieked as he fell out of the mine. Blinded by the dawn, he scrambled on hands and knees away from the black doorway, his mind silent.

An inhuman shriek split the sky, and the ram-horned creature stepped into the light. As it stalked toward him, twisting shadows clung to it, defying the sun. Its eyes burned with the green flame of the braziers, and Matt suffocated in them, all thoughts of resistance melting into the jade light. *I am yours*, he thought, while his soul raged against its imprisonment. The creature grabbed him by the throat and lifted him from the ground, and against his will he joined the whispers as they begged it for death.

Conor appeared behind it, sword flashing in the rising sun. He sheared off one wing with a single sweep of his katana, and as the ghostly metallic feathers disappeared in a shower of sparks he turned and embedded the blade into the creature's back. It leapt and spun, tearing the sword from his grasp as it threw Matt to the side. It crushed Conor into the rock wall with a massive fist, sword still wedged next to its spine. Conor coughed up blood as a pair of knives appeared in his hands, and he cartwheeled over the thing's shoulders as it reared back for another strike.

He jammed the blades into the sides of its head. One skittered off of solid bone, and the other lopped off the top of an ear as it embedded in the skull. As he flipped over top of the beast, he let go of the knives and grabbed his katana two-handed, using his momentum to tear it free in a shower of steaming blood.

Dazed, Matt fell to a sitting position. His head swam. Part of him worried; he recovered from concussions faster than this. A darker part worried that he hadn't suffered a concussion. A memory of a thought tickled his mind. *I am yours.* He scowled and shook the nonsensical phrase away. The mine entrance faded from the black of nothingness to just dark. Light flashed in that darkness. Loud light.

Blossom backed out of the tunnel next to Garrett, both targeting tight bursts through the opening. The bonks that had flanked the altar charged out, roaring. Blossom dove, firing her assault rifle up into one's groin as she rolled through its legs. The other wrapped Garrett in a tackle and landed on top of him.

Conor spun his whole body in two fluid motions, and deep red lines appeared across the winged creature's calves. It leapt into the air, whole-again wings spread to block out the blood-red sky. In an instant it disappeared, washed out by the rising sun. Matt's identity struggled back into his consciousness.

Conor shrieked at the sky. "GIVE ME BACK MY KNIFE, YOU SON OF A BITCH!"

"Matt," Jeff said in Matt's ear. "Are you okay?"

Matt's automatic assessment kicked in with the help of an implanted medical chip. BP 110/60, pulse 58, regenerates not triggered, no major trauma. "Yeah." The feeling of submission had faded to a dull, yearning ache. "I'm fine."

He picked up his combat shotgun and realized he had no clear targets.

Garrett lifted a bonk by the knee and thrust it sideways, then shot it in the groin while it stumbled. Blossom and Conor flashed around the second, their movements traceable only by the lines of blood that appeared on its thick, gnarled hide. The thing raised a knee, and Conor flew sideways in a spray of blood, his face a ruined mass of pulped meat. Undeterred, Blossom jammed a carbon-fiber knife into its back and wrenched the blade sidewise. She snarled as the bonk's legs collapsed, dodged a clumsy grapple attempt, and pulled the knife out, to bury it halfway into its temple.

It grabbed her wrist with one hand and squeezed, crushing bone, then shook her like a rag doll. She screamed and tried in vain to twist out of the monstrous grip as it smashed her onto Conor. Matt bolted forward and leapt, slamming his shoulder into the pommel of the knife. It punched through thickened skull and into the bonk's brain. It let go of Blossom. She stumbled to the side and collapsed. The bonk fell on its face.

It twitched. Matt placed the combat shotgun against the back of its head and fired. The microgrenade blew its skull to pieces in a splatter of brains and blood. He looked up just in time to see Conor sever the other bonk's spine, grab its hair as it dropped to its knees, saw back and forth across its neck with his katana, and tear the head from the body. Steaming red gore fountained from the massive neck as Conor stepped back and flicked blood from his blade in a single, efficient motion.

"Fucking brilliant," he said, beaming through a broken jaw, his face a massive, bloody bruise. He helped Blossom up. He carried the head to Matt, dropped it at his feet, and clapped him on the shoulder. "Done is done is fun, am I right?"

"Status?" Jeff asked in his ear.

As Matt formulated a reply, people stumbled out of the mine, jaws slack, eyes vacant. Dozens of them. "Uh . . . ." They stank of body odor and piss and Jade, and shuffled their feet through the dirt. "I . . . ."

Blossom saved him from having to reply. Her brow scrunched in worry, she spoke into her helmet. "One augmented subject escaped. Multiple injuries, nothing serious."

Garrett and Akash stumbled up to him. Akash, his face a worried mask, held Garrett up with an arm around his waist. Dark blood stained the giant marine's abdomen, a stark contrast to his pallid face. Behind them, more slack-jawed civilians emerged.

"What the hell just happened?" Matt asked.

Garrett grunted and pushed himself off Akash's shoulder. He spat toward the severed head. "I got in that thing's way, and it likes to hug. I'll be fine"—he stumbled and dropped to one knee—"in a few minutes." For whatever reason, Garrett healed slower and not quite as well as the rest of the team, despite the same regenerates.

Jeff's order came through the ear-bud. "Secure the civilians."

Blossom and Conor corralled the perps, pulling off their filthy, hooded capes and herding the naked group into a rough human conglomerate. They complied with dazed expressions and offered not the slightest resistance. Matt frowned. Even before a full bonk-out, Jade could induce violent schizophrenia in severe addicts and a cocaine-like manic happiness in the casual user. This looked more like too much heroin.

A middle-aged man wandered away from the group, toward the desert. Conor put a hand on his chest. "Sir, you need to stop." The group dropped to their knees, vacant eyes forward, mouths open. As one they groaned.

Garrett clucked his tongue. "Recommend neutraliz—"

"Belay that," Matt interrupted. "Civilians are cooperating and docile."

"Proceed, Sergeant Rowley," Jeff said.

Garrett gave him a flat, unblinking stare, then turned away to light up a landing site with phosphorous flares. Even in the broadening daylight, the UV signature would pop on the pilots' heads-up displays.

Akash raised an eyebrow at Matt. "Kill them all? When did that become okay?"

Conor clapped him on the shoulder. "Guy's a bit shook up is all, and their little zombie act freaked him out a bit." He followed Akash's look to Matt. "Well?"

Matt gave the order, and his team zip-tied the wrists and ankles of every man and woman. They didn't have enough for the children, but that didn't matter. Not one person protested, resisted, or spoke. As Conor and Blossom led the shuffling civilians toward the LZ, Matt and Garrett approached the mine entrance.

Worm holes pitted the crumbling, bone-dry wood of the entranceway. Beyond, a narrow tunnel of rough-hewn rock reached no more than ten feet before ending in a cave-in of boulders and rubble. Dusty footprints littered the rock floor, leading right up to it.

"Sorry about the mess," Garrett said. "That thing wouldn't take 'die' for an answer."

Matt reached down and picked up a scarf's length of leather from in front of the cave-in. As his eyes passed over the tattooed glyphs and sigils, his augmented mind connected them to those on the boy kneeling in front of the altar. The whispers tittered in bloodthirsty glee. He dropped the leather strip and took a sharp step back, wiping his fingers on his shirt.

"Yeah," Garrett said. "That sucks."

Matt couldn't shake his confusion. "What the hell happened here? I mean, to us?"

Garrett shrugged, grabbed a wooden beam, and heaved it out of the way. "Don't know, but I want to find out."

Rotors thrummed in the distance. By the time the team made it through the rubble, every civilian had been evacuated by government helicopter. Matt stepped deeper into the cave, careful to avoid the leather strip—*skin*—he'd dropped. He ran his hands along the walls, and the white he first mistook for marble came off on his fingertips, revealing wood and gray stone beneath. He smelled it and wiped the chalk on his pants.

Once inside, he turned on his flashlight and looked around. A kitchen table served as the dais, with chipped white paint showing cheap wood underneath, and instead of obsidian braziers, cast-iron frying pans held piles of Jade over wood coals. A pile of black, cold ash smeared across the floor in front of the table, and in it were chunks of burnt bone. He put a hand over them. Cold.

He looked at Garrett sidelong. "Is it just me—"

"Nope," Garrett said. "I saw it, too. This place was a lot fancier a few minutes ago."

"Hours," Matt muttered. "It's past dawn. We were in here for hours."

They didn't say anything. Nothing they could say would make sense. They stepped back outside and waited for the forensics team. As the civilians did their work, they set up an ambush for the winged bonk, just in case it came back.

They waited three days and filed an action report that nobody would believe. Jeff sure didn't, though he said he'd sign off on their account of events anyway. The winged shadow didn't return.

* * *

Matt carried the overfilled tumbler of whiskey to their booth, careful not to spill any. Conor took it with a nod, downed the alcohol in three massive gulps, upended the glass on the table, and belched. Akash rolled his eyes. Garrett chuckled. Second-generation regenerates had to drink fast to get a buzz, and even so, it wouldn't last more than a couple minutes.

Conor had dominated the conversation thus far, and it contented Matt to let him.

"Look, mate," Conor said to Garrett, jerking a thumb Matt's way. "I'm not saying he owes me his life, I'm just saying I saved it. Mister Flappy had him dead to rights, and he just stood there having a piss. The thing picked him up by the neck, and he didn't even struggle. One squish and he'd be done as done."

Garrett waved to the bartender, pointed to the table, and held up two fingers. "Well, I at least owe you a drink. That bonk crushed my ribs like a beer can and would have kept going if you hadn't intervened."

Conor grinned as the server arrived with another round, setting down the drinks and scooping up the empty glasses. "Just doing my job." He chugged his, then narrowed his eyes at Akash. "You got something to say, eh? Irish stereotypes and all that, right?"

Akash raised his hands in mock defense. "No, no, sorry. I wouldn't dream of smearing the good Irishman's name by tying it to your behavior."

Conor clinked his empty glass against Akash's full one, then nodded toward Blossom, reading an ebook at the end of the bar and sipping a cup of tea. "Having a cuppa at a pub. It's unnatural. She too good to drink with us?"

"She doesn't drink," Matt said. "And she doesn't like bars."

"Or celebrations," Garrett said. "Or people."

"Then why's she here, eh?" Akash asked him.

"Matt invited her. And in Japanese culture, you don't turn down an invite without good reason. It'd be a huge insult even if he wasn't her boss."

"Brilliant," Conor said. "In Irish culture, you don't turn down an invite to a pub, period. And if someone pussies out, that's more for the rest of us."

The server brought the next round. Matt sat back and thought of home. His mind returned to the conversation when Akash said, "If that were really an angel, we'd all be dead. No one withstands the wrath of God. Not you, not me. Nobody." Matt wiped away the symbol he'd traced in the condensation on the table, the bisected circle with an 'S' in each half.

Garrett nodded. "Some fights you can't win."

Conor grinned at Akash. "Aren't you a Hindu?"

Akash rolled his eyes. "No. Are you a Catholic?"

"'Course," he replied, and chugged another whiskey. "Protestants don't use katanas." He slammed the glass down. "It's why I know an angel when I see one. Glowy eyes, big wings, shiny. Angel is as angel does."

Matt frowned. "What would an angel be doing in a cave in New Mexico?"

"I was too busy saving your sorry ass," Conor said, pointing both index fingers at Matt, "so I didn't get a chance to ask."

Blossom spoke from the end of the bar. "No such thing, anyway."

"It speaks!" Conor said. "You going to join us, Sakura?"

She shook her head and turned back to her book.

Akash frowned. "She's right, though. It's just a big bonk."

"With wings," Conor said. "Don't forget the shiny, metal-feathered wings." He popped half out of his chair and flashed his eyes at the waitress. "And speaking of wings, gentlemen, Hot Buffalo or Raspberry-Habanero?"

"Sweet and Sour," Matt said, to a chorus of insults that brought his manhood into question with various levels of vulgarity. He waved them off as he got up, then approached Blossom. She looked up from her e-reader and set it down when he sat. He kept his voice low to keep the conversation between them. "You don't think it was an angel?"

She held up her hands. "More like someone who wants his worshippers to think he was. Makes more sense than proof of angels after all these years."

"Do you believe in God?" He didn't know why he'd asked it, but couldn't take it back once it left his mouth.

She sighed. "I grew up in the traditions of *kami-no-michi*, but even to my parents it was more culture than belief. So, no. You?"

"Sure."

"Sure?" She chuckled, and covered her mouth with her hand, the dainty gesture at odds with her typical dour, mannish affect. "That's your belief? Sure?"

He chuckled with her, but didn't feel it. "Sure."

She looked back at her reader but didn't wake up the screen. In the reflection, her smile turned to a frown as she pulled her hand away. "When I was fourteen I wanted to believe in ancestor spirits, that my parents were still with me, but no matter what I wanted I knew it wasn't true."

Shit, Matt thought. He didn't mean to turn the conversation to that. He scrambled for what to say, and came up with, "Weren't you working for Tokyo Metro when you were fourteen?"

She blinked. "Ah, that's not in my file."

He raised his eyebrows and nodded. "Yeah, it is. It's in the file Jeff gave me. Said you were an informant after your parents passed, from twelve to sixteen."

Her scowl turned murderous. "That's not supposed to be in my file. They said only my police work goes to ICAP."

"I'm sorry, forget I brought it up."

"No, I will not forget." She hopped off the stool, snatched up her reader, and walked out.

Matt texted Jeff to let him know he might have slipped up, then went back to the others.

* * *

"So," Monica said. "It was an angel?" She kicked the dishwasher closed with her foot and fiddled with the cross at her neck. "A real angel with wings and everything?"

Matt tried not to roll his eyes. Monica's responding snort told him he hadn't quite succeeded. "No, of course not. I mean, it had wings, but . . . . No."

"Maybe Conor's right. Why couldn't it be an angel?"

Matt took a moment to choose his words carefully—too far down the wrong road and he'd end up somewhere he didn't want to be. "I don't know, babe. Angels aren't something that modern people see, you know? Jeff figures it's some kind of bonk we've never seen before. With everything else we've seen, big wings ain't out of the realm of possibility."

She scowled while drying her hands on the dish towel. "I wish you wouldn't use that word. They're not bonkers, they're addicts."

They're both, Matt thought. Bonks who snapped were definitely bonkers, and people who augged themselves to the point of risking GIP were, too, but Matt didn't need precognitive therapy to see the warning signs in her scowl. He held up his hands in supplication. "I'm sorry, you're right. It's hard not to . . . you know." He wasn't sure if she understood his point, or even if he did, but he hoped it mollified her enough.

She smiled her sad recovering-addict smile, then wrapped her arms around his neck. She smelled of jasmine and strawberries. He wrapped her in his arms and cursed his augs. *Are you sure you want to—*

She nuzzled his neck. "Are you sure you want to do this? That thing . . . that man, I mean. He could have killed you."

Matt closed his eyes and bathed in her scent. It wasn't fair. ICAP held no more danger for him than the army or the troopers, maybe even less with second-generation regenerates, and she'd wanted him to take the job as much as he had. "Yeah, babe, he could have. But he didn't." He squeezed just a little tighter. "I'm a lot tougher than I used to be." *You said Garrett and—*

"You said Garrett and Conor got pretty messed up."

"They were. Then they weren't." She didn't understand. That bear hug had left Corporal Garrett with six broken ribs, a punctured lung, a fractured tibia and a bruised stomach. Conor had multiple skull fractures and massive bleeding on his brain.

Conor hadn't even slowed down, and ten minutes later they were both right as rain. "We bounce back pretty fast."

She kissed him on the lips. "I don't like that you're in so much danger. Your job with the state—"

"—was safer," he finished. They'd been through this a thousand times in the past three years. After pushing him to accept the ICAP job, and beaming with pride at his acceptance and subsequent promotions, she couldn't accept the risk. They both appreciated the tripled salary, though, plus ten percent since his promotion. "I know, babe. But it's not just that they need me. I need to do this."

Matt thought about the dozens of people they'd rescued from the mine. Jade addicts, doomed to a lifetime of recidivism and struggle, who because of his team at least had a chance to live a normal life, the chance to slough off the shadow they called the Servant. And that counted just his team, just this week.

Thus far, rehabilitation wasn't promising. The initial interviews had gone nowhere. The captives couldn't even be bothered to use the toilet, much less answer questions. After thirty hours or so they'd begun to cry, all of them. An hour or two later they wailed for the Servant and begged to be released to serve her. By the time Matt's team had left New Mexico, they were twitchy and morose, the classic signs of Jade withdrawal, but behaving for the most part like regular junkies. None had come out of it enough to give a statement.

The week since had been a disappointing denouement. Between debriefs and interrogations, a team of normals had brought in fancy equipment to check out the mine. Their results were conclusive: it contained no ornate stairs, no marble, no obsidian. The idea of an entire team sharing a hallucination bothered Jeff, but Matt couldn't shake the certainty that it hadn't been in their minds: it had been real. If anything, that bothered him more.

The inscriptions on the hide had been marker, and forensics had confirmed the skin as human, but they were still waiting on DNA. The report from Linguistics said they were gibberish, meaningless symbols culled from occult books and old horror movies.

The delicate arms around his neck tightened just a little. "You're a thousand miles away, baby." She kissed his sternum.

He shook his head to clear it. "Yeah, sorry. I was thinking about how we'd pay for this place if I left ICAP." He felt bad at the cheap blow, but at some point Monica needed to see the financial truth and accept it. Quitting ICAP meant losing their home.

He felt wetness on his chest. Monica sniffled. "I just don't want to lose you."

"You're not going—" His work phone chirped. He stepped back and looked at the screen. *Jeff.* "Excuse me," he said, disentangling himself from her arms before answering. "Rowley. Go ahead."

Monica leaned back against the kitchen counter.

"Matt, we got a mitochondrial DNA match on that skin you found. Close kin of the Alvarez family, who disappeared last month." Matt stepped onto the porch, slid the glass door closed, and popped in his ear bud. Monica dabbed her eyes with a tissue, then watched him pace on the deck. "We might have some of them in custody, but it's hard to tell. We've only got seven fingerprint matches out of the lot, and three are from a forensics merit badge project in White Sands from 1988."

"Still no cooperation from the perps?" Above him, a squirrel chittered in the pines. A cone landed at his feet, and tree litter drifted down around him.

"Um . . . they're eating at least."

Matt closed his eyes and listened to the wind through the trees. "That's something. So what's next?"

"Well, assuming some of them start talking—"

"I mean for my team." A wet nose nuzzled his ankle. He bent down and scooped Ted into his arms. The Basset tensed on the way up, then relaxed as he settled against Matt's chest, his tail thumping against the deck railing. "Dawkins. What's our next step?"

Jeff answered without hesitation. "I don't know if you're up on just how much that bust roiled the market. That was maybe fifteen, twenty percent of global production for the year. Street prices have skyrocketed, especially in the Southeast. Someone's got to be taking advantage of the supply vacuum."

Matt tried to play out the ramifications in his head. There were too many, so he scratched Ted between the ears instead. "Alright, let's start there."

Chapter 4

Akash Rastogi led them down the cobblestone alley, past rickety shacks displaying pirate-themed knickknacks made for the most part of plastic or carved wood. Despite the proximity to the Atlantic, sweat streamed from Matt's pores in St. Augustine's merciless humidity. The whole city smelled of sweating humanity, dead fish, and salt.

Garrett Johnson voiced Matt's unspoken thought. "Where are we going, again?"

With one irritated glance back, Akash pushed through a beaded curtain and into a dark building whose reek of incense bestowed a small mercy on Matt's nostrils. While his regular vision adjusted, his infrared and ultraviolet sight processed the tens, maybe hundreds of thousands of angel figurines, statues, carvings, and paintings that covered every available surface. A narrow aisle stretched between them, just wide enough to accommodate a man.

"Rastogi," Matt said, "I thought this was about Jade." Akash disappeared around the corner and reappeared with a large, angelic doll. The ancient wood had crumbled in places, and a bent copper frame held wings of sparse tinsel on its back. Whatever had served as its eyes had long since disappeared, as evidenced by the mildew-stained, empty sockets that stared back at him. The whispers babbled their nonsense as Akash lifted the fraying, moth-eaten robe to reveal a sexless, crude body of the same rotting wood. Matt stopped in shock.

Carved into the doll's chest lay the symbol from the angel's—the winged bonk's—forehead. He reached for it but stepped back as the proprietor came into view around the corner. A gaunt man, too tall, too skinny, and too pale, with rotting brown teeth, smiled down at him.

"I'm sorry, sirs, that figure isn't for sale." He wiped his hands on a faded purple V-neck and looked up at Garrett. "My, ain't you a big one." His accent seemed to Matt to be more southern Georgia than northern Florida coast.

"Why not?" Matt said. He'd meant to ask, "What can you tell me about it?"

The shopkeeper lifted the doll from Akash with both hands and placed it back on the shelf, pushing back several other figurines to make room. "She's too fragile for you to be handling her. I'm afraid she hasn't held up well in the Florida humidity." Akash muttered an apology as the owner continued. "She was the first to grace this shop with her presence, and the inspiration for my collection."

"Neat piece. How long have you had her?" Garrett asked.

"I bought the shop thirty-four years ago, meant to open a vacuum-cleaner store. That was before this area became overrun with pirate mania, mind. I found her in the corner in a pile of broken furniture and other rubbish. She seemed so lonely I got her friends. Before I knew it I had this." He held out his hands to the cramped space.

"What do you know about her?" Matt asked. "About the symbol on her chest?"

His smile broadened. "An interesting question, but not as interesting as how your friend here knew about her." He turned, not just his head but his whole body, to peer down at Akash.

Akash put his hands in his pockets and shrugged at the man. "I saw it maybe fifteen years ago when I was visiting with my family." He looked at Matt and Garrett. "I remembered it the second I saw the symbol, thought you guys might want to see it."

"Symbol?" the man asked.

Akash pulled a piece of paper out of his pocket and unfolded it to reveal a close-up shot of the symbol, black marker on pale brown leather, taken from the discarded skin of the Alvarez boy. "It's the same as on the doll, isn't it?"

"Yes," the man and Matt answered simultaneously. Matt continued, "Do you know what it means?"

He nodded. "Yes. But no. No one knows what it means." His eyes fluttered closed. He licked his cracked lips. "To the Aztecs, it symbolized a great sundering, a separation of the Quetzalcoatl from himself. The ancient Greeks used a glyph like that to represent Nyx, the goddess of night who, content with the dark half of eternity, took no followers and coveted nothing of Earth for herself." He ran his tongue over his teeth. "But that thing there also represented the Henostic creation of Demiurge from Monad's overflowing and self-reflection. Heck, even the Zoroastrians, they used it to represent the eternal conflict between Ahura Mazda and Angra Mainyu, wisdom and destruction." He shrugged and opened his eyes. "You might say it means too much to too many, so it don't mean nothing to me."

Matt spoke before Akash could. "Does it show up in Judeo-Christian, um, lore or whatever?" *Shit, that was elegant.*

Impossibly, the proprietor's lips stretched wider, revealing gums pockmarked with bleeding sores. "Not even once." The whispers entwined the words with malicious laughter as Matt watched that rotten grin.

"Does it have a name?" Akash asked.

"I've always called it Ul." The guttural syllable sounded something like "ool," but throatier. For a moment, something slithered behind the man's eyes, the shadow of barbed tentacles.

Matt stepped back into Garrett, blinked, and the whatever-it-was disappeared.

"You're augmented?" the man asked.

The change of subject caught Matt off-guard. "Uh, yes. We work for ICAP."

The man stiffened, and his smile faded to a grimace. "And you encountered the Ul in your work?"

"Yes," Matt said. "Can't really talk about where." To deflect the man's curiosity he asked a follow-up. "Are you an expert on angels, then?"

He shrugged and crossed his arms. "I guess, as far as anyone can be. You won't find two books that agree on nothing, much less two religions or cultures."

"Are there any with wings of smoke and silver feathers?"

He sighed and gave a pointed look to the exit. "Look, *friend*," he emphasized the word so that it meant anything but, "there ain't nothing I can tell you that you can't find on Wikipedia. If you ain't buying, I got other things to do."

"Thanks for your time." Matt tried to walk out, but had to wait for Garrett. If he tried to sidle past, he'd knock a bunch of figurines over. The proprietor said nothing as they left one-by-one, but never stopped watching them. Once outside, Matt gasped in a breath of "fresh" air. Oddly enough, the stink of salt water, fish, and over-concentrated humanity made a welcome reprieve from the oppressive incense.

"That was weird," Garrett said as they walked back toward the car.

"There was something very . . . off about that guy," Matt said. He glanced to the side at a writhing, slithering shadow, but as his eyes focused on it the image resolved as flags flapping in the breeze. *Shit, I'm jumpy today.* He took a deep breath and tried not to think about PTSD.

"He freaked me out as a kid, too," Akash said. "But I thought maybe he'd know more than what we could find poking around online."

Garrett frowned as he got in the front seat of the SUV. "I can't even remember whatever gibberish he said."

"You're not eidetic?" Akash asked, his eyebrows raised.

Garrett shook his head. "Under the new guidelines, it was that or reflex enhancements. I know my strengths." Matt didn't bother to remind him that he'd chosen Garrett more for his tactical mind than his physical prowess; he saw no point in testing the man's modesty. "As it is, I sometimes feel this weird pressure . . . ."

Matt locked eyes with Akash through the rearview mirror. They looked away, but too late.

"What?" Garrett said. "I'm not saying I'm about to bonk or anything."

Matt started the car, and sighed. "You know I'm going to have to report that comment." He waited for a cab to pass, then pulled out into the light traffic.

Garrett shook his head. "No you don't. I didn't mean anything by it. It's just stress."

Akash leaned forward and clapped Garrett on both shoulders. "Yes he does, and if he didn't, I'd have to, eh? There's no policy tighter than that one."

"Give me a break, guys. I didn't mean anything by it."

Matt swerved to the right and jerked to a stop, one tire against the curb. He locked eyes with Garrett as the SUV behind them blew its horn. "You can be sorry you said it, but think about this. If you were me, what choice would you have?"

Garrett glared at him. "I'd be faithful to the men under my command. Always."

Knowing it wasn't what Garrett wanted to hear, Matt said, "I'm glad you understand." He put the car in gear and hit the gas.

* * *

When they got back to their temporary office—a two-room suite at the Best Western Miami—Matt searched the internet for "ool" and "Ul" and "Ewl" and every other spelling he could think of, and came up blank. *Well I'm sure as hell not going back to ask him.*

He shivered and turned as a shadow blocked the light from the window.

Blossom Sakura nodded at the screen. "What are you looking for?"

"That guy Akash told you about? He said the symbol had a name, but I can't find it anywhere."

"Show me." She crouched next to his chair and turned the laptop so she could type. After a few minutes, she gave up, and they discussed the Florida operation. They had to postpone if they wanted Garrett in the field; he had to fly back to D.C. for a full psychological evaluation. In time, conversation again turned to the winged bonk.

Blossom gave him a short bow from her waist and dropped her gaze to the floor. "I can't say it any better. There's no such thing."

Matt sat down, his legs in as casual a pose as he could manage. "Aren't Kami angels?"

Blossom flopped down across from him. "No. Kami aren't angels. And they don't exist, either. Shinto is culture, not religion."

"Are you sure?"

She gave him a withering look. "I'm sure. Maybe some from Japan aren't sure, but I'm sure. There is no more evidence for Kami than for unicorns."

Matt smiled, conceding defeat. "So you don't believe in the supernatural. What do you believe in?"

Blossom froze for a split second, then disappeared. A moment later she sat on the edge of the couch next to his outstretched left foot, a framed picture in her hand. "Her. I believe in Kazuko, that she will make her mother proud."

A Japanese girl, no more than eight years old, sat on a swing, her innocent smile dominating the otherwise plain picture of a little girl in a white blouse and blue plaid skirt. "Beautiful name," Matt said. "What does it mean?"

"It means she is the only child I will have, and the debt I owe her is greater than her obligation to me."

Matt didn't know how to respond, so he nodded. She gave another curt bow and disappeared.

* * *

Two days later, the psychology department cleared Garrett for duty, and he flew back to Miami. Matt accepted his wounded, defiant looks with stoic indifference and planned the next phase of their mission. To his credit, Garrett's professional behavior didn't change a bit, though waves of resentment emanated from him.

That night Matt got a private memo, an addendum to Garrett's personnel file. Psyche screening maintained that he operated at safe levels, but empathy had dropped to borderline levels. They recommended that Brian keep Garrett's solo actions to a minimum, and flagged his file for further scrutiny over the next few weeks' tests.

Chapter 5

"I don't understand why Rastogi's making the buy," Garrett said.

Matt didn't turn away from the computer screen. "Because Sakura, you, and I smell like bacon so hard nobody would ever sell to any of us, Conor can't act his way out of a paper bag, and Akash looks like a college student. Now hush."

Matt knew the real reason for Garrett's foul mood. The video and audio from the digital camera and parabolic microphone were excellent in all the ways that sweating in a van under the Miami sun wasn't. The drone hovered a hundred feet overhead, at that distance indistinguishable from a dragonfly. An uncommon insect for this time of year, but even if the city-bound Miami drug dealer noticed, he wouldn't know better. Or so Matt hoped.

"In position," Blossom's voice said in his headset. The playground at the end of the block bustled with children playing and hollering in the sprinklers, except for three youths loitering on bicycles, who paid too much attention to everything around them and not enough to each other.

"Hit it," Matt said into the microphone.

Akash rolled past the playground down the hill and pulled the Prius up to the curb, his arm out the window, forty dollars held between his index and middle finger. The dealer, a scrawny African American male in his late teens or early twenties, wandered up to the car and took the cash.

"What you want?"

"Hey there," Akash said, his voice too loud in the microphone. "I'm looking for something green."

"Yeah yeah yeah," the guy said, looking both ways down the street. "But it's sixty."

"Seriously?" Akash produced another twenty. It disappeared with the others.

"Times is hard, brother." The dealer leaned against the car, and the juvenile on the red bike coasted down from the playground, pulling up next to the car with a plastic bag the size of a Splenda packet. Akash took it and pulled away without another word. The dealer went back to his stoop while the kid rode around the block.

"This stuff is shit, eh," Akash said. "It's shit for forty bucks, it's definitely shit for sixty."

"Explain," Matt said.

"It's cloudy, and the crystals aren't even all green. This is low, low grade, probably cut with meth or crack. Or Pop Rocks."

"Or drain cleaner," Garrett said.

"Classic cartel," Matt said. "Get it to the lab so we can trace the chemistry, find out who Dawkins is buying from."

"How do we know that's one of Dawkins's guys?" Garrett asked.

"Miami Metro Vice," Matt said. "They arrested him four times selling Dawkins's product, on that playground, before the Keys bust. He's still there, so whatever's going on, it ain't an escalating turf war."

"So what do you figure?" Akash asked over the radio.

"I figure Dawkins is buying from someone else, someone who sells cheap crap cut with cheaper crap, so he can maintain his supply lines for when he's back in product. Given the volume, we're looking at the Chinese, the Russians, the Mexicans, or all of the above. The specific chemistry should tell us which."

"Based on this crap," Akash said, "I'll bet you anything it's Mexican, eh?"

"Be patient," Matt said. "In a week or so the lab guys can tell us exactly where it came from, and we can move up the chain of command."

"What do we do once we find them?" Garrett asked.

Matt sighed. "We make them an offer they can't refuse."

* * *

"Oh, what now?" Garrett asked as they pulled up to 801 Broadway in Nashville. The massive, blocky Estes Kefauver Federal

Building and Courthouse Annex shared a parking lot with the First Lutheran Church, and together they occupied an entire city block. A crowd packed the church lot to standing room only, waving placards and hollering chants.

Red-on-yellow "Humans for Humanity" signs dominated, but "Legalize It," "No GMO Crops," and "Occupy Nashville" peppered the throng as well. Smaller knots of protesters dotted the sidewalk all the way around the buildings.

Matt rolled his eyes. "Apparently our presence at this fine facility has been noticed."

"Brilliant," Conor said. "Only took them what? A month? And us toting this giant sack of black around." He jerked a thumb at Garrett.

Matt parked down the block, but they had no way to avoid notice on the way in. Garrett took point, blazing a path down the sidewalk with his massive frame and impressive scowl. A Bible-waving, disheveled preacher in filthy clothes and a red-and-yellow stole stepped in their way, thought better of it, and stumbled to the side as Garrett stalked past. The crowd boiled out of the parking lot, but not fast enough.

Garrett pulled open the door, let the others through, then followed behind as the edge of the crowd reached the steps, shrieking and bellowing their rage. To their credit, they stopped the court-mandated twenty feet away.

Jeff met the team as they walked past the guards, hand extended for shakes all around.

"How long have they been here?" Matt asked him.

"Two days. They didn't seem to realize you guys were out of town." He led them to the elevator.

"Nothing an LRAD and some pepper bullets wouldn't fix," Conor said. "They tried this crap in Ireland and learned to regret it."

"I don't understand," Blossom said. "They don't want protection?"

Akash shook his head. "They're under the delusion that ICAP isn't needed to control the threat. They think regular law enforcement can deal with the likes of, well, us."

Garrett snorted. "Only if they catch us by surprise." He looked at Matt. "And good luck with that on the precogs."

"I'd have to be sleeping," Matt said. "Which is unlikely if I'm committing a crime."

Blossom furrowed her brow. "What's wrong with safe levels of augs? These people don't make sense."

"Of course they don't make sense," Akash said. "They're Americans, eh?"

They got out on the fifth floor, wandered past a maze of cubicles and into Matt's new office. The view of downtown Nashville would make any country fan jealous, and Matt kept the massive wood desk for the most part clutter-free, except for his laptop, a notepad, and a box of blue pens. The six of them made a crowd, and with only two chairs Jeff kept the briefing short and under two minutes.

"You flew all this way to tell us that?" Matt asked.

Jeff shrugged. "Last performance review they dinged me on visibility, buddy."

Garrett sighed. "Tax dollars at work."

* * *

Majestic pines and towering oaks dominated the mountainous skyline as Conor weaved the Jeep down the unpaved forest road. Matt grunted as a chipmunk crossed in front of them. The two-lane tunnel of trees through dappled sunlight smelled of pine and decomposing leaves, and the only man-made sound came from their engine. "This could almost be Tennessee."

"Not bloody likely," Conor said. "It's so hot you work a sweat just having a piss."

That wasn't quite true, but Coahuila's Indian summer spiked well hotter than Tennessee in late September, even halfway up the Sierra Madre Orientals. Still, if he didn't know his location, he'd never have guessed Mexico. They splashed through a puddle twenty feet across as they rounded the next corner. A young man stood in the middle of the road, hand outstretched, fingers splayed, an assault rifle slung across his back. His Mexican military uniform bore no patches or insignia.

He approached at a casual walk as they slid to a stop, asking questions in rapid-fire Spanish. As Conor responded, Matt's infrared vision picked up seven red-and-orange blotches hidden in the foliage. The man spoke into a shoulder mic, patted the hood, then stepped out of the way.

"He told me to go slow," Conor said. "We're almost there."

A half-mile further, the road opened up. A huge, well-manicured yard surrounded a stone-and-mortar, single-story mansion, more porch than house, with a terra-cotta roof and a large in-ground pool. The guards didn't bother to hide themselves, and for the first time Matt missed his combat shotgun and helmet. And Garrett, Blossom, and Akash, who waited at the airport as per the arrangement; two men in, no weapons.

A man watched their approach from the front of the house, leaning against a pillar, his arms crossed. Matt recognized Onofre Garza from the pictures in his file. Five-three, too thin, with a pencil mustache and pale brown skin, he didn't fit the popular image of a cartel overlord. The blue-and-yellow Hawaiian shirt, khaki cargo shorts and bare feet didn't help. A firm grip with calloused hands accompanied his welcome in near-perfect English.

"Welcome to my home, gentlemen. Come inside, before the day gets too hot." His gums and tongue were stained red, a vestige of an impoverished childhood spent chewing achiote. He turned his back on them and led the way up the stairs. His shirt bulged at his waistline in the telltale sign of a pistol tucked down the back of his shorts. The spacious interior, teak floors, and sparse mahogany furniture looked more like a gallery than a home. An empty gallery. Aside from dark plum drapes with brass finials, nothing adorned, cluttered, or otherwise occupied the walls.

They sat at a small table. Matt ran his hands over the mahogany, admiring the craftsmanship. A dark-skinned tween girl with long black hair carried in a silver tray. She poured them coffee in delicate china cups, set out sugar cubes and a pitcher of cream, accepted their thanks with a nod, and disappeared through a doorway. Garza toasted in her direction, then took a sip. "My daughter, Aracelia. Beautiful girl, like her mother."

"You're a lucky man," Conor said, dropping two sugars and a huge drizzle of cream into his cup.

Matt's black coffee tasted as good as it smelled, strong and just bitter enough.

"Yes," Garza replied. "Forgive me, but I have much to do today, so let us get straight to business. Your superiors said you have an offer for me."

Matt ran his tongue over his front teeth. As an investigator for the Tennessee State Police, he'd cut dozens of deals with criminals for one reason or another, but none of those criminals were drug lords. The man across from him wasn't a two-bit thug selling dime bags on the corner. Busting a syndicate boss like Onofre Garza would make a policeman's career. Hell, it would make the head of the DEA's career. Garza had enough outstanding warrants that the only hard part about arresting him would be dealing with the Mexican authorities, and under UN treaty, ICAP had wide latitude when prosecuting the Jade market.

Matt suppressed the thought and the accompanying sigh. Conor had tagged along just in case he needed a translator en route, but Garza spoke perfect English, so it fell to Matt to make the deal, no matter how slimy it made him feel.

"Senor Garza, thank you for your hospitality." He took another sip. "As you know, ICAP's main goal is the containment of Gerstner technologies, in particular Jade, and above and beyond that we have a vested interest in apprehending and prosecuting Dawkins. We're looking for information: who he is, where he operates, known associates. He's made this personal, and we're inclined to take him up on it."

Garza smiled. "This distinction between business and personal is for the movies, no? Business is livelihood, livelihood is personal." He shook off the thought. "No matter. The real question is why I would do such a thing for you. As they say, what's in it for me?" He smiled his red smile.

Conor folded his hands under his chin. "What do you want?" Matt suppressed an annoyed grunt. Conor wasn't trained in negotiation, and his instructions were to keep his trap shut.

Garza sighed and leaned back in his chair. "What do any of us want? Money? Power? Beautiful women? The freedom to live in a paradise of my own making? I have these things already."

Then why aren't you retired? Conor opened his mouth to ask.

Matt cut him off before he could start. "I'm sure there's something of value to your business interests that we could provide. A foothold in Florida?"

"Senor Dawkins has provided this already. Your adventure in the Keys cost him a great deal of money but has made me more still. Money doesn't disappear, it just goes elsewhere. To me and my associates, for example. This drug war is not a winnable fight for your—"

Conor cut him off. "As soon as he's up and running again, you're out of Florida. The only way that's not true is if—"

Matt grabbed him by the arm and dragged him to the entrance, his vision flushing red. Through clenched teeth he said, "If you can't keep your goddamned mouth shut, wait outside." He opened the door, shoved Conor through, and shut it. He walked back to the table, where Garza looked at him with raised eyebrows. "I'm sorry, Senor Garza, for my colleague's behavior. If we may continue?"

Garza gestured to the chair, so Matt sat.

"As I was saying, my organization already has a foothold in Florida because of the supply vacuum you so graciously created. Dawkins will like this territory back, to be sure, but that does not mean we will surrender what we have gained, and he knows it. We have the matter well in hand and are confident that our plans going forward do not require your assistance. Let's not dance around with these petty offerings. What do you have that I want?"

"Hernando," Matt said.

Garza froze. "What about him?"

"Depending on the level of cooperation, we could arrange a transfer from ADX Florence to house arrest somewhere in the United States." A former warden once described the "supermax" prison as a "cleaner version of Hell," and Hernando Garza had earned his place there as his brother's chief enforcer north of the border. According to his dossier, Onofre had a tendency to murder anyone who reminded him of this fact. "He could see his family, and we'd allow supervised, monitored phone calls."

Garza's shrug revealed nothing. "Prison is prison. Freedom is freedom. I will consider helping you in exchange for my brother's extradition to Mexico."

"I don't think that's going to happen."

Garza slammed his cup onto the table, sloshing scalding coffee over his fingers. "Ask." His killer's eyes bored into Matt's, every hint of hospitality burned away. "Call them, or get out." His eyes flicked to the door, then down to his hand. He picked up a cotton napkin, wiped the table and his fingers, then set it down next to the cup.

"Excuse me a moment." Matt stepped away and pulled out his cell phone. The satellite uplink would work anywhere in the world, but the four bars of local service surprised him. He stared out the window as he talked to Jeff, who in turn had to call someone else in

Washington. The forested mountains out the window stood taller and perhaps more majestic than home but were no more beautiful. After a lengthy conversation he returned to the table.

"We'll consider extradition in exchange for Dawkins's whereabouts leading to his capture. We get him, you get Hernando."

"No. Verified whereabouts only, not guarantee of capture. You want Senor Dawkins brought back to the fold, that's up to you. I mean no offense, but recent successes aside, I'll not bet my brother's freedom on your agency's competence."

A dozen replies went through Matt's mind. "Um . . . What do you mean, 'back to the fold?'"

Garza smirked. "Surely your superiors have told you. Senor Dawkins was one of yours. An ICAP agent."

Matt's heart pounded. "Excuse me?"

Garza gave a dismissive wave of his hand. "It doesn't matter. What your superiors choose not to tell you is not my problem. Do we have a deal?" He'd walked halfway to the door by the time Matt replied.

"Yes." The idea of freeing a man like Hernando Garza sickened him, but bagging Dawkins would be worth the price. Maybe.

Garza smiled, one hand on the doorknob. "Excellent. I will be contacting you through a surrogate within the month. Good day, Senor Rowley." He opened the door.

The porch glistened with bright, wet redness, and the air smelled of iron and shit. A red-blue, ropy garland hung between the main columns. *Intestines.*

Matt reached for a sidearm that wasn't there.

Garza pulled the pistol from his shorts and ducked behind the door. "What is the meaning of this?"

Matt admired the gun, an Obregon .45 ACP, with mother-of-pearl grips and gold etching on the barrel. A seven-shot semi-automatic. At this range a center-of-mass shot would make a mess of him, regenerates or no. A hit to the head or heart would kill him, no question. Matt decided to tell the truth.

"I don't know."

Garza spat out a string of Spanish. Matt caught *puta* and nothing else. Whispers rejoiced in the muzzle flash the instant before it happened. He dove to the left, and the report followed him through the kitchen door.

Aracelia sat at the counter, mouth agape, a half-sliced apple in one hand, a paring knife in the other. He ducked past her, grabbed a rolling pin from the counter, and grunted in pain. The girl had driven the knife into his kidney. He backhanded her off the stool and hurled the pin toward the door, pulling the throw so the impact would be non-lethal. It took Garza in the forehead just as he peeked around the corner. Aracelia rebounded off a cupboard, and the bodies collapsed together. Grunting, Matt pulled out the knife and dropped it.

His third step pinned Garza's wrist to the floor. He plucked up the .45 and checked the magazine. Six, plus one in the chamber. Garza's eyes lost their glaze, so Matt pointed the gun at his forehead. The wound in his side itched as his kidney knitted together.

"Onofre, I'm not trying to hurt you, but I will if I have to. Can I help you up?" He held out his left hand. Garza looked from the hand to the gun and back, then reached up. Matt pulled him up. He spun the pistol so that it faced Garza grip-first. "You need that more than I do. Don't shoot at me again."

Garza took it, then knelt by his daughter, semi-conscious and babbling in Spanish. "What happened?"

"She'll be okay. She stabbed me. Where the hell are your guards?"

Garza shook his head. "They should be here by now. Dozens of them."

No one moved on the lawn, and he heard no footsteps. "Do you have somewhere to hide?" Garza nodded to a door behind Matt.

Matt yanked it open. Wine cellar. "Get in there. Don't come out until I give the all-clear. Where's your security feed?"

Garza shook his head as he cradled his daughter in his arms. "Off-site. Helicopters will be coming."

Matt ducked into the cellar with them and pulled out his phone. He called Conor. It picked up on the third ring. Conor said nothing, so Matt kept his voice low. "Flynn. What's your status?"

A sloppy gurgle answered him, almost a voice. It sounded like Conor, but low, guttural.

"What the hell is going on?"

The line went dead. He tried Jeff. The phone rang once, and Jeff picked up. "Mexican military choppers are inbound on your position. A lot of them. What's your status?"

Matt hesitated. "I think Flynn bonked out."

"That's ridiculous. He passed his psych screen two days ago, same as the rest of you."

"Fire the goddamned shrink. And get me an evac." He hung up the phone and turned to Garza, who sat on the floor with his daughter's head in his lap, stroking her hair. "Do you have any weapons down here?"

Garza patted the pistol, on the floor next to him. "Just this."

"Keep it," Matt said. He stepped out the door and closed it behind him with as much stealth as he could manage. Crouching low, he peered through the dining room. Outside in the grass, a uniformed man lay on his back, but with his head face down. He saw no sign of the other guards he'd seen on the way in—the heat of the day obscured Matt's infra-red vision, and even with UV augmentation he couldn't see more than a few feet into the foliage.

He grabbed a pair of chef's knives from the kitchen, each one a nine-inch blade of razor-sharp steel, and crept from room to room, searching the house for any sign of Conor. Chunks of meat lay scattered across the side veranda in an ocean of steaming blood, with only a single hand to identify it as human. Or humans. He closed his eyes.

Breathing in the next room, sharp and frantic. The scent of jasmine mingled with blood and sweat and urine, and under that, aftershave. Conor always used classic Old Spice.

Matt opened his eyes. Muscles taut, he turned the corner.

Conor crouched naked over a crying woman, one hand on her shoulder, the other easing a ropy coil of intestine from her abdomen. Words Matt didn't understand crisscrossed Conor's body in a red-brown tattoo, a jumble of runes and letters—Roman, Gaelic, Cyrillic, Sanskrit, Chinese, Arabic . . . .

For the moment, the woman lived, her entrails intact. If he could stop Conor, she might survive.

"Conor," he said. "Can we talk?"

The woman continued her sharp, short breaths as Conor pulled another foot of bowel from her stomach. She would have been pretty, with chocolate skin and stunning eyes the same tan as her silk sundress. Instead she looked broken, covered in blood, face bathed in terror and pain. Her eyes rose at his voice but looked through him.

"It was an ambush," Conor said. "They were going to kill us." He didn't let go, and Matt couldn't risk violence while he still held her. His neck twitched. "Try. They were going to try."

"Fair enough. But you got them. It's over."

Conor didn't move.

"You want to get going?"

"No," he said. "I'm busy." He turned to smile at Matt, his face dripping with blood and offal. "There are three left." He let go of the woman, and Matt lunged.

The whispers clawed through his mind, pushing him to rejoice in murder but warning him of every strike before it came. He stepped over Conor's sweep, blocked the heart strike with his left hand, and slashed his right across the naked man's throat. Conor's blood drenched Matt in sticky, salty heat. The impact of Conor's fist carried him through the wall, his ribs on fire. He hit the ground and rolled to his feet, then dove sideways without looking, striking out with his left hand.

Conor sailed past, into a table. The knife ripped out of Matt's grip, the hilt buried between Conor's ribs.

Matt winced as he caught the blade an inch from his face, all four fingers cut to the bone. His left foot crunched into Conor's throat, and the man stumbled back, no longer bleeding. The blade slid out of Matt's hand and clattered to the floor. He flexed his fingers. Stiff and unresponsive—the nerves would need another moment.

"You can't win," Matt said, buying time. Conor's augmented reflexes were no match for precognition, but he out-muscled Matt by a good ten percent and healed just a shred faster.

"No," Conor said, his naked, tattooed, blood-drenched body whole and unblemished. Matt wasn't sure if Conor was agreeing with him or not.

The window shattered as he carried Conor through it, jamming a shard of glass past his eye and into his brain. Conor's fist broke his jaw even as Matt brought the second knife down. The steel split Conor's skull. He twisted it sideways, pulled it halfway out, and jammed it in again.

Conor bit through his sleeve and tore a chunk of his bicep off with his teeth. Matt grunted as Conor grabbed his left thigh, crushed his femur with a punch, and tore his leg off above the knee. Everything went numb.

Conor laughed and spit a chuck of meat into Matt's face.

Matt dug his fingers into either side of the knife, then pulled. Conor's skull came apart, revealing pink-gray jelly glistening with blood and cerebral fluid. Conor jammed his fingers into Matt's stomach and tore out a chunk of viscera. Matt brought his palms together, pulping Conor's brain between them.

The world faded to red, then black.

Chapter 6

The world reverberated, impossibly loud. Matt's leg spasmed with searing pain, and his stomach burned. He tried to sit up, to move his arms, to lift his head. Strapped down, he couldn't. He opened his eyes. A Hispanic man in a blood-streaked white coat and earmuffs with a microphone smiled down at him. The man's lips moved, but Matt heard nothing over the thundering rotors of the helicopter.

Akash's voice rang in his ears. "Look, I'm not saying it doesn't suck, but there's no way they could let you back. They banned Ethridge for life, and all he had was what, a little adrenal boost and level one musculoskeletal? And he wrecked people. Even if the league allowed it, you'd kill someone. Everyone."

Matt shook off his confusion and realized he had headphones on.

"I'd kill a normal, sure," Garrett's voice responded. "But how cool would a gridiron full of augs be? Can you imagine the playbooks? The *hits*?"

"Guys?" Matt asked.

Akash appeared over him, a smile on his face. "Hey, look who's awake!"

"Is the woman—"

"Housekeeper. She'll live, we think." His smile disappeared as he transitioned from down-time to go-time. "Your guts are good. Jaw feeling better?"

Matt relaxed with a deep sigh, opened his mouth, and flexed it side to side. The muscles pinched, too tight, but everything seemed to be in working order. "Yeah. How's my leg?"

"Still knitting. We had to keep cutting off the muscle until the bone healed."

"But—"

"You're fine. Give it an hour or two, eh?"

Garrett broke in. "Glad to have you back, Sergeant."

"Thanks, Garrett." He locked eyes with Akash. "Flynn?"

His smile vanished. "Dead. Very dead. Bonked, did he?"

Matt gritted his teeth against the millions of needles shredding his thigh. "Yeah. No. He went crazy, but it wasn't . . . normal. He spoke to me."

He blinked, and Blossom appeared, scowling at him. "Once a bonk snaps, he doesn't talk. Just kills."

"I know, but he did. It wasn't a psychotic rage. He was downright calm." In his mind's eye, the woman's intestines spilled out on the floor into a circle, cut by a line. *Did it happen that way?* His enhanced, eidetic memory fuzzed on the detail.

Her frown deepened. "What he say?" She unbuckled his head strap and pulled the steel-reinforced leather off of him.

Matt cracked his neck as she worked on his torso restraints. "He said it was an ambush and they were going to kill us."

"Was it?" Garrett asked.

Matt thought for a moment. The guards hadn't been tense, nor had Onofre. "No. Even if Garza had augs on standby, there's no way he'd plan an ambush with his daughter serving coffee."

"Don't sit up yet," Blossom said. "We're keeping your leg secure for a half hour." She looked down at it. "Maybe longer. Don't wiggle."

He lay back, and tears sprang unbidden to his eyes.

"I know," Akash said, patting his shoulder. "He was my friend, too."

* * *

When they touched down in Texas, Matt could put weight on the leg, but he didn't get off the plane. Instead he brooded out the window, his dark thoughts at odds with the clear blue sky. Conor's psychological break bothered him, but somehow less so than Garza's statement that Dawkins had been an ICAP agent.

Jeff boarded, and Matt let him get situated before weighing into him. Jeff put his bags in the overhead compartment, then spoke as he flopped down.

"That was a hell of a thing, huh?"

Matt looked out the window. "That's one way to put it."

Jeff patted his shoulder in an odd echo of Akash's gesture. *Is that what you do to the traumatized? Pat their shoulder?* "Well you just relax, buddy, and we'll deal with the debrief stuff later."

Akash checked his brace. "You'll be right as rain in no time. We can probably pull the brace off mid-flight." Considering how much his leg itched, Matt figured it had to be healing in record time. That, or it'd fall off any second.

Garrett tossed a pair of ICAP-issue urban camouflage pants in his lap. "Then you can put these on, and stop showing off to the world." He sat next to Akash.

"Thanks." Matt rolled his head to the side so he could look at Jeff. "So Garza said something that's got me . . . I don't know." Jeff raised his eyebrows and smirked, so he just blurted it out. "Was Dawkins ICAP?"

All talk on the plane stopped. Jeff opened his mouth, closed it, then licked his lips. "Uh . . . what makes you ask that?"

"Was he?" Blossom asked from behind them.

Jeff's eyes widened. "No, no of course not." He patted Matt on the shoulder again. "Why, did Garza say something like that, buddy?"

Matt hated it when Jeff patronized him. "Yeah. He said something about us 'bringing him back into the fold.' Just before all hell broke loose."

Jeff grinned. "He's just messing with you, man. Just because he's willing to cooperate to get his brother back doesn't mean he likes us any. He knows we'll bring him down when the time comes, so he's getting his licks in where he can." He shifted in his seat. "Excuse me, I got to hit the head." Jeff got up and walked to the front of the plane, where he slipped into the bathroom.

Blossom sat next to him in a flash, her gaze boring holes in his head. "He said that. Garza."

Matt nodded.

"Did you believe him?"

Matt shrugged. "I think he thought it was true."

"What would make him believe that Dawkins was ICAP?"

He shrugged again. "I don't have any answers. That's why I asked Jeff."

Akash half-turned in his seat, and kept his voice low. "Sorry, but anyone else not quite buy Jeff's ignorance act?"

Garrett scowled. "Why would he lie? He's always got that used-car-salesman smirk, makes it seem like he's hiding something, but there's nothing here to hide. If Dawkins used to be ICAP, that'd be just one more reason to take him down, yeah?"

"I guess so," Matt said. "Still, it's a pretty weird thing to say."

Jeff came out of the bathroom, hand in his pocket. Matt couldn't quite shake the notion that his question had prompted Jeff to make a phone call.

* * *

He walked off the plane in Tennessee. His leg itched like hell as he drove home in the dimming light, and he went easy on the old truck's accelerator. He rounded the bend, pulled into his driveway, and killed the engine. Monica met him at the door with a cup of tea in her hands and a broad smile.

"I'm sorry, mister, but my husband won't be back until Tuesday, and he don't like me letting strangers in the house."

He quirked a grin. "Can't say I blame him, ma'am. If I had a wife as beautiful as you . . . ."

She looked delicious in a threadbare SheDaisy T-shirt as old as the hills and sheer enough that it'd cause a scandal if she wore it into town. Her athletic legs were still firm under the yellow stretch pants but showed traces of pregnant pudge.

She raised an eyebrow and affected her best Scarlett O'Hara as she set her cup on the end table inside the door. "I am immune to such flattery, sir." She stepped forward, pressing her chest into his, then slid her hands into his back pockets. Nibbling his chin, she pulled him inside. "Well, maybe I won't tell him, just this once." She had his shirt off before he'd taken three steps, and dropped to her knees to undo his belt. If any part of his injury still showed, she didn't react to it.

When they'd finished, Monica's skin glistened, and she collapsed beside him, panting. She tickled the sparse tuft of hair on his chest, and he felt her heart racing as he rested his hand on the growing mound of her belly. His heart thundered on at its steady pace, an atomic clock of augmented meat. He hadn't even broken a sweat.

"Well," she said. "This is a nice surprise."

He recognized the question in her cautious statement. "Yeah. We finished up in Mexico faster than we thought." She didn't reply, so he added, "I have to fly to D.C. tomorrow morning for a meeting, but I'll be home in the afternoon. Not sure what the schedule is from there." He felt no need to tell her that the 'meeting' consisted of Conor Flynn's autopsy.

"If you want to come to Momma's on Sunday, she could use a hand with that gutter after service."

He kissed her nose. "Can't promise, but I'll see what I can do."

She squeezed him, then lay cradled under his arm, the tension draining from her. As her breaths turned to soft snores, he stared at the ceiling and fought off dreams of Conor, laughing at him as he tore his skull in half.

The whispers startled him from sleep, and he opened his eyes to an empty ceiling. He reached over to an empty pillow.

Monica screamed.

He rolled off the bed and raced to the bathroom, leaping over Ted as the Basset sat up in the hall. Monica stared into the toilet with tear-filled eyes, the water pink. Her hand, slick with blood, grabbed her abdomen. She winced and hunched over. "Nonononono . . . ."

He swept her pajama bottoms from the floor, grabbed a roll of toilet paper out of the cupboard, and cradled her in his arms. "It'll be okay." He carried her outside, set her in the truck, jammed the stick into reverse, and gunned the gas. He buried the speedometer, with only an occasional sniffle from Monica or growl from a passing car to break the drone of the engine. They were halfway to the hospital before he realized he wore only his boxers and that he'd left his phone and wallet on the nightstand.

There were two people in the Emergency Room when he carried Monica through the automatic doors: a black triage nurse and a bleach-blonde secretary, both of whom sprang to their feet. He stepped to the nurse. "I think my wife is having a mis—"

"Don't you say it," Monica snapped. "Don't you fucking say it."

"—a problem with her baby."

The nurse nodded to her right. "Room one." As she followed them in, Matt heard over the PA, "Doctor Savard to the ED. Doctor Savard to the ED."

He set Monica on the bed, and the nurse shooed him out of the room, after drawing the curtain to block his view. Monica's blood streaked his forearm. Numb, he went into the bathroom and scrubbed it off, watching until the last pink streak swirled down the drain, then took a seat in the waiting room. A long hour went by, worse than the wait before a firefight. After another forty-five minutes, he stood as a middle-aged woman in a white coat came out. Gray streaked her blonde hair, which she'd pulled up in a bun held with chopsticks.

"Mister Rowley?" She offered her hand. He shook it. Her smooth hands had not a trace of callous, and her fingernails were painted a green so faint it almost looked natural. Her green eyes locked onto his, though she had to crane her neck to do so. He sighed in relief the moment before she spoke, her voice a pleasant Mississippi drawl. "Everything's okay. The baby's fine, your wife's fine."

"What happened?"

She sat down, and motioned to the empty chair beside her. He fell into it.

"Well," she said. "Your wife had what's called a subchorionic hematoma. The symptoms are a bit like a miscarriage—vaginal bleeding, mild cramping—and it some cases it can lead to an increased risk." His heart caught in his throat. "This hematoma was small, and carries little elevated risk."

"Little," he said.

She nodded. "Yes. Really no more than a normal pregnancy. We're going to keep her for observation overnight and recommend limited bed rest for the next week. No heavy lifting, no exercise, but she can move around the house a bit."

"Can I see her?"

Her smile softened. "You can, but we had to sedate her, bless her heart. She'll sleep some hours now."

"You're sure she's fine? And the baby?"

"I'm sure. A bit shook up is all."

"I have to catch a flight at eight. Do you know when she'll wake up?"

She patted his wrist. "Oh, well after that. Why don't you go on in, give her a kiss, and get on home? We'll call you when she wakes up. She's in good hands here."

He exhaled, and only then realized he'd been holding his breath.

* * *

The morgue smelled of polished steel and bleach. Conor Flynn's body lay on the cold metal slab, his head an unrecognizable flap of skin and cartilage. The coroner, an obese man with a bad comb-over, took pictures of the red-brown tattoos that covered the body, a stark contrast to Conor's pale skin. They looked amateur, almost primitive. Matt didn't recognize a single word. Given the look on his face, Jeff didn't either.

An Asian man who looked no older than thirteen cut tiny samples from several of the tattoos and carried them to a lab station against the wall. Matt couldn't place the meandering tune the technician hummed, but the cheery melody struck him as out of place. Matt wished he'd stop.

"Do you think he did those himself?" Matt asked.

Jeff grunted. "What makes you think that?"

Matt rolled the corpse on its side to expose Conor's back, ignoring the coroner's disapproving cluck. "Look. The letters on his back are much sloppier than the letters on his front. If a tattoo artist did them, they'd be more consistent. Cleaner."

The coroner grunted. "Why would a man tattoo himself with gibberish?"

Matt shrugged. "Why would a man let someone else tattoo him with gibberish? It doesn't make sense either way."

"True," Jeff said. "But we're shopping these pictures around the local parlors and police stations just in case. I think maybe you're right, but that's no reason not to check other options."

"Well," the coroner said, "preliminary analysis says there's nothing overly strange, nothing physically abnormal beyond standard ICAP Augmentations. Cranial abnormalities are of course impossible to assess, though we might get some brain chemistry from some of the larger pieces, drugs or whatnot. Bath salts, maybe."

"Nah," Matt said. "Drugs pass through my system so fast there's no point, and Conor's regenerates were even more effective than mine. He'd have to take bath salts every minute to sustain a high, and it wouldn't do any long-term damage."

"Well, we'll check anyway." Without preamble the doctor picked up a rotary saw and cut through Conor's sternum—it took twice as long as with a regular man, and the scent of burning bone reminded Matt of the dentist's office. The chest spreader split Conor's rib cage to expose glistening internal organs. Matt's biology education stopped at his freshman year in college, but everything looked normal to him.

Jeff pulled him aside. "Maybe it was PCP or something, something his regenerates didn't respond to. We've never seen brain abnormalities in a bonk anyway, and this behavior wasn't exactly textbook." He handed Matt a manila folder labeled "Flynn, Conor."

Opening it, Matt leafed through Conor's psychological profiles over the previous five years. There were no significant changes from one to the next, except for a spate of mild depression three years earlier when his eighteen-year-old dog passed away.

"I told you," Jeff said. "He was as sane as you or me this time last week."

The humming technician looked up from his lab station. "Mister Hannes?" They turned to him. "These tattoos are blood."

Jeff raised an eyebrow. "How do you know?"

"Chromatography indicated that it was possible, so I ran a Takayama test. Pyridine forms pink crystals when it reacts with hemoglobin." He gestured toward the microscope, and Jeff took a look.

His eyes buried in the lenses, Jeff asked, "Is it human?"

The man shrugged. "That takes a lot longer to figure out. The lab should have results in a week or two."

While Matt looked, Jeff spoke to the tech. "Well, tell them to step on it. And if it's human, I want DNA."

As promised, pink crystals impregnated the whitish background of the microscope slide.

"Will do," the tech replied.

A pleasant female voice broke over the PA. "Mr. Hannes, I have linguistics on line three."

"That was fast," Matt said, stepping away from the microscope.

Jeff picked up the phone, identified himself, and jotted notes in a small notepad. Matt spent a few minutes avoiding the autopsy table, while the coroner harvested and weighed organs, speaking for the benefit of the microphone. Jeff hung up the phone. "Well, that's fucked up."

"Gibberish?" Matt said.

Jeff shook his head. "On the contrary, there are sixty-seven unique tattoos, and every single one says a variation on the same thing: 'Be ready. The master is coming.' The most interesting one is on his left ribs. Cindy called it, 'Uruk proto-cuneiform.' It's early Bronze Age, like six thousand years ago."

Matt flipped to Conor's résumé in the front of the file. "Conor knew, what, nine languages?"

Jeff shrugged. "But not Uruk proto-cuneiform. He was a polyglot, not a linguist. He never studied any dead languages."

"That we know of."

Jeff shrugged. "That we know of."

Matt tapped the coroner on the shoulder. "Hey, we know how old these tattoos are?"

The man's jowls shook as he nodded. "Regenerates make it impossible to tell based on healing rate or anything of the sort, but knowing that he used blood for ink allows us to narrow it down quite a bit." He leaned in for a closer look, hemmed and hawed for a minute, then stood to his full height. "Based on the limited photobleaching and strong pigmentation, let's call the oldest ones no more than two years or so, but no newer than a year."

Jeff asked, "When's the most recent?"

He chuckled. "It's not that accurate. As far as I know it could have been this morning."

"Can you tell the time between them?"

He shrugged. "I can't. But I'd be confident testifying that they spread out over at least a year."

Matt handed the folder of psychological profiles back to Jeff. "So much for these."

Jeff set the folder on the table and threw up his hands. "You can't just ignore the evidence. This incident shouldn't have happened."

"Right, he didn't bonk," Matt said. "It wasn't like that at all. It wasn't mindless rage." He laughed, a soulless, lost bark. "It wasn't even rage. He acted like he wanted more cream in his coffee or had decided to clean the garage. Only he decided to slaughter eighteen people instead." Matt ran his hands through his hair. "And 'The master is coming'? I can't be the only person thinking this is related to our winged friend back in New Mexico."

Jeff shrugged. "That was 'The Servant,' buddy. Maybe they work in the same office."

"Not funny."

Jeff turned to look at Conor's headless, now empty torso. "No. No, it's not."

* * *

By the time Matt flew back to Tennessee and drove to the hospital, Monica had woken up and taken a cab home, against medical advice. They handed him an envelope containing her cross and wedding ring, which they'd removed during her examination, and gave him more than his share of admonishing looks.

"She promised that she'd take it easy," the doctor told him.

He lead-footed it home, then pulled in the driveway at a crawl. He eased the door shut after he got out. He tiptoed to the deck so as to not disturb her rest.

He crept up the steps, skipping the third, and swore under his breath when the screen door creaked. The latch on the door to the deck clicked as he stepped inside. *Oh, good,* he thought. *She's not asleep.* He stepped around the corner to the kitchen, just as she backed out of the pantry. "Baby, you really shouldn't have—"

She turned to him with guilty eyes, always a terrible liar even before she'd said anything. *I was just getting some lunch—*

"I was just getting some lunch—"

He stepped forward and interrupted her with a kiss, ashy and unpleasant. Nudging her to the side, he opened the pantry and scanned the shelves. She burst into tears as he picked up the can of Folgers and tore off the lid. Upending the grounds into the sink, he picked out the half-full pack of Marlboros and crushed them in his fist. He closed his eyes without turning around.

She sobbed. "I'm sorry, baby, I just—" She yelped as his fist shattered the countertop.

Blood dripped from his knuckles onto the broken stone. He flexed as the skin healed over the exposed bone, then took a better look at the counter. The marble slab had broken into four large chunks, the drawer underneath cracked in two. *Better it than her.*

His temper in check, he took a deep breath and turned around. "You were saying?"

She wrapped her arms around him and buried her face in his chest. He held her, patting her hair as she cried. One minute. Two. Five. When she'd cried herself out, he scooped her off her feet and carried her to the couch. By the time he sat, she'd already fallen asleep.

He picked up the remote and turned on the TV. With *Sharktopus vs. Mansquito* the most compelling option, he pulled up the previous week's Titan's game on DVR. Ted made it onto the couch on his third try, and lay down half on Monica, his head on Matt's thigh. His tail thumped the cushion as Matt scratched his head, and he snored his way through the fourth play. Monica woke up in the third quarter, curled around Ted to use him as a body pillow, and they watched the rest of the game in silence. When it ended—28-17 over the Texans—he turned off the TV.

"The whole time?" he asked.

She shook her head without lifting it. "No. Just this past week. Only one a day. Sometimes two. Never more than that."

He sighed. "Just cigarettes?"

Her head jiggled by way of reply, but he couldn't make out a "yes" or a "no."

"Weed?" He didn't want to say it. "Meth?"

"Just cigs. I ain't done anything in three years, you know that."

"Drink?"

Ted gave a happy whine as she squeezed him, and licked her arm. "I'm still on that wagon. There's nothing in the house, and Momma makes sure there's nothing there, neither." Matt sighed again, this time in relief. They sat in silence for a while. He knew she wanted something else, or she'd have gotten up to do something. He didn't know what it could be, so he waited.

"Matt?"

"I'm here, Mon."

"Aren't you going to ask?"

He rolled his eyes, thankful she couldn't see his face, and shifted his weight to disguise the gesture. "I'm precognitive, baby, not telepathic. What am I supposed to ask?"

She sat up, dumping Ted on the floor. He shook off the sleep, trotted three steps, and collapsed under the coffee table. Monica's face crumbled into tears as she looked Matt in the eyes. "You're supposed to ask why."

Matt had assumed the near-miscarriage had triggered the relapse, but in retrospect the timing didn't fit. He realized then that he didn't care why. He loved his wife and would do anything for her, but when it came to this . . . junkies lie. That's what they'd always said on the force. She couldn't produce an excuse good enough, nothing that would justify smoking while pregnant with their son . . . and yet she needed something, something she didn't have and he wasn't sure how to give. Hell, he didn't even know what to give, much less how. So he asked.

"Why?"

"I don't know." She sobbed and hugged him again and rambled into his chest. He caught something about distance and being lonely and worried and afraid, so he held her and uttered reassurances he felt but didn't mean until she fell asleep again. She didn't wake up when he moved her from the couch to the bed.

He lay there, restless, listening to a loon's mournful cry in the distance. He knew it wasn't sad, but it sure sounded like it. The clock on the wall read one o'clock. He sat up, shifted Ted off his feet, and got dressed.

Eight minutes later he pulled into Tony's, a former garage, the only place in White Spruce open this late. Ten years back, Tony's sandwiches had started selling better than his maintenance, so Matt's high school buddy had stopped working on cars and converted the garage to a BBQ Bar and Grill. Matt walked through the Old West-style swinging doors to the sound of Brooks & Dunn's *Neon Moon*.

Two gray-bearded men sat at the bar, local handyman Jedd Callaway and thirty-year-mayor-turned-layabout, defeated in the last two elections two-to-one, Sawyer Wilkinson. Both looked worse for the wear, nursing a Coors Light and some kind of brown liquor on the rocks, respectively. Neither looked at him as he bellied up to the bar in front of Tony.

Matt suppressed a surprised grunt. Sawyer had never forgiven him for escaping White Spruce even for a few years, and had always blamed him for stealing Monica. That she'd shown Sawyer not the slightest interest did nothing to dispel his delusions. As pleasant as being ignored could be, Matt didn't expect it to last.

Bald, obese, and always smiling, Tony Palermo stood all of five-one in thick shoes, and to Matt's knowledge he'd never skipped a meal or a beer his whole life. "Hey, Matt. What brings you down here this time of night?"

"Same old same old, I guess." He opened his mouth to order a beer but Sawyer cut him off with a snort.

"Your kind don't even drink, Rowley."

Tony raised an eyebrow.

Matt gave him the barest hint of a shrug and swiveled on the stool to face his accuser. "My kind?"

Sawyer stirred his drink with his finger so that the ice clinked against the side. "Yeah. You left-wing, one-world government, too-good-for-your-own traitor bonks. Your kind."

A dozen replies flashed through his mind, from pointing out the stupidity of that statement, to defending his decisions, to smashing Sawyer's head to a pulp between his palms. He turned to Tony and pointed at the taps. "I'll take a Bosco Rye."

"I'M TALKING TO YOU," Sawyer said, glaring daggers at Matt.

"I know," Matt said, as Tony poured him a pint. "But I ain't listening."

Sawyer stumbled back from the bar, steadied himself on a table, and put his hand at his waist—on the holster of a Colt .380 Mustang Pocketlite. Matt just succeeded in not rolling his eyes. A drunk normal with a pea shooter constituted not the slightest threat to him at twenty feet, much less five.

Jedd stood and backed toward the other end of the bar, sliding his beer across the polished wood the whole way. Tony froze, eyes wide.

Matt reached out, grabbed his beer, and pulled it over. Eyes on Tony, he lifted it to his mouth and took a long pull. He savored the mingled sweet and bitter flavor even as his regenerates attacked the ethanol. He set it down, wiped his mouth with the back of his hand, and dropped a ten-dollar bill on the counter.

"Thanks, Tony." He got up and walked toward the door.

He made it halfway to the door before Sawyer screamed, "I SAID I WAS TALKING TO YOU, ROWLEY!"

He turned around and walked back, straight at the former mayor, shoulders squared for maximum intimidation. Sawyer's hand quivered over the gun as he came nearer, and he gripped it with white knuckles as Matt invaded the drunk's personal space. Three feet away, Matt flashed forward and put his hand on Sawyer's wrist even as the other man tried to clear the holster. It wasn't unlike trying to wrestle a teddy bear as he kept the weapon holstered and used his own fingers to block Sawyer from reaching the trigger.

He stared down into bloodshot eyes and felt more exasperation and heartache than rage. "You wanted to talk to me, mayor?"

Sawyer snarled and jerked upward, resulting in a tumble to his ass. Matt followed him to the ground, dropping to his knees and pinning the Colt to the floor.

"You clear that weapon I might have to get violent," Matt said. "And there's only one way that ends. I ain't trained to wound."

Bloodshot eyes wide with fear, Sawyer relaxed his grip. Matt snatched up the gun and tossed it to Tony without releasing his gaze.

"So you were talking to me. Talk."

Sawyer turned his head and spat. "I ain't got nothing to say to the likes of you."

Matt let go of the mayor's hand and leaned in nose-to-nose. "No. I didn't think so."

He got up and walked out into the chilly night air.

As he opened his truck door, Tony called out.

"Hey! Matt!"

Matt turned and, seeing Tony's look of distress, gave the man his best disarming smile. "Sorry about that, Tony."

Tony's brief nod punctuated his next sentence. "I'm sorry about that." He looked back to the bar, then at Matt. "Maybe it's best you don't come around here no more."

An unaugmented man might have blushed with anger, might have yelled something inappropriate. With no adrenal flush at all, Matt returned the nod. "Reckon not, Tony. Have a good night."

He got in, slammed the door, and drove home, angry at his inability to feel proper anger.

Ted met him at the door, tail wagging, so he sat on the deck while the dog rustled around in the undergrowth. A few minutes later he peed and wandered up the deck to lick Matt's hand. Matt scratched his ears a minute, then let them both inside.

Monica lay in the same position he'd left her. She slept through the night, and in the morning he left her again for D.C.

Chapter 7

Matt walked up the sidewalk of the blue-sided colonial, flanked by Garrett and Blossom, with Akash trailing behind. Garrett held an Irish flag, Blossom the UN flag. Matt held the letter notifying Jessica Flynn of the death of her husband, a useless faux-vellum lie about duty and service and honor. The haggard lawn needed a good mowing and raking, and there were no lights on inside. A silver Lexus SUV sat in the driveway, a garden hose coiled next to it.

Matt steeled himself and jammed the buzzer with his thumb. He heard the chime through the door, but saw no sign of movement. He tried again. Nothing.

"Nobody home, eh?" Akash said.

A screen door creaked on the house to the left. A middle aged woman in a pink bathrobe surveyed them from her porch. "No one's been home for days. Jessie missed book club last night, too. Didn't call or anything."

"Okay, thanks," Matt said.

She went back inside without another word.

Next to him, Garrett mumbled, "Does anybody else feel that?"

Matt closed his eyes. His feet tingled. He touched the door with his fingertips, and they tingled, too. "Yeah. And what's that smell?" Underneath the grass, wood stain, and goldenrod crept the faint, sweet smell of decay, mixed with a hint of sulfur. He opened his eyes. Garrett and Blossom nodded. Akash breathed in, then grimaced.

"Could be a raccoon, eh?" He didn't sound like he believed himself.

Garrett tried the doorknob. Locked.

"Rastogi," Matt said, "check the back door. Sakura, with him." As they circled around the house, Matt shielded his eyes from the afternoon sun and peered in the windows. Aside from mid-range wooden furniture and wall-to-wall carpeting, nothing struck him as out of the ordinary. "See anything?"

"Nope," Garrett said. "Real clean, though."

Not just clean—immaculate. Perhaps a trace of dust, but not the slightest bit of clutter. Nothing on the tables, the stand by the door, or the sideboard in the dining room. His desk notwithstanding, Matt's house had never been that neat.

Blossom appeared next to them, so fast she may as well have teleported. "Door's locked. Windows, too."

Garrett spoke as Akash came around the corner. "I don't suppose anyone brought any lockpicks?" Nobody had.

Matt took a step back and looked at the house. "What about the second floor?"

Blossom grabbed the porch column and flipped herself onto the roof in a single fluid motion. She lifted the screen of the closest window, then used her fingertips to slide the window up. She disappeared inside, and a moment later opened the front door, unleashing a downright pungent aroma.

"I really hope that's a raccoon," Akash said. Garrett grunted.

The open floor plan made it easy to clear the house. The upstairs bedrooms and bathroom held no surprises, nor did the ground floor. A check of the small, unfinished basement confirmed that the furnace had been turned off, as had the air conditioning, which left the source of the hum a mystery. And the smell.

"There's something here," Matt said. "Find it."

They knocked on walls and stomped on floors, raising a frustrated, methodical ruckus until Blossom called out. Matt rushed to the dining room and stopped just behind Akash.

On her hands and knees, Blossom pressed her face against the floor and closed one eye as she looked under the china cabinet. Akash helped her up as Garrett lifted the cabinet and moved it to one side. The door behind it had a deadbolt lock but no knob, and blended so well with the wall that Matt doubted he'd ever have noticed it.

"Cute," Garrett said. "Anyone see a key?"

Matt tried the cabinet. Halfway down a stack of Wedgwood bowls he found one. It fit, vibrating in his hand as it slid in, and the bolt clicked open.

"Shouldn't we be armed?" Akash asked.

Matt frowned. "There's a sidearm in my glove box." He relocked the door and waited until Akash got back. Blossom found a cricket bat in the front closet. Garrett contented himself with his hands. The whispers shrieked as Matt opened the door.

A black cloud boiled out. It enveloped Matt as he stumbled backward, suffocating him with buzzing, squirming filth. He sucked in a breath through clenched teeth, the vapor wriggling in his mouth as he hit the ground. He heard a door slam. Someone grabbed his hand and helped him to his feet. He spat, then opened his eyes.

Thousands of flies buzzed around the room. The rotten smell twisted his gut and wouldn't let go. His squad mates brushed at and swatted flies as they backed into the living room.

Akash put his hand over his mouth and spoke through his fingers. "Am I the only one with a good, bad idea of what's behind that door?"

Blossom scowled. "People or animals?"

"Akash," Matt said. "Get the masks out of the car, please."

Gas masks were utter overkill, designed for tear gas or biological weapons, but they'd do the job. Putting them on outside would attract much more attention than he wanted at this point, so they retreated to the foyer to wait for Akash. The cloud dispersed through the house, covering drapes and windowsills and furniture with wriggling black bodies.

Matt hated the claustrophobic feeling as he pulled the rubber over his face, but it beat flies in his mouth and eyes. Several trapped insects wriggled against his head and in his clothes.

Geared-up, the team opened the door.

Every surface writhed. He'd never seen so many flies. There had to be millions of them. They crawled into his uniform, covered his head, squirmed into his ears. He had to wipe them off his lenses to see as he descended steep, narrow steps of poured concrete, each step a slippery, crunching mess of mashed insects.

"Holy shit," Garrett said, his voice muffled by the mask. Matt stepped around him, and bile rose in his throat.

The brown, sticky floor writhed with maggots, plump and white. For a fleeting second they formed an image, a circle bisected, sinuous curves in each half. He blinked and it disappeared, his eidetic memory now hazy on the details. "Did you just see—"

"Matt," Akash said, and put his hand on Matt's wrist.

He raised his eyes.

Eight bodies hung from the walls, crucified with razor wire on the naked studs. The farthest body, blonde, female, her lips, ears, and eyes missing, wore a simple gold band and Jessica Flynn's engagement ring, a silver claddagh set with tiny emeralds. The closest corpse consisted of no more than a skeleton, almost held together with strips of dried meat and tendon. Even through the mask, the flies overwhelmed Matt's hearing, the buzz almost primeval. Behind him, someone threw up and retreated up the stairs.

A white ceramic bowl sat on a wooden bench to the left, the only clean area in the room. Matt scattered the flies with a brush of his hand to get a better look. Next to the bowl lay a small, wooden mallet and a stick with the end whittled down to a point. Under the table, rows of small, white cylinders filled a set of shelves. Behind a small glass door, they were the only things in the room not covered with flies. He almost left his dress shoe in the muck as he stepped forward to get a closer look.

The white tubes were no more than two inches long and a quarter inch in diameter. Tiny letters etched into each one spelled gibberish that Matt recognized from Conor's tattoos. He plucked one from the shelf, examined it, then handed it to Blossom.

Her brow furrowed through her mask. "Bone. Largest toe." He handed her another. "This one, too." She gave the next the same pronouncement, and the next. Dozens of bones filled the shelf, yet none of the bodies on the wall were missing their toes.

"He didn't bonk out," Akash said. "He was insane."

Matt didn't say anything. He couldn't reconcile the man he knew with the scene before him. But he had a duty to perform. He swallowed an uncomprehending scream and said, "Yeah. Fall back."

They left their shoes at the top of the stairs, the treads caked in maggot-riddled, red-brown, sticky gunk. Matt stumbled out the front door, tore off his mask, and vomited in the grass. He gasped in a breath of air, the fallen leaves and grass smothered by rot and lit matches and the contents of his stomach. The smell clung to his clothes, and trapped flies still buzzed against his skin. His stomach churned again, but he held it in.

Akash leaned against the car, vomit spatters on his pants, gas mask in the grass at his feet. He ignored the neighbor, gaping wide-eyed at them from her porch, and spoke into his ICAP-issued phone in terse replies to questions Matt couldn't hear. "Yeah. At least eight, maybe a lot more. Jessica was one of them. On the wall. Yes. Yes. We'll hold here." He pressed "end" and put the phone in his pocket.

"Jeff?" Matt asked.

"Yep. Seemed a good idea to get forensics here stat, eh?"

Matt nodded. "When the techs get here, tell them to take as many samples as they can. I want a cross-check on DNA from the basement and Flynn's tattoos."

"All of them?" Akash asked. "That'll cost a fortune."

"Eight bodies on the wall, fifty-nine bones on the shelf. Do the math."

"Sixty-seven tattoos."

* * *

Hours later, Matt sat at a booth and stirred weak diner coffee, black without sugar; the motion served no culinary purpose. Screaming himself hoarse had served no purpose, either, but he'd done that, too.

"I don't get it," Akash muttered from across the booth. "You think you know a guy, but you just don't." He carved off a piece of omelet with a fork, smeared it in the maple syrup on his plate, and shoved it into his mouth.

Matt closed his eyes. "Is it weird I feel better?"

"What do you mean?"

"I killed him. He was my friend, and I killed him. But I don't think I'll lose any more sleep about it." The whispers gibbered and cooed; they wanted him to kill Akash, too, and the waitress, and the guy bellied up to the counter shoveling a week's worth of pancakes into his gullet. "His family, though. I might not ever sleep again."

"He was my friend, too. But yeah, I hear you."

Matt opened his eyes. "When I walked downstairs, I saw . . . ." He didn't want to say it, didn't want to invite the unending string of psychologists and scrutiny and Gerstner-Induced Psychosis experts poking around in his psyche. He didn't want to admit that he might be going crazy.

"The rune," Akash finished. He pushed his half-full plate away and they locked eyes. Akash looked as uncertain as Matt felt.

"You saw it, too?"

Akash nodded, then averted his gaze. "Just for a second. It was crazy. It's not like those flies on her face would make that exact pattern on purpose."

"Wait, seriously? On her face?"

He froze. "Yeah. Where'd you see it, eh?"

"On the floor. But it's weird, I can't recall it."

"Yeah," Akash nodded. "Me, neither. Blossom said I imagined it, told me to see a shrink. Garrett said he didn't see anything."

"Do you think he did?"

Akash shrugged. "He said he didn't. I don't think he'd lie about it."

Matt knew Akash well enough to smell doubt when he heard it. The rift in trust between Matt and Garrett hadn't gotten any better since he'd been duty-bound to report the "pressure."

"What the hell is happening to us?" Matt asked.

Akash took a slurp of Coke. "I don't know. It's weird and it's messed up and I don't like that I don't have a good handle on it. I'd worry it's all in my head, but you saw it, too. In that mine, everyone saw it. Even Sakura."

"So what do we do?"

Akash's sad smile echoed his own. "We let the investigators do their jobs, and we nail Dawkins to the wall."

* * *

Matt pulled open the front door and stepped inside. Monica sat on the couch, watching a home-improvement show over a pint of Ben and Jerry's.

She pulled the spoon out of her mouth. "How'd it go?"

He shook his head by way of reply, hung his keys on the hook, and walked into the bedroom. He'd stripped to his underwear by the time she poked her head around the corner. "I'm sorry, baby. Course it was shitty. Nobody takes news like that well." He didn't say anything. "You think I should call her?"

Matt sat on the bed, then fell back against his pillow. "No."

"Are you sure? Maybe a friendly—"

"No."

"But couldn't I just—"

"She's dead, babe." He closed his eyes. "I don't want you to call her because Conor killed her. And a lot of other people."

He felt the bed shift as she sat next to him. Despite their husbands being coworkers and friends, Monica had met Jessie just two weeks before, at a picnic party Conor had thrown Matt to congratulate him on his promotion. Monica usually had a hard time making friends, but they'd hit it off and had promised to get together soon.

A minute or two later Monica got up, and the door closed with a click. Thirty seconds after that sleep took him.

His eyes snapped open at 4:26 am, according to the red glare of the alarm clock. Monica spooned into him, her body dwarfed in his arms. His left leg lay trapped under Ted, the hot, dead weight a loving comfort.

She tensed. "You okay, baby?"

He thought about it, hating that she lay there awake for worry of him. "Yeah. No. I guess I never really knew the guy."

"Do you want to talk about it?"

He kissed her behind the ear. "I can't. The investigation—"

"—is ongoing." They said it together. She'd heard the line a thousand times when he worked for the state troopers, and he admired her resilience in the face of "need to know" that she never needed to know. "Are you sure it was him?"

He grunted. "I still can't talk about it. But yeah. We're pretty darned sure." He closed his eyes and inhaled the scent of her hair, strawberry shampoo and something unique to her, feminine and loving and strong and brittle. His mind twisted it to a maggot-swarmed charnel house, and he tried not to gag. He rolled off the bed, stepped into the bathroom, and closed the door.

His clear, flawless eyes held no hint of bloodshot or bags, and he could run a marathon on the minute. Haggard and emotionally spent, it struck him at that moment just how inhuman he'd become, unable to even look or feel as exhausted as his mind knew he should be. He splashed water on his face, then brushed his teeth. By the time he got out of the shower, Monica was asleep.

* * *

It took almost three weeks to complete the paperwork on Conor, and by that time the DNA had come in. Sixty-seven exact matches between the tattoos and the bodies, the etchings on the bone identical to the tattoos on Conor's corpse. The victims ranged from drifters and truckers to people from the neighborhood to Conor's wife and four-year-old son, most of whom had been reported missing in the past year, a few not at all. They had no correlation in age, sex, race, religion, sexual preference, or any other demographic.

Under the filth, investigators discovered a ten-foot pentagram etched into the concrete floor, a crude, rough-hewn symbol that looked in photographs to almost be an afterthought. The cupboard behind the bones contained scraps of paper scrawled with what might or might not be gibberish, crystals, powders, and the bronzed skulls of several rodents. Investigators tagged and bagged it all, and took it back to HQ for further research.

Forensics found no sign of an accomplice. The intel weenies couldn't pull up anything on the tattoos; "Be ready. The master is coming!" came from the Book of Matthew, but other than that they had no leads. The profilers at DHS labeled Conor Flynn an "organized, sociopathic mass killer with possible religious motives," which meant exactly nothing.

Chapter 8

Under his cowboy hat, Warden Miner glowered down at Onofre Garza with all the hostility that Matt felt but couldn't show. For his part, Garza seemed to pretend that the giant man next to him didn't exist, and kept his focus on Jeff Hannes. Matt's boss wore a bright red prison jumpsuit, the first time Matt had ever seen him in something other than a suit and tie. The guards had confiscated everything at the entrance to ADX Florence, given them prison garb to change into—while being watched—and only then allowed them through an airport style body scanner.

The warden led them down a narrow, concrete hallway with tall, four-inch-wide windows that showed nothing but sky. Cameras tracked every move, and every door operated by remote. The shiny, polyester fabric restricted Matt's movements; they didn't have a spare quite big enough, and one flex would shred the thing. It added to his general feeling of claustrophobia, a drop of discomfort lost in an ocean of concrete.

"The guards inside carry no keys," Miner explained, his chest puffed up as he gave them an unasked-for tour. Matt couldn't place his accent beyond somewhere in the Midwest. "They can't let anyone out, or in. No firearms, either. They're restricted to batons and pepper spray while on the prison blocks, and they surrender their uniforms daily. The idea is that you'd need at least three people to smuggle anything in or out, and that's too big a conspiracy to try." They stopped at a red bulkhead-style door. It unlocked, and he led them through.

Red doors lined both sides of the hall, each with a window blind secured on the outside.

"The complex is designed so that prisoners don't know where they are and don't know who's in the cells next to them. The cell blocks and hallways are identical, and at no time can an inmate see anything outside other than sky or ceiling." He seemed oblivious to Onofre Garza's furious glare as he led them through several more cell blocks, yammering non-stop about what made the Supermax prison the United States' most secure facility for non-augged humans. By the time they got to the visitation room, Matt had no idea how to get to the exit but felt confident that he could tear his way through the walls until he made it outside.

The door opened to reveal a concrete room bisected by a thick pane of bullet-proof polycarbonate. On this side sat a table with three chairs, on the other a single concrete slab serving as a desk, with a concrete cylinder for a stool. The guards had shackled Hernando Garza's ankles to the stool and his wrists to the desk. Clean-shaven and too thin, he looked nothing like his wooly, Che Guevara-like FBI's Most Wanted pictures. Matt couldn't reconcile this scrawny, cowed little man with an enforcer who had killed dozens of people, including three prison guards.

Hernando's eyes widened at Onofre, and he babbled something in Spanish.

"English," the warden said.

Hernando stopped mid-sentence and looked down at the table, hands shaking. "I so sorry, warden. I forget myself." Unlike his brother, Hernando's thick accent reflected his destitute Mexican background. He looked up at Onofre, but his body language remained cowed. "Brother, why you come here? This place, it's no good."

Onofre's face betrayed not the slightest hint of emotion. "I wanted to see you, brother. Make sure you're all right. Tell you that Emma and—"

Hernando quivered. "This place, they never going let you out. I so, so sorry you here." He leaned forward so he could wipe a tear from his eye with his shackled hands. "This place—"

Onofre cleared his throat. "I've seen enough."

Patrick Freivald

The warden hit a button on the wall. The door behind Hernando Garza opened to admit two guards. They used the keypads on his shackles to unlock his left hand from the desk. He put his hand behind his back without the slightest hint of resistance, where they locked it to a ring on his jumpsuit. They did the same with his right. They unhooked his ankles and then locked them together with eight inches of chain. He shuffled out of the room, his head hanging.

The moment the door closed Onofre whirled on Jeff. "We have a deal."

Jeff reached down for a briefcase that wasn't there, then wiped his hand on his jumpsuit. "The paperwork's in the lobby."

* * *

"Look at this," the technician said, pushing the paper across Matt's desk. Matt picked it up and held it in front of his face. The massive string of chemical symbols meant nothing to him.

"What am I looking at?"

"The crazy shit we found in Flynn's basement. Mushrooms, MDMA precursors, some radium, cesium, radioactive potassium isotopes . . . I looked up the various mixtures, and I got a couple of hits that were interesting if useless. It's all a mish-mash of everything you could imagine out of a paranoid 1970's spy novel, real *Manchurian Candidate* stuff."

"I have no idea what you're talking about," Matt said. He wanted to slap the blond man's pleased smile right off his face.

"The powders in Conor Flynn's dungeon. All kinds of crazy stuff. MKULTRA mixtures from the internet, ancient voodoo-zombie mind-control crap, Aztec sacred-trance mixtures." He tapped one entry. "Hell, you know what that is?"

Matt shook his head.

"Yeah, neither did I, until I borrowed some time on the NSA's data-crunchers. Some Damaran king in the seventeen-eighties tried to achieve apotheosis—"

"Apo-what?"

~ 85 ~

"Apotheosis. He tried to become a god. And this is the mixture he came up with. Legend says he could see the future and would have lived forever if jealous priests hadn't cut off his head within the month."

"Huh," Matt said. "Guess he couldn't see it very well."

The tech removed another paper from the manila envelope, set it on the desk, and lined it up with the first one. "The computer stumbled upon this, too."

Matt compared the list of compounds and mixtures. "Same list?"

"The acid in Flynn's stuff is more modern, but other than that, yeah. Same list."

Matt sat up straight. "So, the chance of this being a coincidence is . . . ?"

"As close to zero as you can get."

"And where'd this come from?"

"I had to circumvent some firewalls to figure it out, but that same mixture of chemicals was pulled from a bombed-out Nazi bunker under Dresden in the nineteen-fifties."

"I thought Hitler hated religion," Matt said. "Why would he be messing around with this kind of stuff?"

"Philipp Lenard, his chief scientist, got into all kinds of crazy shit. Haven't you seen *Raiders of the Lost Ark*? The Deutsch Physik guys thought that with proper geometries and machines and stuff they could channel God's power to whatever they wanted; open doors to Hell or Heaven, summon demons or angels, call down the Wrath of God on the impure races. Some really fucked up shit."

Matt tried not to seem too interested at the mention of angels. "Did any of it work?"

He snorted. "Of course not."

Matt sat back.

"There were rumors, of course. Secret laboratories in secret bunkers, black masses in churches desecrated by human sacrifice, *Übermenschen* imbued with divine Aryan power . . . some conspiracy-minded folks say that was the whole reason for the concentration camps. But all that mystic hoo-hah didn't stop Patton, did it?"

"Yeah." Matt leaned back. "Don't know why I asked."

"Still," said the tech. "It tells you just how fucked in the head Flynn was."

Matt prided himself on his lack of a murder record, so he didn't snap the little guy's neck. "So Conor just followed random crazy rumors from the web?"

The tech shrugged. "I'm just a research chemist. I have no idea where he got it from . . . but that bunker's still there."

* * *

They pulled up to the Brulische Terassen on the Elbe River at ten-fifteen local time in a pair of rented BMWs. The cobblestone streets had made for a loud, vibrational ride, and Matt shook the numbness out of his limbs as he got out of the car. Akash let out a low whistle at the architecture. The brick-and-stone Standehaus had been restored to how it looked before being utterly flattened by allied bombing in 1945, and every building in the vicinity looked like a riverside palace.

Brian Frahm sat in the back, his hands on this thighs, talking to Jeff Hannes in a low voice. Brian had asked for a ride-along, and once his boss decided to go, Jeff couldn't help but tag along. For his part, Matt wasn't even sure what any of them were doing there, but in good conscience he couldn't pass up a lead, no matter how odd and unlikely.

They got out as a gray-haired man in a brown suit approached their cars, eyebrows raised in expectation. "Herr Rowley?"

"That's me," Matt said, and stuck out his hand. "Thanks for agreeing to meet with us, Herr Gottschalk." He recognized the curator's voice from their conversation the day before.

"It's the least I could do, given that you've come all this way." Matt had an easier time navigating his thick accent in person than over the phone. "Though I wonder what it is you expect to find."

"Me, too," Matt replied.

Gottschalk gave Brian a puzzled look, which he returned. Instead of speaking, he led them on foot under a masonry arch, through a small iron portcullis, and into a hallway lined with faded, yellow-brown tile. "It's not often we get requests to see the *Reichbunkersystem*. Tourists don't know of it, and most German citizens would prefer to forget." He ran his fingertips along the wall as he walked. "Even after the war there were no records of it, and its discovery in 1957 took the restoration workers, and everyone else, by surprise."

He reached an unstained oak door and turned around, hands clasped at his waist. Matt turned with him and surveyed his team. Akash's eyes wandered, though what he expected to see on the blank walls Matt could only guess. Blossom's eyes didn't leave Gottschalk. Garrett stared at the door, and both Jeff and Brian looked at Matt.

"Excuse me, Herr . . . Frahm, is it?" Gottschalk asked. Brian raised his eyebrows at him. "Have we met before?"

Brian shrugged, a small grin on his face. "I don't think so. I've never been to Dresden."

"You look familiar."

Brian shrugged again. "I get that a lot, actually. Common genes, I guess."

"No matter," Gottschalk said. He gestured to the door two-handed, reminding Matt of Vanna White. "This is the entrance. The bunker is deep, the only reason we have not yet restored it and turned it into some kind of museum. The excavation crew took most everything decades ago. I'm afraid there's not much to see."

He opened the door to reveal an unadorned concrete stairway with flat concrete walls. He heaved a large, Frankenstein's-lab-type switch up, and an orange-white glow struggled to illuminate the featureless stairs from periodic, naked bulbs hanging from black iron fixtures, connected by a long black cable that dangled as far down as Matt could see.

Gottschalk touched the cable with one finger, then pulled away. "In 1969 they moved the lights up here for convenience."

They said nothing as they descended, until five flights down they encountered a massive swastika inlayed into the wall, bright red ceramic on a painted white background, surrounded in a ring by German words in gold filigree. Even after most of a century, to see the symbol not in a book or movie but on a wall raised goosebumps on Matt's arms.

"What's it say?" Blossom asked.

"For the glory of the Fuhrer and the Thousand Years Reich, today's work echoes to eternity." Gottschalk dropped his eyes and continued down into the gloom. The whispers mourned the optimistic lie.

"Tell that to the US Army," Garrett muttered in Matt's ear.

Six more flights, these with murder holes in the walls of every landing, and they reached the bottom. The weight of all the earth above them pressed on Matt's mind, and the thought of bombs sealing them in chilled his spirit. That he recognized the fear as a psychological trick didn't help.

Jeff breathed a sigh of relief as he stepped off the last stair. "Ow."

"Wait until we have to go back up," Matt said.

Jeff's second sigh held no relief.

The massive steel door to the bunker complex lay on the floor, the deep, jagged cuts through its hinges caked with old rust. Ten feet behind it the hall took an abrupt right turn, exposing two more murder holes five feet off the ground.

"You'd think they wanted to keep people out, eh?" Akash asked.

"Imagine the number of people you'd lose just taking the stairs," Garrett said. "A dozen men could hold this place forever, if they had enough ammo and stores."

Blossom stooped to run her finger along the floor, and held it up to examine the dry, gray dust. "I expected mold."

Gottshalk nodded. "Yes, when it was uncovered they scoured a great deal of mold from every surface. The museum installed enormous dehumidifiers to control the problem, and they've run ever since."

Gottschalk produced a massive flashlight and led them through the facility, a complex warren of dusty, empty rooms, not counting the narrow ladders that climbed up six floors to each of the pill boxes overlooking the stairs. "The team that uncovered the *Reichsbunkersystem* found many skeletons. The stairs had to be excavated, with many tons of rock and broken concrete burying the only entrance . . . best guess is that the occupants committed suicide when they learned they had been buried alive."

Good riddance, Matt thought, but he said, "Were any of the bodies identified?"

"No," Gottschalk shook his head. "Most of what we know came from their uniforms. Among the bodies were an *Oberarzst*, a chief surgeon, and strangely enough an *Heeresoberpfarrer*, a senior army Chaplain. Many of the bodies wore the uniforms of the SS, but investigators found no records to indicate who these men were or what they were doing here—not one scrap of paper." He stepped into an enormous room and spread his arms wide as if to banish the shadows from the vacant corners. "This was the main theater, and documents say it was full of medical devices, cots, surgical suites . . . ." He turned to Matt. "As I told you on the telephone, there is nothing to see."

As Matt followed Gottschalk through the empty chamber and into the next, a rising sense of frustration crawled through him. The vacant warren of concrete rooms held no clues to Conor's psychopathy. He had trailed Gottschalk through the next room, and the next, when he noticed that Jeff and Brian were no longer with them.

He leaned over to Akash and whispered in his ear. "Where'd the bosses go?"

Akash looked behind them, brow furrowed. "No idea."

"I'll be right back," Matt said.

He let their guide lead the rest of them into the next room, then turned around and retraced their steps. In the darkness of the huge room, his infrared vision picked up two heat blobs, human figures standing toward the back next to a metal square in the wall that shimmered with their reflected heat.

He crept forward, taking care not to be heard, but they stopped talking before he got close enough to hear. He stood back as Jeff helped Brian to his feet. *But why had he been kneeling in the first place?* Jeff opened his phone and bathed them in the pale screen light. Behind them, the metal square on the wall read *VERBRENNUNGSOFEN* in faded crimson.

Brian dusted off his knees, and they walked toward the rest of the group. "We'd better get back."

Matt cut around them, avoiding the light from the phone, using the infrared spectrum to navigate the concrete chambers. He joined the others moments before Jeff and Brian did. Gottschalk, still walking and talking, didn't seem to have noticed.

Blossom stared daggers at Matt, but her eyes flicked to Brian and Jeff and she said nothing.

Matt reached out to cut off Akash before he spoke, but didn't get there in time.

"Where'd you two go, eh?"

Gottschalk stopped talking in mid-sentence and turned around, mouth still open.

Brian's eyes flicked to Matt for a near-imperceptible moment, then to Jeff. "My shoe came untied."

"Ah," Akash said. "Don't want to trip in a place like this, you'll get filthy." He nodded to Brian's dusty knees.

Brian gave him a sheepish grin. "It'll wash out."

A few minutes later they arrived back at the entrance. Gottschalk turned off the light and gave an apologetic smile. "That's all there is to it, unless you wish to peruse the pillboxes." He knocked on the metal ladder leading up into the darkness.

"I think I'm about walked-out," Jeff said, ignoring the stairs with vigor. Brian nodded in agreement.

"I'd like to see them," Blossom said. "But don't need a guide." She grabbed the rung and disappeared up the ladder.

"Me, too," Matt said and climbed up after her, eyes squinting against rust that flaked off in her wake.

She waited for him three floors up, peering out the horizontal slit onto the stairs. She spoke softly, without preamble and without turning to look at him. "Where were they?"

"The big room, next to a metal door with a word I don't know," he said. "*Verbrennungsofen*." He knew his accent couldn't be helping, so he spelled it. "What's it mean?"

She frowned out at the stairwell. "It means 'incinerator.'" She glanced down the ladder toward the group below, who paid them no mind. "Frahm knows you went back for them. Was he tying his shoe?"

"Um . . . I don't know. He was on his knees, but they were a good twelve meters from where we were walking."

"And he didn't say, 'wait.' Something's funny."

"Yup," he replied. *But what?*

They climbed up the rest of the way, saw nothing other than more empty concrete rooms, and climbed back down.

"Anything exciting?" Garrett asked as Matt's foot hit the floor.

"No," Blossom said.

Jeff looked at the massive staircase. His theatrical sigh echoed through the complex.

"I know you're thinking 'piggy back,' eh?" Akash said. "But that's not going to happen."

* * *

On the flight back to D.C., Matt couldn't figure out a way to breach the subject without calling his bosses liars. He settled into a disturbed slumber to the droning of jet engines.

Chapter 9

Matt shifted Ted off his lap and picked up his cell phone on the second ring. "Rowley speaking." 8:02 am wasn't quite too early to call on a Tuesday.

"Morning," Janet LaLonde said. Director of Information and Computing at ICAP, Janet's job reached into every dark corner of the international organization. "You ever heard of Lake Barnacle, Georgia?"

"What do I win if I have?"

She didn't reply.

"No, I haven't. What's up?"

"You put in a requisition for warrants on Conor Flynn's financial activity. The warrant cleared, and we pulled up his info. The only thing interesting is several credit-card purchases from Lake Barnacle. He spent three days at the Alligator Moon Motel four years ago February, or at least his credit cards did, and in that time he spent almost a grand on food, drink, and hardware supplies. Mostly the latter."

"Where is this place?"

"Not too far outside Forsyth, off Route 83."

He drew a blank trying to bring it to mind. "Nope. Not ringing a bell."

"The internet's pretty spotty on it, too. Population eighty, no post office, no church, no stores. A commune, they're Ben Case's 'family,' who moved there after being ousted from Savannah in '89." He could downright hear the quotations around "family."

"Why does 'Ben Case' sound familiar?"

"He claimed he was the love child of Dennis Wilson of the Beach Boys and Marnie Reeves, whose real name is Patricia Krenwinkel."

"Krenwinkle. You mean Katie Krenwinkle?"

"That's right."

Patricia "Katie" Krenwinkel had killed several people, including Abigail Folger of coffee fame, on the orders of Charles Manson in the late nineteen-sixties. "So this guy's a whackjob, and Flynn spent time with him?"

"Nobody stays at Lake Barnacle without his permission. It's a closed commune."

"Of whackjobs," Matt said.

"Not my place to judge," Janet replied.

"Are these guys dangerous?"

"Doesn't look like it. No complaints, no warrants for anything serious besides a tax evasion case back in '94, which they resolved peacefully."

"But they're a Manson cult, right?"

"No, not really. They rejected Helter Skelter in favor of something called the Process Church of the Final Judgment, a Scientology spinoff Manson incorporated but ultimately rejected. You know it?"

"Never heard of it."

"Well, you'll have to Google it, then. Apparently Case left the Process Church to form his own splinter in the mid-eighties — extreme pacifists, vegans, mostly harmless. That's all I got."

"Thanks," Matt said, and hung up. He called operations and booked a flight to Atlanta for 6:10 the next morning. His phone rang forty minutes later while he read up on the Process Church. The Caller ID said, "Hannes, Jeff."

He hit Talk. "Hello."

"Hey, buddy. I just got a requisition for a solo flight to Atlanta?"

"Yup, you did."

"All right. What am I putting on the paperwork?"

Matt thought about it for a moment. "Tell them I'm following a lead on Conor Flynn's psychotic break."

Silence, then, "Is that what you're doing?"

"Yeah. I and C just got word that Flynn spent three days with Ben Case down in Georgia four years ago. I'm going to go check it out."

"Ben Case the Manson kid?"

"That's the one."

"Why the hell would Flynn—"

"That's what I'm going to find out."

"You really think that's a good use of your time? We've got Dawkins intel—"

"Yeah, I do. Dawkins can wait a couple days."

"You sure, buddy?"

"I wouldn't have booked the flight if I wasn't."

"All right. I'll sign it."

* * *

Matt touched down in Atlanta at 8:32 am, grabbed his duffel out of the overhead compartment, and headed to the Hertz desk. He took the rented XTerra south into wooded nothing, following the GPS to Lake Barnacle. Just outside of town he came to a one-lane bridge, blocked by a chain, over a tiny splash of water not quite worthy of the name "creek."

He got out to read the sign that hung from it, letting the engine idle.

> Welcome to Lake Barnacle Commune.
> This land is the property of Benjamin Case, Lord Processean and Prophet of Jehovah, Lucifer, and Satan, may they be Reconciled on the last of days.
> Visitors wait to be admitted.

Matt leaned against the hood of the car and pretended he didn't see the heat signatures of the two people lurking in the brush on the other side. A few minutes later, a man pulled up in an old Jeep with peeling army-green paint. He got out and stood so that the door obscured most of his body, but his disheveled, curly red hair and beard stood out over it.

"Help you?"

"Morning," Matt said, hands in his pockets. "I was hoping to talk to Mr. Case—"

"PROPHET Case," the man corrected.

"Prophet Case. I don't have an appointment."

"Yes, you do. All supplicants are welcome to the presence of the prophet."

"All right, then." Matt got back in the rental car while the man unlocked the chain and dragged it to the side of the road. His drab clothes were made of hemp or some other natural fiber, a crude weave you might find on a frontier doll, and he moved with the urgency of a snail on Nyquil.

Matt followed the Jeep at five miles an hour down a winding dirt path that almost counted as a road, through a forest of chalk maple and sourwood, the roadside and occasional clearing overgrown with bright, orange-yellow goldenrod. They passed an abandoned farm, the old barn caved in and bristling with saplings, the sad two-story colonial devoid of paint, the door a black gash open to the elements.

They came to another gate, just two concrete pylons connected with a chain. Beyond it sat a huge pond populated by hundreds of sea gulls, the shore scattered with dozens of multicolored tents. Naked children ran through the grass, kicking a ball in a game Matt didn't recognize, and maybe a hundred adults crowded around an oak tree, long-ago shattered by lighting or some other calamity. Next to it stood three massive crosses, one upright, one even like a plus sign, and one inverted. Each bore the same carving.

The Ul.

At the behest of his guide, Matt stood to the side and waited. Case sat in a rickety, sun-faded, aluminum-and-plastic lawn chair. His followers ringed around him, lounging on blankets or sitting Indian-style in the trodden grass. They wore the same natural-fabric smock-like things, had unkempt hair, no makeup, and, judging by the smell, no deodorant. In his jeans and black T-shirt, Matt felt overdressed.

Case spoke to his flock in a chaotic mix of Spanglish, Pig Latin, and what had to be made-up words. They stared at him with rapturous eyes and responded to each pronouncement with a murmured, "Eh-la eh-la." Matt couldn't quite get over Case's hair, a giant, dirty-blond, white man's afro that just might fit through a door.

Twenty minutes later, Case finished, and the adults moved off to other activities: tending children, cooking, weeding the enormous garden on the far side of the pond, a few staying where they were to copulate in plain view of everyone. Aside from a few curious glances, nobody paid Matt any attention.

His guide whispered in Case's ear, burying his face in the massive 'fro to get close enough. Case raised his dark blue eyes and beckoned Matt forward. Matt decided against shaking hands, and Case made no move to do so as he sized Matt up with the same bland expression he'd worn since Matt got there.

Case twitched a finger, and the guide walked away.

"Good morning," Matt said.

Case's expression didn't change. "They always are. What brings you before the Prophet today?"

Matt pulled a photocopy of Conor's family portrait from his pocket, unfolded it, and handed it to Case. The prophet bit his fingernails, despite the dirt caked beneath them. "Do you know these people?"

Case tapped Conor's face. "This man, yes, he came to us some time ago. The woman and child, no." He handed the paper back. "Who asks, and why do you want to know?"

"He was my friend, and he's passed away. I'm trying to figure out why. He did some awful things," he nodded toward the crosses, "and that symbol had something to do with it."

"And you believe that his visitation with the Three Gods led him to do these things?"

Matt had read about the Process Church's three gods: Jehovah, who demanded stern adherence to morality; Lucifer, who encouraged peace and harmony and living life to the fullest; and Satan, whose dual natures were asceticism and violent hedonism. "Flynn had a . . . visitation?"

"As you are now, brother . . . ?"

"Matt. Matt Rowley."

Case stood from the chair and walked away from the scattered couples on the lawn. Matt followed as he wandered to the shoreline; and without seeming to scatter, everyone gave them a wide berth, even the children. "Brother Rowley, Conor Flynn came to us seeking knowledge, and we are duty-bound to provide it when we can. But he came to us filled with too much of the Satan-pattern's darkness, and took into himself yet more before he left us."

"What did he want to know?"

Case picked up a flat rock and skipped it across the choppy water. "Why do you want to know what he wanted to know?"

Matt weighed the value of telling the truth. "Because he was my friend, and he murdered a lot of people, and forced me to kill him to keep him from killing more."

They walked in silence for a minute, distancing themselves further from the raucous noise of children at play. On the far side of the pond, the land sloped downward to reveal a hidden garden, several acres wide, of neat, well-ordered winter crops. "That is a dark thing. One cannot kill without dying. It is why we eat of no flesh, possess no weapons, take no drugs or alcohol, and live in harmony even with the thetan spirits that seek to corrupt from within and without."

"So?" Matt asked. "What is it Conor wanted to know?"

Something thrashed in the water behind them, and the world erupted with the cries of gulls. Matt turned. Bloody ripples spread from a point fifty feet from shore, and a few white feathers bobbed on them. The rest of the gulls had taken to the air, screaming their distress to the blue sky.

"Alligators?" Matt asked.

"Conor sought knowledge of bridges," Ben said, ignoring his second question. He continued walking. Matt followed, one eye on the shore.

"Bridges?"

"Between this realm and others. He sought the Old Way, where man and demon and angel are not separate but are one. He refused to accept that this will not happen before the Reconciliation, and would not rejoice with us in the Lucifer-pattern's hospitality." They rounded a thicket of blackberry brambles and came to a simple graveyard, each mound of earth pierced with the three crosses. Case dropped to his knees beside one and placed his hands on the mound. "He fell to the Satan-pattern's darker nature, and my darling Katie paid the price for it. After, we asked him to leave. He went."

"I'm sorry. Who was she?"

"All who give of their womanhood to join with the Prophet are Katie, as she was and will be from Genesis to the forever beyond, eh-la eh-la."

That didn't make any sense, so Matt asked, "What did Flynn do to her?"

Case bowed his head. "Too much and not fast enough, without the barest shred of human mercy. We beseeched him to stop, but he took her blood and her toe and left her skin beside her on the ground."

"You didn't try to stop him?"

Case stood from the grave and grabbed Matt on the back of the neck, an earnest, fraternal gesture. He stared deep into his eyes. "Brother Rowley, we no sooner harm a man than we harm our own spirit."

"So you let him torture and kill this woman—"

"Not just a woman. A Katie."

"—this Katie, because you wouldn't hurt him to stop him?"

"It is not our place to lead a man away from where the Three God-patterns have led him."

Matt jerked back, out of his grip, and didn't try to mask his disgust. "It's not your place to stop a man from torturing and killing—"

"That is what I said."

"Did you report it? To the police?"

Case shook his head. "We answer to no external authority and do not invite them to meddle in the Three God-patterns' affairs."

"Jesus."

"No. It was the dark nature of the Satan-pattern working in Conor Flynn, and He has not yet Reconciled with the Emissary."

"So if I call the cops? Tell them there's a murder victim here?"

Case held up his hands as if in supplication and closed his eyes. "If that is where the Jehovah-pattern leads you, el-ah el-ah."

"You'll go to jail. You can't just not report a murder."

"Those who embody the Jehovah-pattern of course contain the Lucifer-pattern and Satan-pattern, and we will not be well treated by the men outside. If that is the enduring legacy of Conor Flynn's brutality, we will accept it as the Jehovah-pattern demands."

"Her family deserves to know what happened to her."

"When a woman becomes Katie we are her family, and we know too well."

"What about her parents?"

"Katies have no parents."

Matt sighed.

"Is there anything else you can tell me about Conor Flynn?"

"I have no truths you would hear." He turned and headed back toward the other side of the shore.

"The symbol on those crosses, what can you tell me about it?"

"Nothing."

"Why not?"

"Those crosses are the reason I chose this place for our sacred home. They predate us, and the original Barnacle farm, which you passed on the way in, and the earliest records of the settlers. But when I saw them, I knew this place was meant for the Katies and Bens."

"Are all the men here named Ben?"

"Of course."

* * *

On his way out of town, Matt pulled over into the parking lot of the Alligator Moon Motel, or that's what he assumed given the crescent-alligator flag and the neon VACANCY sign. The dilapidated, periwinkle-blue, one-story structure had all of three rooms, plus a tiny office. He called 911, reported what Case had told him about "Katie's" murder, left his contact information, and drove back to the airport.

He typed his report on the plane, then put it away to focus on their next operation: killing Dawkins and dismantling his Jade empire to the last brick.

Chapter 10

Matt hit the clicker, and the smart board projected an image onto the wall of conference room B of the Nashville Federal Building. Centered between Rwanda and the Congo, a large island sat in the middle of a massive lake.

"What are we looking at, sir?" Garrett asked.

"That'd be central Africa, corporal," Akash said with a grin.

Garrett flipped him the bird, and Matt stifled a sigh.

"That," Matt said, "is Idjwi Island in Lake Kivu, on the border of the Democratic Republic of Congo and Rwanda. Jungle not that long ago, now it's three hundred and forty square kilometers of clear-cut subsistence farms for a quarter-million half-starved refugees. Except for this." He hit the button and the picture changed to a construction site on the shore, where dozens of bulldozers and cranes cleared land and erected buildings. "Two years ago the DRC broke ground on a series of two-megawatt power plants to compete with the Rwandan operation on the eastern shore." The next slide showed a series of smoke stacks jutting into the sky. "The first three facilities went online a few months ago, and they anticipate at least six more over the next decade."

Akash raised a hand, and Matt nodded to him. "Go ahead."

"Why build power plants in a warzone? That doesn't make any sense."

"It does," Matt said. "First, it ain't much of a warzone anymore, and Idjwi is in firm control of the Congolese army. Second, Lake Kivu is a so-called 'explosive lake.' It's got enormous amounts of dissolved methane a hundred meters down. They pump it up from the bottom, it bubbles out of the water in the lower pressure, and they burn it. They use the heat to boil the water, spin some turbines with it, and there you go. The water goes back into the lake, they get electricity for next to free, and it makes the lake less likely to explode again. It's a win-win for everyone."

Matt let the conversation wander to the hows and whys of exploding lakes and the unwise decision to live on or near one before clicking to the next slide: the front of the facility, a large brick edifice complete with a marquee emblazoned "Idjwi Power Inc." in bold, six-foot letters. "IPI is a privately-held firm incorporated in DRC that seems to have greased all the right palms. We're not sure who's the owner or owners, but it sprang out of nowhere three years ago and now owns half the Idjwi coastline. Their contractors are French, Swiss, and Japanese, all reliable construction firms and all on the up-and-up. IPI have gone way out of its way to ease the concerns of environmentalists and have created a state-of-the-art lab to monitor and minimize the impact of their operation on the ecosystem."

A series of slides showed satellite photos of forklifts offloading pallets from ferries and bringing them into a large octagonal building. "One of the primary concerns is algal blooms from the returned water, and as such they've purchased billions of dollars of algal vats, centrifuges, dehydrators, glassware . . . ." He let the list sink in. A state-of-the-art biochemistry lab that size could produce a lot of Jade.

"So," Garrett said. "Dawkins?"

Matt nodded. "According to Onofre Garza, it's the seat of his global operations. The power plant's a perfect cover. The political instability means he can carve out a place and stock it with goons, and the location gives him easy access to the Congo, the Nile, and land in any direction." He clicked to the next slide, a small airfield, not much more than a pair of dirt runways half-concealed with camouflage netting. "Not to mention millions of square kilometers of virtually unmonitored air space." The next slide showed a pair of tanks, old Soviet T-55s under inadequate camouflage. "And the DRC army at his beck and call."

Akash rubbed his hands. "When do we go in?"

Garrett grunted. Matt raised an eyebrow at him.

"I think 'how' is a better question," Garrett said. "We've got no means of entry they won't see coming. They've got huge fields of fire in every direction, and we'd be fools to assume he doesn't have radar."

"Right," Matt said. "I've got pictures of the radar installations on a later slide. It's outdated Chinese kit but good enough for most purposes."

Blossom spoke up. "No bombs because of lake, yes?"

Matt nodded. "Right. We don't think an air strike would trigger the lake, even with the pumps running, but we aren't confident enough to risk it."

"So what if it did?" Garrett asked. "That'd take care of the problem, wouldn't it?"

Matt flipped through several slides until he found the one he wanted, a closer satellite image of the lake and all of the surrounding cities. "It's like shaking a Coke bottle. If the lake erupts, the explosion wouldn't be that big of a deal unless you live right near shore. But the lake's on high ground, and carbon dioxide is heavier than air. Once released, it'll flow downhill and suffocate everything for dozens of clicks. Two million people, give or take."

"Well," Garrett said, "that's inconvenient."

"Almost like he picked the spot on purpose," Akash said, irony dripping from every word. "So how do we go in?"

"We need goals first," Blossom said. "'Why' is first, before 'how' or 'when.'"

"Right," Matt said. "I've talked this over with Jeff. Our mission parameters are a targeted assassination. Go in, kill him, trash the facility, and get out." He set down the clicker and met their eyes, one by one. "But that's not what we're going to do." He ticked points off on his fingers. "So as far as you're concerned, our primary objective is the apprehension of Dawkins, alive. Secondary objectives include gathering intelligence on his operation and destroying the Jade processing capabilities of the facility. Tertiary objectives are eliminating product and capturing targets of opportunity."

Nobody said anything.

"Look," Matt said. "The facility ain't going anywhere, so there's no major hurry. If we verify he's there, we grab him. Somehow. Let the bigwigs worry about the rest of it."

"Great," Akash said. "So we go in, bag the bastard, and get out. Like Garrett said, how do we do that, eh?"

* * *

"THIS IS INSANE!" Akash shouted over the C130's droning engine, his oxygen mask muffling the scream to a bare murmur. The fuselage pitched in the turbulence, and the engines whined in protest at the punishment of 350 knots at 32,000 feet. The air drop into Rwanda couldn't slow down or change course without drawing attention, so the HALO jump had to be at speeds that would kill normal paratroopers. To avoid a suspicious change in radar profile, they couldn't even jump out the back.

Matt patted Akash's shoulder and grabbed the door handle. Muscles straining, he wrenched the unwilling metal toward the back of the plane. The roar of the freezing wind made verbal communication impossible as the wispy clouds under them came into view. He returned Akash's wide-eyed stare with a thumbs-up as the door locked into place.

Akash rolled his eyes and jumped, body tucked around the REC7 assault rifle strapped to his abdomen. Garrett and Blossom followed. Matt braced himself, bit down on the oxygen tube, and leapt.

The wind broke him. He screamed as tendons shredded from the impact with the air. The world flashed dark and light as he tumbled, but he used the dusk sun to orient himself straight up and down in a pencil dive. As his body knitted back together, he felt the itch on his face as frostbitten skin healed and refroze, healed and refroze. Looking down, his augmented vision picked out the three specks that were Garrett, Akash, and Blossom, already formed up in a dive toward the western shore of Lake Kivu.

His joints ached as what little nitrogen remaining in his blood boiled. Between hypoxia, the bends, and frostbite, they'd all be ravenous by the time they hit the ground. *Speaking of which . . . .* His altimeter read 26,000 feet and dropped fast. He kept the pencil dive until he formed up with the others, spread out just enough to match their speed, and then they dove together.

At six thousand feet they jettisoned their oxygen masks, tucked into balls, then lengthened back out, belly to earth. Matt took the lead, activating his wingpack. A compact, jet-powered glider patterned on the ESG Gryphon, the carbon-fiber ICAP pattern unfolded just fast enough to level them out eighty feet above the water. He couldn't help but laugh. *To infinity, and beyond!*

With the setting sun at their backs, they zoomed toward Dawkins's compound at two hundred kilometers an hour. In radio silence they unholstered their weapons, the latter three with silenced REC7s, Matt with a brace of Beretta M9A1 pistols, also silenced. The AA-12 combat shotgun strapped to his thigh would stay out of play unless stealth failed them. Computer-guided, fin-stabilized micro-grenades couldn't be silenced when they went off. Matt dropped his visor.

The HUD highlighted hostiles in orange double-triangles. Consistent with the satellite imagery, four men sat on each roof, machine-gunners hunkered behind sandbag emplacements. Akash took his shots first, and blips dropped off of Matt's HUD. Garrett and Blossom opened fire as they zipped overhead. Garrett's target remained until Blossom fired again, neutralizing the last guard.

They banked straight up, retracted the glider wings at the top of the arc. Two hundred feet above the top of the buildings, they stalled and fell, pulling their reserve chutes at the last second. As his boots crunched on the gravel roof, Matt popped the harness, and the entire pack fell away, pulling the oxygen tank with it. The others followed suit, then formed up in front of the roof-access door.

Blossom signed, too fast for Matt to follow. Garrett flipped her the bird.

A wooden shim propped the door open a crack, through which Matt could see a metal staircase. He smelled lamb curry, and Justin Bieber sang in the distance through tinny, low-quality speakers. Blossom took point, then Matt, then Akash, with Garrett covering the rear. Intel had Dawkins's office on the second floor, above the lobby. They jammed steel bars through door handles as they descended two levels to the correct landing.

Video camera, Akash signed. *Covers the whole hallway.* Doors lined both sides of the thirty-foot hall. The camera perched at the far end, and if Matt had to guess another just like it lurked above them, just inside the door.

Below us, too, Blossom signed. Matt looked. A security camera covered the stairs to the first floor.

The information scrolling across Matt's HUD hadn't changed; Dawkins hadn't left his office, thick bars precluded any escape out the windows, and they stood at the only exit. *On three,* he signed. *One . . . Two . . . Go!*

Blossom had made it halfway down the hall when a massive hand punched through the wall and grabbed her arm. Her REC7 fell from her grip as the bonk yanked her through in a spray of imploding plaster. Her machine pistol fired two short bursts, then she flew into the hallway and rebounded off the far wall, weaponless. As Akash advanced, Matt tossed a flash-bang grenade, then choked up the AA12.

Their visors blocked most of the light, and their ears recovered from the bang in a split second. It wouldn't do any good against a bonk, but any normals in the area were another story. Garrett fired when the farthest door opened, and a figure ducked out of sight. Akash tossed a fragmentation grenade through the hole in the wall, but the massive aug broke into the hallway before it went off. Matt's ears rang, and shrapnel peppered the ten-foot wall of uniformed muscle without slowing it down.

Akash pulled the trigger, and blood erupted from its neck. He ducked the bonk's haymaker, then caught a knee to the helmet. With Akash prone, Matt opened fire. The combat shotgun bucked as three explosive shells plunged through muscle into the bonk's abdomen. It roared as entrails coated the wall and kicked Akash ten feet, into Matt. Matt rolled to the side and fired again, but his shots just bounced off its armored chest.

A REC7 chattered behind him. "Company," Garrett said. AK fire answered him up the stairwell. "Normals. I'll hold them."

The giant dragged Blossom to her feet, then backhanded her through the wall. Matt's shot ricocheted off its skull, but the next blew a chunk from its neck. He advanced. It dropped to one knee, steadying itself on the wall until Matt blew off its elbow with another volley. Three more shots knocked it on its back. Dropping to one knee to get a shot under its chin, he pulled the trigger and the microgrenade went off inside its skull.

"Status?" he said into his helmet. Radio silence earned them nothing at this point. He snapped another 20-round drum of 19 mm HEAB rounds into the shotgun as his team reported in.

"At least a dozen below us, pinned down," Garrett said. "Upper stairwell still clear."

"Minute, sir," Akash said.

"Alive," Blossom reported, her voice slurred. "Pretty broke up."

Jeff's voice spoke over the radio. "You have DRC troops closing on your position. Kill him and get to the extraction point. Marine support ETA ten minutes, and it's going to be close."

"Mister Dawkins?" Matt shouted toward the end of the hall. "You're under arrest on the authority of the International Council on Augmented Phenomena. Come out with your hands on your head. Or don't, and we'll kill you, which my boss would prefer. You've got three seconds."

Dawkins's voice held a hint of England but otherwise sounded all Middle America. "The DRC recognizes neither UN nor NATO authority, Sergeant Rowley. ICAP has no jurisdiction here."

Matt grunted. "We don't care. One."

The floor shook as a grenade went off in the stairwell. Akash hobbled up next to him and fired a round into the bonk's ruined, bloody eye. "Just in case."

Matt ignored him. "Two." He triggered the AA12's range finder at the doorway and flipped the thumb switch so that the HEAB round would explode to the left. "Th—"

A grenade skittered out the door. Akash dove, covering the explosive, his body jerking as it went off. Matt rounded the corner, firing. Explosive rounds tore into computers, filing cabinets, and a cheap metal desk. Whispers roiled across his brain, and he stepped back.

Feet caught him in the chest as Dawkins dropped from the ceiling. A palm strike knocked the shotgun from his hands. Another pounded his helmet, dazing him. Matt blocked the next two strikes, then countered with an uppercut. Dawkins spun to the side, past Akash's body, and sprinted down the hall. Matt took three steps and dove, hooking Dawkins's ankle as he scrambled over the dead bonk.

Dawkins caught himself before he fell prone, but Matt yanked him back and delivered a knife-hand chop to his groin. Dawkins deflected some of the blow with a roll to the side and Matt just managed to block a crushing strike to his throat.

"I'm hit," Garrett said. "Flesh wound." His assault rifle chattered as Dawkins pressed the attack.

Matt anticipated every strike, but could barely keep up. Almost as fast as Blossom, Dawkins wielded iron-like hands that hurt like hell even when blocked. Dawkins took a helmet to the face and laughed through bloody teeth. A flurry of blows forced Matt down the hall, over the dead bonk and past Akash's body. *He's too fast.*

Helmetless, Blossom appeared behind Dawkins. She'd found a claw hammer somewhere, which she swung two-handed at the side of his head. He ducked without turning around, then snap-kicked her leg. She gasped as her knee bent sideways, then dropped as he drove his palms into her temples.

Matt drew his combat knife and lunged at Dawkins's back. A finger strike shattered his visor and broke his nose, and a snap-kick to the face backed him up another step. Dawkins wrenched the knife from his hand and stabbed it through his shoulder, the monofilament blade punching through armor, muscle, and bone.

Dawkins grinned through bloody teeth. "I guess you're not the one, Rowley." Matt tried to lift his arm and couldn't. Dawkins yanked out the knife and reversed his grip on it.

An assault rifle fired and Dawkins dropped, clutching his right leg. Still prone, Blossom fired again, the second burst tearing into his left leg at point blank range. Dawkins spasmed as she switched to full auto, emptying the magazine into his calves and thighs.

Matt crushed Dawkins's throat with his knee, then flipped him onto his back with his good arm. Dawkins's mouth opened and closed, but no words came out as Matt hogtied him with steel-reinforced zip ties. Matt's arm regained more use with every passing second. He looked down at Akash, still face down on the floor.

"You alive, Rastogi?"

Akash didn't move. Matt rolled him over and hissed through his teeth. Steaming blood and viscera mingled with Akash's body armor, his neck a ruin of blackened flesh. Matt knelt, then exhaled in relief. Akash's exposed arteries pumped, and air wheezed through his throat.

Blossom dragged herself upright, spared them a glance, then picked up Akash's REC7 and joined Garrett at the door. She took a few shots, enabling him to reload. "Going up. Cover me." She tossed a pair of grenades out the door and disappeared into the stairwell. Garrett's weapon barked.

"Sorry," Matt said. "This is going to hurt." He grabbed Akash's combat harness in his left hand and Dawkins's shirt in his right and dragged them toward the exit. He handed off Akash to Garrett, who cradled him in his arms.

"Up!" Blossom yelled. "Go!"

Garrett shouldered through the door. Blossom stood at the edge of the landing, her weapon trained on the first floor. "Clear to the roof," she said. Matt's lungs burned with cordite and gunpowder as he took the stairs three at a time, Blossom backing up behind him. Before they could make it to the top the building rocked, brick dust falling from the ceiling.

"What the hell was that?" Garrett asked.

"Tanks," Jeff said. "DRC. Marines'll distract them. Proceed to the extraction point."

Whispers begged him to die as he stepped onto the roof. He ducked behind the stairwell just before machine gun fire blasted chunks out of the brick next to where he'd been standing. He triggered his radio as his squad took cover. "Jeff, we've got a 67-2 on the opposite roof pinning us down. Are we on our own for this?"

"We see them," Jeff said. "Give us a minute."

They crouched at the top of the stairwell in an unrelenting hail of brick chips, and took occasional shots down the stairs to discourage pursuit. Thirty seconds later a streak of fire hit the far roof and the pillbox exploded.

Blossom whooped.

"Thank you, Marines," Garrett said. As if on cue, a cacophonous legion of small-arms fire erupted from the beach.

They ran to the edge and punched pneumatic crampons into the brick facade. Carrying Dawkins, Garrett rappelled down first. Matt followed with Akash. Blossom took the rear. The building shook as another tank round hit it, and Javelin missiles streaked overhead in response. Matt stumbled as his thigh erupted in pain but kept sprinting. As he carried Akash to the beach, a hundred pinpoints of firing automatic weapons filled his vision.

The colonel in charge of the operation gave a perfunctory salute and rushed them to the evac boats. The LCAC hovercrafts spit bullets up the beach, covering their retreat into the water. In moments they made it out of range of hostile fire. Matt checked his leg. Through and through, the bullet wound had already closed.

Once aboard, the colonel yelled to them over the giant fan propellers. "Air support has us covered all the way to the Rwandan shore. Once there, you'll head north-west to a small air field. Mr. Hannes will send the coordinates to your helmets." He glanced at

Matt's shattered visor, and Blossom's helmetless head. "From there it's a fast jump to Saudi Arabia. You'll be home before you know it."

Matt patted Akash on the shoulder. "You going to live?" The question wasn't necessary; with second-generation regenerates, ICAP agents would survive anything that didn't kill them outright. A ruined, gory mess, he grinned through bloody teeth.

"You're one ballsy asshole," Garrett said. Akash gave him a weak thumbs-up.

* * *

As the WWII-era troop transport made its way through the dark Rwandan mountains, Matt checked Dawkins's bonds for the millionth time. The banded steel had cut through the skin of his wrists and ankles, which had healed around them. Dawkins stared at him, and the whispers muttered every time their eyes met.

A rugged man in his mid-forties, Dawkins had dark brown hair that matched his eyes. Like everyone with second-generation regenerates, his perfect skin held no blemish, scar, or wrinkle. He blinked in the dust of the road, then resumed staring.

"Do I know you?" Matt asked.

Blossom glared at him. "You not supposed to talk—"

He cut her off with an upraised hand and looked back at Dawkins.

"No," Dawkins said. "We've never met. But I've read your dossier, twice."

"Twice?"

"Once when you were recruited and again when you were assigned my case." He clucked his tongue. "Not very distinguished, I'm afraid."

Matt refused to take the bait. "That's what I told them." *Keep him talking, and maybe he'll slip up and reveal his source.* "And yet," he grabbed Dawkins's restraints and shook. "Here you are."

"What if I'm here because I wanted to talk to you, Sergeant Rowley?"

Akash snorted, then let out a tiny groan. "You're here because we kicked your ass and dragged you back with us, eh?" He rubbed the fresh, pink skin on his throat and chest.

Dawkins looked at Akash for a moment, then turned back to Matt. "You left the C130 at 4:42 pm local time, just as it crossed the western shore of Lake Kivu. Using the cover of the setting sun, you approached on ICAP-pattern ESG powered gliders—"

"Enough," Matt said. "You've made your point."

Dawkins looked back at Akash. "What you need to ask yourself, Mr. Rastogi, is if I knew all that, why didn't I ambush you on the way in? A flak cannon would have ruined that pretty face in a moment. So why weren't mine manned?"

"Were you going to talk before or after you tried to kill us in the hallway?" Akash asked.

Dawkins rolled his eyes. "My plan was to capture Sergeant Rowley, not the other way around." He smiled at Akash. "And the rest of you were expendable."

Matt exchanged looks with his team, then looked at Dawkins. "Okay, you want to talk to me? Go—" He gasped as the whispers slithered through his mind, strangling conscious thought. Pinpricks of white pain drove through his skull. He put the heel of his hand to his head and groaned through a clenched jaw. "Ahh—" Next to him, Blossom clutched her head with both hands. Dawkins's eyes rolled into the back of his head.

A blinding flash lit the sky behind them. The truck swerved and skidded sideways, pitching Matt to the floor, and came to rest, diesel engine idling at a low rumble.

"What the fuck was that?" Garrett said through gritted teeth, pulling himself from the floor.

Behind them, the atmosphere burned. A column of smoke and white steam boiled skyward.

"My God," Akash said. He got out and gaped at the horizon.

Matt followed him. As the whispers faded, he spoke. "Kivu."

Garrett dragged Dawkins out of the truck by the throat. "What did you do?" he snarled.

The shockwave blasted them to the ground, and rocked the truck up on two wheels. By the time Matt regained his feet, a mushroom cloud filled the horizon. He turned back to the group and cried out.

Garrett's fist sprayed blood as he pulled back and punched again, caving in Dawkins's cheek bone.

"JOHNSON," Matt screamed. "STAND DOWN!"

Garrett pulled back for another punch, but Blossom appeared in front of him, a twelve-inch knife at his temple.

"You won't hit again."

Garrett snarled, shaking, his bloody fingers digging into Dawkins's throat. "He killed . . . Millions. Millions of innocent people."

Blossom didn't twitch. "Drop him."

Garrett dropped him. Dawkins collapsed and rolled to his side. Garrett spat on him, glared at Matt, and got in the truck.

Matt stepped up to the hog-tied prisoner. He tried to speak, couldn't, and tried again. His raspy voice quavered, but he got out the word. "Why?"

Dawkins spat, then shook his head.

Matt lifted him and slammed his mushy, ruined face against the side of the truck. "I asked you a question."

He froze. Dawkins's torn collar exposed part of a tattoo, a line of pictographic text defaced with a brown cross over the top. Matt couldn't read it, but he recognized it. *Uruk proto-cuneiform,* the linguistics department had said. *Be ready. The master is coming.*

Dawkins pushed a bloody tooth out of his mouth. He said something impossible to decipher through his swollen tongue and shattered jaw. He tried again, and the gurgling wet noise sounded something like, "Wasn't me."

They locked eyes. Matt saw no deceit in them, but if his years as a trooper had taught him anything, he made a terrible judge of honesty.

* * *

By the time Jeff met them at the thin strip of packed earth that passed for an airfield, the flames over the mountains had faded to a dull yellow that still washed out the single, dim beacon on the control tower. Two small, single-propeller planes with French tags waited beside a red-and-white civilian helicopter.

Akash got out with help from Blossom, still hesitant on his feet. Jeff intercepted Garrett as he carried Dawkins toward the plane, redirecting him to the helicopter. An armored figure sat in the back, unrecognizable with his combat visor down, hands on his thighs. *Frahm.*

As Matt approached, Jeff stuck out his hand. They shook.

"Great job, Sergeant. Looked dicey for a minute there. I didn't expect you to take him alive."

"Thanks," Matt said, his eyes on Dawkins. "But Sakura took him down without killing him, and I couldn't pass up an opportunity like that." He met Jeff's gaze. "How'd the marines fare?"

"They lost a chopper when the lake exploded. Nine casualties. But they were in full evac, and everyone else got away. It could have been a lot worse."

Matt paused. "What the hell happened back there?"

Jeff shrugged, his gaze sliding back to the chopper. "Booby trap is my guess. We might be able to find out, if DRC cooperates. I wouldn't count on it, buddy. They just lost a whole lot of soldiers, and radio chatter suggests they know that ICAP led the hit."

"Jesus." Matt nodded toward the chopper. "He's not going with us?"

Jeff clapped his shoulder. "He's in good hands, Matt. We—"

"Not a good idea. He's . . . crafty. Don't underestimate him."

Jeff's patronizing smile didn't instill confidence. "It's all good, buddy. See you stateside."

Matt opened his mouth to protest, then frowned at Jeff's back as he walked away. Jeff climbed into the chopper's front seat and it lifted off, propellers flashing black and orange in the light of the rising fireball.

"Sergeant?" their driver asked.

"What?"

He gestured toward the runway. "We're taking off, if you'd hop in."

"Yeah." With one last glance at the helicopter, he followed the marine to the plane.

What did you want to tell me, Dawkins?

He ascended the stairs, ducked his head through the door, and sat down in the canvas bucket seat next to Akash, who looked at the door in surprise.

"Where's the prisoner?" he asked.

"Jeff took him," Garrett said.

Blossom buckled her safety harness. "Where?"

Matt shrugged. "I don't know. What was I supposed to do, stop him?"

"Yes," Blossom said. "You said it yourself. Something here isn't right."

"But he's still our boss."

"Maybe you screwed up," Garrett said. "Maybe we should have followed orders in the first place. Maybe Jeff knows what he's doing, and we're grunts for a reason."

"Shit, guys," Akash said, palms pressed to his temples. "We got him. Nailed him to the wall. He's in custody. The good guys won. We can be happy about that, eh?"

Chapter 11

Matt dropped his keys on the table next to the door and picked up the note.

At Kate's. Call when you get in. —Monica

He grabbed a Coke out of the fridge, filled Ted's water dish, and went into the bedroom to change. He stripped off his undershirt and looked at himself in the full-length mirror behind the door. The raw gash where Dawkins had plunged the knife into his shoulder had faded to a pink line. There'd be no trace of it by morning.

He worried about Akash. The tactically smart decision to dive on the grenade, and thus shield the rest of the team from the blast, could well have killed him. Matt thanked God for the miracle that instantaneous trauma of that magnitude hadn't, and cursed Akash for his recklessness. Heads-up Boy Scout heroics had their place, but on an all-augged team they weren't necessary in most situations.

He sighed and emptied his pockets onto the dresser. Some loose change, two pens, his wallet . . . and a flash drive that wasn't his. Frowning, he picked it up. Etched on the back in tiny letters, it read, "Disconnect your network, then watch me. Use headphones."

Matt snatched Monica's netbook off of the kitchen table, sat on the bed, disabled the WiFi, and plugged in the drive. It held two files, a spreadsheet and a video entitled "Watch Me First." He took a swig of Coke and popped the ear buds in, then helped Ted up onto his lap. The antivirus software gave the okay, so he opened the video. A window popped up with a question. "What is Ted's birthday? MM/DD/YYYY"

He scratched Ted behind the ear, then typed in "11/26/2011" and hit "Enter."

He grunted when Dawkins appeared on the screen. *How the heck would he know that?* Without a single brown hair out of place, Dawkins looked like a businessman in an Armani suit. He didn't smile.

"Sergeant Rowley, ICAP is lying to you. To everyone. There are no safe levels of Gerstner Augmentations, and they know it. The technology is . . . ." He sighed. "Parasitic. It feeds off of life, off of sanity. It breaks people, consumes them. There's something . . . I don't . . . ."

He ran a hand through his hair. So much for the perfect look.

"The chemistry doesn't make sense. I mean it works, but there's no reason it should. And ICAP. They own it, they control it. Not me. Every gram of Jade, every boost, every aug, the Gerstner carbon comes from them . . . and all they have to do to stop it is get rid of the source. But they don't. Instead, they flood the market and make it easy for monsters like me to poison people for money. They created you and pretend that you and people like you are the solution. You're not. You're just a puppet."

The camera panned out to reveal Dawkins's IPI office on Idjwi, his desk piled with bags of Jade.

"I don't know their end-game. Why do this? Why not just shut it down? When they find out you didn't assassinate me, they're going to kill millions to destroy my computers at Kivu, just to keep what I know from getting to the wrong people. You, for example." He folded his hands and rested his head on his knuckles.

"I had to kill a lot of people to get this information to you. Some of those people were your friends, and you're right to hate me. But understand this: they were dead anyway. So am I. So are you. They made sure of that, the day they gave you your first aug. Gerstner-Induced Psychosis is inevitable, only a matter of time and who you kill on the way out."

He sat back. "So before you die, I'm going to use you to bring the whole game crashing down. And you're going to do it, because it's the right thing to do. You don't have a lot of time, so make it count."

Dawkins reached toward the keyboard, then pulled his hand back.

"And one more thing. Things are about to get very bad for you. I'm sorry. You'll have my help where I can give it."

He hit a key and the video stopped.

Matt stared at the frozen screen for a long time, then looked at the date on the file. Dawkins had made the video two weeks before they'd landed on Idjwi, before Onofre Garza had even told them about it. So either Dawkins had access to much better precognitive therapies than Matt did, or he blew up the lake himself and wanted Matt to think ICAP had done it. *Does he think I'm that dumb, or does he know I'm not?*

He looked at the other file. Scrolling through the mass of numbers, he looked for anything that made sense in the jumble of columns and blank spaces. He found his ICAP ID number, and next to it a string of dates—the dates of each augmentation. Using his own information, he figured out that the top row showed codes for the type of augmentation, which explained the gaps in the other rows. Not every agent had every aug, and he confirmed his suspicion with Akash, Garrett, Blossom, and Conor's entries.

The last column in his row held a date thirty-nine months out. He deleted the date for his late-second precognitive therapy, and it increased to eighty-four months. He put it back, and the date reverted.

He logged into the ICAP servers using his smart phone, and pulled up the employee numbers for his team and for several agents who'd bonked out. Mark Carroll went bonk fourteen months after his first augmentation, two months before the final date on his entry. Liam Salt succumbed to GIP fifty-four months after his, and the spreadsheet read fifty-one. He checked another eighteen bonked agents, and only one erred by more than four months. Connor Flynn wasn't set to bonk out for another year and change.

He checked Blossom, Garrett, and Akash. Eighteen, forty-one, and twenty-two. He checked his own again. Thirty-nine months. Just over three years. *If it's true.*

He jumped as his phone rang. *Hannes, Jeff.* He hit "Send."

"Rowley."

"Hey, Matt. What's up?"

He hesitated. "Not sure what you mean. Just winding down. Monica's at Kate's, I'm having a Coke and kicking back."

"So that's not you poking around our employee files?"

"Uh, yeah, that's me. Just looking up some employee numbers."

"May I ask why?"

Matt looked at Ted, at the screen, and back at the dog. Ted wagged his tail and licked Matt's stomach. "We know Dawkins knows way too much. I have a hunch on where he gets his information."

"You think there's a mole?"

"I'm not ready to share yet. I'll let you know if it pans out to anything. Hey, when's the interrogation?"

"Sorry?"

"I assume we're interrogating Dawkins sometime soon."

"Let us handle that. I need you to supervise the Garza transfer. His brother's getting out of Supermax tomorrow, and Onofre wants you there. Says he trusts you to make the delivery."

"Who the hell cares what Onofre Garza wants? He's getting his brother, which is more than either of them deserves."

"We've already booked you a flight—"

"So cancel it. I'll be in D.C. tomorrow for the Dawkins interrogation."

Now Jeff hesitated. "Dawkins isn't in D.C."

"Well, where the hell is he?"

Nothing. Then, "Capturing him was more than we could have hoped for. You did a great job. Now let other people do their jobs."

"You can't be serious."

"I am. You're a field team, and he's no longer in the field. We'll get you a new assignment once we're done with operational debriefs on the Kivu operation."

"Begging your pardon, Jeff, but this is a steaming pile right here. Did you see his tattoos? At least one matches Conor—"

"I know, buddy. It's messed up, but we'll get to the bottom of it. We want to figure this out just as badly as you do. But it's not your skill set. Let it go."

Matt opened his mouth, then thought better of it. He thought he trusted Jeff, but not necessarily over the phone.

"I want your report by the end of the week," Jeff said.

"You'll have it."

He hung up, logged out of both systems, and pocketed the flash drive. Lying back on the bed, he wrapped his arms around Ted. "What now, Ted?"

Ted whined and licked his face.

* * *

Matt spent the flight from Mexico City to Washington in a black rage. The congratulatory hug between Hernando and Onofre Garza brought bile up his throat, and the thought that he had brokered the deal brought him nothing but anger and sorrow. The Garzas were killers, as bad as Dawkins in their own way.

No. In his mind's eye he relived the mushroom cloud that immolated or suffocated two million innocent Africans, and he refused to believe that ICAP would do that. The joint UN-NATO venture would never sacrifice that many people for any cause, not after the lessons of the twentieth century. Dawkins killed those men and his team in the Keys, not ICAP.

Matt didn't like being toyed with.

By the time the plane touched down he hadn't slept a wink. Even the fact that he didn't feel any fatigue enraged him. He should be exhausted, from lack of sleep, from the mental effort of keeping the *"What ifs?"* at bay, from the numbing emotional hell of millions of dead clawing at his conscience. Hours on the plane should have left him stiff and sore. And yet, physically he felt great. He could do an Iron Man in record time without even stretching first.

A black Lexus met him outside baggage claim. *Funny how that always happens in D.C., but everywhere else I get a rental.* He carried his own travel bag over the weak protests of the overdressed chauffer, tossing it on the back seat as he got in. "Take your time," Matt said. "If you get lost or stuck in traffic or accidentally drive to Orlando, that's cool, too."

All too soon he arrived at the ICAP stateside offices, an imposing brick building appropriated from some government agency or another after they'd outgrown the UN headquarters in New York. He flashed his badge on the way through the metal detectors, but instead of turning right toward the Operations offices, he took a left and followed the beige marble tiles toward Data Management.

Matt ignored the protests of the desk flunky, walked around the reception area and knocked on Janet LaLonde's door.

"Come in," she said.

He opened the door and stepped inside. Janet pulled her feet off the desk and swiveled to face him. Her legs quit at her neck, and her mid-thigh candy-stripe dress violated dress code, but the powers that be tolerated her antics because she knew her way around the ICAP network like nobody else. Her straight, brown hair hung down to the desk, and she smacked on purple chewing gum with exactly the right amount of low-class sexy that made her Mensa-level IQ dangerous. The aroma of artificial grape flavor permeated the office.

"'Sup, bud?"

"Hey," Matt said. She knew his name, and he presumed that she chose to keep all of her coworkers at a distance. "Can I bother you a minute?"

She scanned her sparse, neat-freak desk, then shrugged. "You already are. So why not?"

He pulled up a chair and sat down. "I'm trying to find a file with some specific data strings." He handed her a flash drive he'd bought at the airport kiosk, which contained fourteen randomly-selected fragments of Dawkins's spreadsheet.

"How soon do you need it?" She blew a bubble, punctured it with her tongue, and sucked it back into her mouth.

"Before I walked in would be nice."

She plugged the drive into an already packed external USB hub, hammered on her keyboard for a minute, then looked up "What's this for?"

Matt shrugged. "I have a hunch." She didn't move so he took a chance. "It involves some ICAP personnel. Could be sensitive."

"Mmm-kay, so where'd you get it?"

Matt should have been prepared for the question, and wasn't. "Um, Santa. I got it from Santa."

Her eyes floated from the monitor to his, and she stopped chewing. "Well," she crossed her legs, "this bad boy's past your payroll, if you know what I mean."

Matt decided to play dumb. "Not really. You mean I can't have it?"

She shot him with her fingers. "Bingo. You're cleared for Level Four. This file is Eight. The freaking POTUS is cleared for Seven." She ejected the drive, rolled it over in her hands for a moment, and tossed it to him.

Still playing dumb, Matt pursed his lips, then nodded. "Fair enough. I'll ask Jeff." He put his hand on the doorknob and turned around. "Keep this between us, yeah?"

She smiled, gum between her teeth, then resumed chewing. "I only report what I have to."

"Thanks!" *That could mean anything.*

He closed her door behind him, waved to the desk flunky shooting daggers out of her eyes at him, and stalked down the hall to Operations. Jeff's office stood in stark contrast to Janet's, with piles of paperwork that threatened avalanche at any wrong move. Jeff had his desk phone to his ear, a smart phone in his lap, and basked in the glow of his desktop monitor. He pointed to a chair when Matt walked in, so Matt moved the stack of papers to the floor and sat.

Jeff, in a gray suit indistinguishable from any other that Matt had seen, backed out of a call from "Bill," fielded another from "Tim," and a third from "Angela." When he finally hung up, his phone rang. He let it go to voicemail and gave Matt an apologetic smile. "What's up?"

"Job's done," Matt said, even though Jeff already knew that. "That wacky Garza family . . . ." He ran out of funny halfway through the comment, so he let it die with a scowl. "I hope it was worth it."

Jeff's grin vanished. "It was."

Matt frowned. "Is his organization crushed? Is Jade off the streets?"

Jeff rolled his eyes. "You know it isn't. But this is huge. Pablo Escobar huge. Huger."

Matt's smirk held no humor. "So, just like Escobar, we can expect rival cartels to pick up the slack, then?"

"Don't be an asshole. There's still a lot of work to do, but we showed them that no matter how big they get, we'll nail them. Nailing the Garzas would be a good next step."

"I'm not interested in—"

"—baby steps," Jeff finished. "I know. Your job sucks. So does mine. There are a bazillion bad guys for every one of us, they don't have rules to follow, and every time you whack-a-mole one, another dozen pop up. But we can at least be happy that we whacked this mole."

Matt said nothing, then closed Jeff's door with his foot.

Jeff raised an eyebrow. When he didn't speak, Jeff did. "What's up, buddy?"

Matt chose his words carefully. "I think this might be bigger than Dawkins." He wasn't sure if Jeff realized how fake his patronizing smile came across or how much it made Matt want to punch him in the face. With a chair. "Much bigger."

Jeff steepled his fingers. "We seized fifteen billion dollars of Jade in a single operation. If there's such thing as bigger than Dawkins, it isn't much bigger. We're half a pube from nailing the entire global operation. We could price most junkies out of the market for years." Jeff smiled.

Matt didn't. "So what's next?"

"Good question," Jeff said. "It might take a while to tease out the necessary intelligence."

"Dawkins," Matt said.

Jeff held up his hands. "Yeah. Dawkins. He's not an easy nut to crack, but we'll squeeze out of him whatever there is to squeeze." With the UN strictures on enhanced interrogation techniques, Matt doubted they could squeeze his Laundromat address out of him. "When we know more, you'll know more."

Matt scoured his brain for the right thing to do and came up empty. "What if I could talk to him?"

"Not going to happen," Jeff said. When Matt opened his mouth to protest, Jeff cut him off. "Look, we talked about this. It's not my call. Your job was to bag him, my job was to help. You bagged him, I helped. The guys upstairs are happy. I'm happy. You should be happy. You'll get a new assignment sometime this week."

Matt set Dawkins's flash drive on top of a pile of papers. "What about this?"

Jeff raised an eyebrow. "What's that?"

"A couple of files. I think Dawkins slipped it into my pocket while we were fighting."

"No shit?" Jeff said. He stared at it for a moment, then reached behind his desk, pulled out the Ethernet cord, and disabled the WiFi. That done, he took the drive and popped it into a USB port. "Can't be too careful."

They watched the video together. Jeff grunted, then opened the spreadsheet. "Holy fucking numbers. What is this?"

"That's what I was looking at the other night." Matt showed him and explained the correlation with bonk timetables.

"You realize that Dawkins could have access to the GIP data and just made all this up to fuck with you? You know he's got an inside line somewhere."

"Yeah," Matt said. "That's why I checked with Janet LaLonde. That file is on our servers, behind confidentiality firewall."

Jeff's smirk vanished. "Janet told you that?"

Matt shook his head. "Not on purpose. I gave her some snippets of the code and asked her for the whole file. She told me it was past my pay grade. Level eight or something. So I told her I'd ask you."

"I see." Jeff sat back.

Matt exhaled. "It's not her fault. You understand that she didn't know what or why, only that I wanted it. But note that she didn't say that no such file existed. She said I couldn't have it, and by doing so admitted that it's there to have. So if Dawkins has a mole, it's a Level Eight mole. Who's got Level Eight clearance?"

"Weird," Jeff said. His smirk returned. "Tell you what, buddy, I'll look into it, see if I can get a better handle on that file. I'm Seven-cleared, so I should be able to sort this out, and if I can't I'll pass it up to Frahm." He stood, walked around the desk, and shook Matt's hand. "Thanks for bringing it to me. I can't overstate how much I appreciate the trust you've put in me. Go home, spend some time with Monica. I'll keep you posted."

"But you'll keep my name out of it."

"Of course," Jeff said. Matt didn't leave, so Jeff leaned back on his desk. "Something else?"

"Conor Flynn was my friend. Or I thought he was." Jeff nodded. "And I want to know what happened to him. Dawkins's tattoo matched Flynn's—"

Jeff cut him off with an upraised hand. "Enough, Matt. We've got good people on it, but it's not something that makes sense for you to be working on. First, you're right. Conor was your friend, so you're emotionally compromised. Second, Dawkins is probably screwing with us, and you're letting him get in your head with this bullshit. Third, you've got a bazillion dollars of Gerstner Augmentations that make you a superhuman ass-kicking machine, and this is desk work. Let the research weenies do their jobs while you go out and kick superhuman ass, and when they know, I'll know. And once I know, you'll know."

"You swear it?"

Jeff frowned. "I don't have to swear it, I'm your boss." Then he smiled. "But yeah, I swear to God there will be people looking into this, and when they get to the bottom of it, you'll know. Now go spend a nice couple of paid days off relaxing with your wife. That's an order, buddy."

"Aye, sir," Matt said, and walked out.

Chapter 12

He grabbed the mail on the way into the house, shuffling through bills and junk mail and stopping at a large manila envelope from Herr Gottschalk in Dresden. He set the rest of the mail on the deck, leaned against the rail, and tore open the envelope.

He pulled out Gottschalk's business card and a scanned, black-and-white photograph. Nine men stood under a giant swastika circled with German words, the enameled frieze from the stairwell to the Dresden bunker. Circled in red marker, a young man in a windbreaker smiled, one hand in his pocket, the other on the shoulder of the man next to him. With his light hair and dark eyes, he had to be Brian Frahm's grandfather. They could have been twins.

Gottschalk hadn't circled the text beneath the photo. "Joint British-American archeological team, Dresden, Germany, 1958. Photo by Tom Hannes." On the back in severe block letters, Gottschalk had written, "I knew he looked familiar. Uncanny!" Matt frowned, stuffed the photo and envelope in his back pocket, and walked inside.

He stepped through the door, scooped up Ted, and sat down on the couch next to Monica. They chatted about nothings in front of *Family Guy* reruns—Bartell's public nuisance hearing, the new cheese counter at the grocery store, winter greens from the farmer's market. He let her presence soothe him into something that resembled but wasn't peace of mind, closed his eyes on an enthusiastic *giggity* and let sleep take him. He woke to the squeak of the deck stair, followed by a strange rumble.

The TV had died. In the pitch black Ted growled again—he'd never done that before—and Monica stretched, groggy. "Is the power out?" The black-and-white ultraviolet mingled with the green infrared background of the house's ambient warmth. The heat registers glowed a modest, fading orange.

"Looks like it," he said, and leaned in close to whisper in her ear. "Something's wrong. Get the shotgun and lock the door. But go easy."

Her eyes glinted in the moonlight, full of worry. She swallowed, then sat up. "I'm going to bed," she said with too much theater. She stretched on her way to the bedroom, hamming it all the way. Ted followed her, still growling, his tail between his legs. Matt followed her, cutting into the bathroom with feigned nonchalance. He didn't turn on the light.

He ran the sink, flushed the toilet, and used the noise to cover his movements. He pulled the .45 ACP from the holster taped under the sink and chambered a round. His late Uncle Jon's model 1911 from Vietnam, a reliable handgun that had never been fired at another human being. He grabbed both spare box magazines and stuffed them into his back pocket, then closed his eyes and listened.

Faint scratches at the deck door. Frantic barking from the bedroom. "Ted, shut up!" Monica yelled, real fear creeping into her fake annoyance.

He eased the door open and looked at their wedding photo in a gold-painted frame on the wall. It held the only place he'd seen Monica's defiant, "bring it on, world" confidence in a long while, and while circumstance had shattered her, she'd been recovering for years and he loved her more than ever. In the fuzzy IR reflection at least two figures crouched on the deck. He held his breath as they picked the lock. The door slid open, and they stepped into the kitchen.

Matt rounded the corner pistol-first and pulled the trigger. The gun roared, and Matt's vision hazed blue in the afterimage. The first shape crumpled as a double-tap took him in the chest. The second staggered backward and fell off the railing, hot blood spraying orange in the infra-red spectrum. Matt dove through the doorway, snatched the fallen man's suppressed REC7 on his way, and rolled off the deck. A suppressed assault rifle chuffed as he hit the ground, bullets tearing through the underbrush.

As he stood, the second commando gasped for breath behind a pair of night-vision goggles, hot red blood leaking through his body armor. Matt crushed his trachea with a brutal stomp, then snatched a pair of grenades from his bandoleer. With an annoyed, curious grunt he pulled the autoinjector from the man's belt and stuffed it into his pocket. He pulled the pin on one of the grenades and tossed it at the oak by the corner of the house. It bounced off of the trunk and out of sight. The explosion shattered the front windows. Someone yelled for his mom in an anguish-filled voice.

The whispers gibbered their murderous nonsense as he circled around the deck. The screaming man's left leg lay three feet from the rest of him, and steaming liquid gushed from ravaged arteries. The iron tang of blood mingled with the earthy smell of gunpowder. Matt shot him center-of-mass, then choked up the REC7 and fired another burst into the house. Bullets tore through a man that leaned around the wall, and the grenade dropped from his hands.

"Pomegranate!" someone yelled. Another burst dropped a man as he fled for the counter, and Matt shot yet another in the thigh as he turned to run. The man stumbled to his knees next to the grenade, cried out as he scrambled for it, and blew sideways in a spray of shrapnel. His weapon scattered across the floor, some kind of strange air gun.

Matt picked it up and pulled back the breach. He caught the small canister as it ejected, a light metal object with a needle on the front. The serial number engraved on the bottom sifted through Matt's mind and landed on its significance: level-six muscle enhancement. If the needle hit him, he'd bonk in minutes at most. He tossed it across the floor, tore out the magazine and stuffed it into his pocket, and kinked the barrel over his knee.

He crouched and looked for movement, taking the time to reload from a dead man's bandoleer. Six dead and not one of them augged. He unscrewed the suppressor from the REC7. *Except for the aug gun, they used standard ICAP issue, and the man who yelled "pomegranate" had to be either French or French Canadian.* Assuming standard tactical doctrine, there were four left in the squad, and at least one more squad on standby. The whispers clawed at his mind, an orgy of desperate bloodshed.

Monica crouched beside the bed, the shotgun trained at the door. Her hands shook, and her lips stretched in a thin line. Ted cowered under the bed as the window exploded inward. She screamed.

Matt shook off the premonition and charged the house. He grunted in pain as a bullet punched through his abdomen, and threw the last grenade left-handed into the living room. Monica screamed as glass shattered in the bedroom, a full five seconds after Matt had seen it. Their shotgun roared even as the grenade went off behind him. He hit the door with his shoulder, splintering it around the lock and catapulting into the room.

A commando sprawled on the floor, his head leaking bright orange in the infrared spectrum, a REC7 on the floor next to him. Ted snarled and worried at his ankle. A second man wrenched Monica's head back by her hair, pressing a black pistol to her neck. A third crouched behind the bed, his assault rifle trained on Matt's center of mass. The shotgun lay on the floor.

Matt froze. Hot blood ran down his stomach, soaking his shirt and jeans. *That's three, plus one in the living room. If he's alive.* Neither of these men held air guns.

The man holding Monica tightened his finger on the trigger. "Drop your weapon and fold your hands on your head and she won't get hurt." His accent struck Matt as either Spanish or Portuguese.

Monica's eyes flicked downward, barely visible in the moonlight.

"Yeah," Matt said.

As she raised her arms and dropped to her knees, her assailant tried and failed to maintain his grip. Matt pulled the trigger. The three-round burst sprayed bits of bloody skull and brains onto the wall. The other man pulled the trigger. Matt snarled as the full-auto barrage caught him in the chest, shredding his lungs as he fell to the carpet.

He caught himself with one hand and sprang forward. Monica snap-kicked the man in the face, tearing off his goggles. She kicked him again as he rebounded off the wall. Coughing blood, Matt fell on the shotgun and choked it up. The man's eyes widened as he looked down the barrel. "*Non!*" he cried.

Matt jammed it into his throat and pulled the trigger, then rolled over, training the gun on the door.

His chest itched, and his breath came in wheezes. He tried to talk and couldn't.

"You okay?" Monica asked.

He nodded, then gestured at the shattered window. As he reloaded the shotgun, she busted out the rest of the glass with her fist, draped a pillow over the sill, and clambered out. He handed the weapon out the window, then picked up Ted and passed him through, gritting his teeth against the agony in his chest. He coughed blood as he dragged himself through and fell to the ground five feet below.

"Walker's," he gasped, standing.

She nodded and whispered to the Bassett. "Ted, heel."

They crept through the woods toward Aaron Walker's tree farm. The old man raised eighty acres of Christmas trees and shipped them across the United States. He once bragged about supplying the White House, and sometimes Rockefeller Center. The story changed based on how much he'd had to drink and whether or not his wife heard it and called him a liar. More importantly, he drove a '92 Dodge pickup and kept the keys in the cab.

Freezing dew soaked through Matt's blood-spattered socks. He looked down at Monica's bare feet and impotent rage consumed him, washing out even the burning itch of his lungs stitching back together. A man who can't protect his family is no man at all. Someone shouted behind them, guttural French carrying through the woods. *No radio?* Matt thought.

He pulled Monica behind a small conifer, kissed her, and leaned in so that his lips almost touched her ear. "Get to the truck," he whispered while reattaching the suppressor to the front of the assault rifle. "Make sure the keys are in it, but don't start it. And don't close the door. Be as quiet as you can." He pulled back and looked into her blue eyes, irises almost black in the moonlight. His heart tore with pride at the determined, fierce look.

She licked her lips, touched them with her fingertips, and looked at them in the moonlight. "You're bleeding."

He took a full breath and didn't want to scream. A good sign. "I know. But I'll be fine. Now go."

She nodded once, scooped up the dog, and took off at a silent trot.

His eyes traced the heat signature of her bare feet on the grass, fading in the cold dew but not fast enough. He bolted across the open space between the tree line and the barn, lifted the latch and heaved open the door. The hinges squeaked, and Buster started baying from inside Walker's house. The collie would bark at anything and everything, and even nothing at all. *C'mon, Ted, stay quiet.* A good dog by nature, obedience classes had reinforced his desire to please, but he could be headstrong when he wanted to and liked to join the chorus. Nobody who owned a Basset hound would accuse them of being smart.

The horses whickered and stomped as he pulled open their stalls, and Walker's three goats bleated in agitation. Once freed they milled about in confused sleepiness, except for the pony he'd harnessed and secured with a loop to the hitching post just inside the entrance. Ducking to the back of the barn, he pulled the pin on a grenade and dropped it in the cistern, then heaved himself up and over the hay loft. The bang shattered his eardrums, and the animals panicked. He dropped to the floor and followed their mad dash into the darkness outside, pulling the pony with him.

Two horses scattered into the lines of trees, and he led his pony after them, masking his heat signature on the line of approach from his house. Someone muttered off to the right—he caught *"pourquoi"* and *"l'animaux"* and nothing else. He dropped to one knee and let off two tight bursts, the second louder than the first. *Suppressor's failing.* He led the horse over to the bodies of the two men, swapped his weapon for one of theirs, and refilled his bandoleer with grenades.

He turned just as a third man rounded a thicket, air gun raised. Matt stepped forward and knocked the barrel to the side as it spat certain madness, and the commando struck him twice in the torso. Matt smiled as the taut wall of muscle absorbed the blows, then head-butted his opponent square in the face. His skull crunched as it caved in, but Matt wasted no time on satisfaction. He closed his grip on the barrel and rounded the shrub, swinging the weapon like a baseball bat. The collapsible metal stock caught the hiding man in the neck, and a geyser of hot blood sprayed from his shredded carotid artery.

As the man's life pumped onto the ground, Matt scanned the tree line. Behind him, Buster's high-pitched, rolling howl got louder, and a screen door banged closed. In front of him, nothing moved in the darkness. If the other six were out there, they had thermal camouflage. He crouched, bent the barrels of both weapons, and listened.

A throaty rumble rose in the darkness. *Helicopter.* He ran for Aaron's truck as Buster made a fantastic ruckus trying to herd the panicky animals toward the barn, bounding through the grass, tail wagging in unfettered glee. Matt jumped behind the wheel as a shotgun blast roared into the air from the porch.

"Hey!" Aaron hollered. "You get out of there!" Walker cocked the gun for effect.

Matt yelled back. "Aaron, get inside and stay there. Don't come out until the cops show up, not for anything. Go!" As the sounds of the rotors got louder, Matt took heart that they had a higher pitch than a typical ICAP transport.

Aaron's brow furrowed, but he lowered the gun. "Matt? That you?"

Matt waved, jammed the stick into drive, and hit the gas. "Sorry!" he yelled over the gravel-spitting tires. He accelerated through the trees as Monica cradled a whimpering Ted.

She squeezed her eyes shut against the darkness. "Jeez, babe, you're going to kill us."

"I can see fine," he said, shifting into fourth. *Just hope I don't hit anything.* He left the lights off. The black-and-white UV overlay helped him drive, and at this speed his mind flooded with precognitive images of countless crashes, which he avoided without slowing down. He bounced through the creek into McMullen's field and ploughed a line straight through the dry feed corn.

"I think I'm going to be sick," Monica said as he veered around the towering oak in the middle of the field, then jerked a hard right to avoid an ancient harvester hidden by the faded yellow stalks.

"Sorry," he said. "Are you hurt?"

She shook her head but threw up before she could get the window down, filling the car with the acrid smell of bile and half-digested macaroni and cheese. Ted whined and licked her face, but she didn't open her eyes. They broke the tree line and barreled through pine boughs, the old growth cut high by generations of McMullen hunters. He risked a glance up and saw nothing but trees, then gritted his teeth as the front right tire hit a large root, bashing his head into the ceiling. The truck veered, tilted, and then came back down on four wheels.

He exhaled a sigh of relief and jammed his foot on the brake. The truck careened to a stop just in front of an ancient pine, one that Matt had used in his pre-ICAP days for a hunter's stand. Monica looked at him with wide, bloodshot eyes. "Why are we stopping?"

"That chopper can't see us through the trees," he said, "but they sure as hell know where we went. I think from here I can find the north road, but we've got gullies funneling us. They're sure to have a map, so can figure out where we're going." He killed the engine. "Wait here."

He heard her *Wait, what?* before she said it and had climbed ten feet up the tree before it left her mouth. The bulky REC7 made it hard to climb, but at least he could breathe again. Thirty feet up, the trees broke enough that he could see stars, and the distant thrum of the helicopter closed in. The sound echoed through the mountains, so he couldn't tell what direction it would come from. If they were smart, they'd circle around to catch them as they exited the far side of the dense pines.

He trained the assault rifle on an empty piece of sky and sucked in a lungful of freezing air. He let it out and took another, happy with his lung function. He frowned. Two squads of commandoes would be massive overkill against a normal threat, and inadequate to the point of stupidity for an aug. But those air guns . . . they were something new. He could only think of one reason to shoot massive doses of GS Augs at a person, and the thought filled him with rage. *They wanted me to bonk, to kill my wife, Ted, my neighbors, so they could put me down like a dog and no one would be the wiser.* He wondered how many agents had fallen the same way and how many people knew about it.

The thudding rotors grew much louder, and Matt forced all stressful thoughts from his mind. He had to relax. He wouldn't get much of a shot, and it had to count. This wasn't the movies, where a good hit to the gas tank would take—*There!* The clear heat signature confirmed his hopes: ICAP used US Army AH-64 Apache attack helicopters, and their standard "Black Hole" infrared suppression system would have muddied his vision. This civilian craft had four or five seats and wouldn't have armor or, hopefully, a bullet-proof canopy.

Matt tried to work through the ramifications as the chopper circled closer. *No augs, wrong helicopter, radio silence. But they used ICAP issue and doctrines.* He breathed out, listened to the whispers gibber their incoherent bloodlust, then pulled the trigger. He fired the second burst a quarter-second later, just to the left of the first. As the glass canopy cracked, the pilot jinked, putting his center of mass right in line with the second volley. The pilot twitched and jittered, and the chopper dropped into a death-spiral.

Matt heard the impact before he reached the ground, skinning his hands on the rough bark. Monica still sat in the truck, upright and rigid, Ted on her lap. Matt got in and wrinkled his nose at the smell, impossibly even worse than before.

"Ted piddled," Monica said, her voice cracking with stress.

"It's okay. We're clear." He turned the key. The engine struggled for a moment before springing to life. "It's too much to hope that Aaron won't report his truck missing, so we'll need another car." The smell hit him anew. "And some fresh clothes."

"Where are we going?"

He popped open the glove box and pulled out Aaron Walker's wallet. There were two credit cards they couldn't use, but Matt stuffed the $87 in cash into his pocket. He hit the gas, drove through a creek bed, and just managed to climb the shallow gulley on the other side. "North. Somewhere they won't think to look."

* * *

The mountainous back roads of Tennessee made it easy to hide, even in a truck. Asphalt roads cut through winding forests broken up by quaint, half-dead coal towns that had run dry a century ago. Matt scanned the neighborhood as they drove through one of many suburbs without a city, then grunted in satisfaction at a lemon-yellow colonial with green trim. They ditched the truck next to a half-dozen decaying vehicles behind an abandoned rail yard, tossed the license plates into the creek, then walked back through the woods into town.

Matt felt a twinge of guilt when he stole a pair of boots and a long overcoat off of a porch, but it didn't stop him. Satisfied that his bloody clothes were well-hidden, he went into Wal-Mart to buy them new ones.

He wanted to replace the boots and coat, but didn't have enough cash. At the last second he grabbed bottled water, a ten-pound bag of dog food, and blonde hair dye. After tax, he had just over two dollars. He tossed their old clothes in the dumpster behind the store while Monica changed, shivering as she scrubbed off filth with the water. The yellow maternity shirt hung a little big on her, but it worked.

He sniffed. "We don't smell good, but it's better." He leaned over and let Ted lick his nose. "You stink." Ted gave a happy chuff and wagged his tail.

They walked through town hand in hand, Ted at their heels, a happy couple and their dog out for a morning stroll. Drivers waved as they drove by, and they waved back. They loitered for a moment as a red Ford pickup passed, then ducked down the driveway of a white split-level. They approached the house from behind, creeping into a well-shaded back yard through the gate in the fence. *Perfect.* Nobody could see them from here, unless they climbed a tree.

He jiggled the handle on the back door. Loose, it rattled but the lock held firm. He took one step back, then kicked. The frame shattered around the deadbolt and the door banged open. Plastic covered the furniture, and the house smelled of dried rose petals and dust. Matt cleared the house, then grabbed two bowls to feed and water Ted.

He surveyed the half-dead street from the shadows of the living room. "I'll check our options while you dye your hair. Don't turn on any lights."

Monica kissed his cheek and swatted his butt on the way past. "Sure."

He heard the shower start as he opened the door to the garage. Dust motes scattered in the sunlight through the scratched Plexiglas windows of the overhead door. As neat and as packed up as the rest of the house, the garage was spotless—every tool had a place, hung on the wall or tucked into a drawer in one of the several tool boxes surrounding the tarp-covered car that dominated the center of the room. Matt removed the cinder blocks from the blue tarp and folded the cover back. He let out a low whistle at the gold-tone 1954 Oldsmobile F-88 convertible, with whitewall tires and cream leather seats.

He popped the hood, examined the engine, then looked around for the keys. He found them hanging on the wall next to the garage door clicker, put them in the ignition, and fired it up. The motor purred without so much as a tick, and the gauges all worked. It even had a quarter tank of gas. He turned it off, got out, and rummaged through the tool boxes. He found a tire iron and a jack, which he put into the trunk, and left the rest in place.

A shadow crossed his vision so he turned toward the door and almost didn't recognize his wife. Monica had cut her platinum blonde hair short, in what he'd have called a dyke cut back in high school. In the yellow shirt she looked so . . . *bright* wasn't the right word. *Ephemeral.* Like a fairy or an elf. "Wow."

"Wow, yourself," she smiled. "That's some car." She hopped down the single step and kissed him on the lips. "Do you like it?"

He shrugged, and wished he could withdraw it when she scowled. "You're beautiful. It's just different is all."

"It's supposed to be. We're in disguise, remember?" She kissed him again.

This isn't a game, he thought.

"So this is our getaway?" She ran her hand down the door and peered at the console. "We could do worse."

"Yep."

"How'd you know it was here?" she asked.

"I didn't. Saw the unmowed lawn and the pile of newspapers on the front porch when we drove by. Figured someone was on vacation, and it'd give us a chance to get cleaned up. I didn't figure they'd leave a car. That was a bonus."

"Well, you did good." She held out a child's Crayon drawing of an older couple. The purple chicken scratch at the bottom read, "See you springtime bam and poppop."

"Snowbirds. Probably won't even miss it until spring."

"Good. I need—"

"There's a lockbox in the bedroom closet. Think you can open it?"

He looked around at the toolboxes. "Probably. But let me shower first."

She bit his shoulder, a little too hard. "Want company?"

He grinned. "Of course, but we'd best not. What if someone came in, or Ted started barking?"

She pouted. "Oh, poop."

"Yep."

* * *

They pulled out of the garage with two thousand dollars in cash stuffed into a stolen purse. Matt vowed to pay "bam and poppop" back when this whole thing ended. *If we live through it.* He tried not to look at Monica as he shoved the thought away—he could psychologically handle his own life in danger, but the moment he dwelled on Monica he froze up. He made a left toward the highway and waved at a couple walking a floppy-eared Doberman.

Monica spoke through her smile. "What if they report us?"

Matt dropped his hand as they passed. "If they know the car, the wave makes us look less suspicious. People tend to write off the friendly. But yeah, we'll ditch it for something less conspicuous when we can."

They filled up the car at the next town, shadowing the highway on back roads, a happy couple making one last drive in the classic car before winter forced it off the road. Monica made small talk with the old gentleman who walked over to admire their ride, and Matt admired how well she lied even as it stabbed at his heart. As they crossed the Kentucky border, Monica rubbed his thigh over the top of Ted, who had dropped from exhaustion after hours of ecstatic overstimulation with his head in the wind.

"You sure about this?"

"You trust him." He kept his eyes on the road. "And I trust him to keep you safe."

"But—"

He put his hand over hers and squeezed. "Stop it, Mon. You were in pain, you got drunk, he got drunk. What happened, happened. I can't forgive you without forgiving him. What's important is that he loves you, and that love will keep you safe while I deal with this. Ancient history is ancient history. And besides, he's not exactly on the dating scene anymore."

She pulled her hand out of his grip, then set it on top of his. "But you haven't talked to him in eight years. Not since . . . ."

Not since you went to him for solace after your first miscarriage.

"Are you sure he'll even talk to us?"

Matt tried not to snarl. "He's going to cooperate, or I'm going to tear off his arm and beat him to death with it."

She squeezed his hand again. "I don't know that this is a good idea."

He sighed. "I can trust you, right?"

"Of course," she said, without the slightest hesitation.

"Then it's a good idea. Nobody would ever imagine I'd leave you with him on purpose."

* * *

St. Martin's website put their Mass schedule at eight and eleven. Matt pulled into the half-full parking lot at eleven forty-five, as parishioners trickled out under the sound of Father Rees's final prayer. The Baptist haven of Franklin, Kentucky, compared with Damascus as a hotbed of ardent Catholicism, and the sparse attendance played that out.

A gaggle of white-clad altar boys went from solemn to roughhousing the moment they left the church, punching and hollering as they looped around toward the side entrance. A chubby woman carrying a red Bible the size of Texas came next, then another boy with a brass candelabra-thingy. Father Rees came last. Jason looked good—thirty years old, with black hair buzzed close to his head to almost hide male-pattern baldness, a healthy, tan complexion and intense, steel-gray eyes. He smiled and waved as his flock dispersed.

Matt stepped in his path, hand extended. "Father."

The priest's genuine smile vanished, replaced with a car salesman's. "Matt!" He shook, squeezing too hard. "Long time, man!" He pumped his arm up and down, placing his left hand atop theirs as his eyes quivered in uncertain fear. "What brings you to Franklin?"

Matt didn't bother with the finger-crushing contest—he had less than nothing to prove about his superhuman physical prowess. He used the grip to turn Jason to his left, where Monica leaned against the brick facade, her cross outside her shirt. One look at her worried face and his cracked to near-panic.

"Can we talk?" Matt asked. "Now?"

"I have an appoin—"

"Cancel it. This is important."

As Rees turned to the Bible-woman his voice shook. "Mary, please give Mr. Elliott my apologies. See if he can reschedule for tomorrow or Tuesday."

"Yes, father," she said, and scurried off, glancing back over her shoulder with a worried frown.

Matt watched her go, then turned to Rees. "Thank you. Got somewhere private?"

He pursed his lips. "How about a diner?"

Matt shook his head. "Something . . . privater." As panic gripped Rees's face, Matt put his hand on his shoulder. "I'm not going to hurt you, father." No matter how much he wanted to.

Rees jerked his head toward the church. "Follow me. There's a Bible study in the Rectory at noon, but I've got an office in the back."

Matt followed him through the door into the church proper. The whispers crushed him, scoured his bones, burned his mind to ash. He gritted his teeth against the onslaught and fell to one knee. The odd symbol throbbed in his vision, the sinuous curves writhing in gore, the bisected circle dripping with gobbets of bloody flesh. He gasped as he fell forward, and the image—and the whispers—vanished. He caught himself inches from the floor. The carpet smelled of Febreeze and burnt matches. He let Jason help him up.

"Are you alright?" the priest asked. "That was a heck of a trip."

Matt frowned, and rejected telling the truth even as the thought sprang to his mind. "I'm fine. Stubbed my toe is all." These whispers had been different. Always on the verge of intelligible, they had had a consistent feel to them, an urgent need for carnage and death. These were anguished, angry . . . and impotent—the rage of a spoiled child denied his favorite toy.

"You sure?"

Matt looked around the church, a modern monstrosity bearing not the slightest resemblance to the dark, gothic, stained-glass festooned edifices you see in the movies. Instead, tall windows looked out into the parking lot on one side, and the Save-A-Lot on the other. The walls, a bland cream that reminded him of a Wal-Mart bathroom, blended with the drab, cushioned pews arranged in a U-shape around the altar. The marble slab stood atop a few short steps, and behind it hung a cross—far from the gory crucifix TV had led him to expect, the cherry-stained mahogany looked almost sterile. "Yeah. I'm good."

Jason—Father Rees—led him past the altar, through a cheap, pre-fab door into an office not much bigger than the Ikea desk crammed into it. Jason offered Matt a chair, sat down, opened a drawer, and pulled out a bottle of scotch and two glasses. He put them both on the desk and hesitated when Matt shook his head. He set the bottle to the side and sat back.

His tan hid the bags under his eyes, but not quite enough. His skin, healthy at first glance, pulled too tight against his face, and his nervous, bloodshot gaze flickered more than once to the bottle as they sat in uncomfortable silence. *Hair of the dog, Jason?*

Matt realized two things: One, that even with no other options, this might be a mistake. Two, that he'd lied to Monica and to himself about forgiveness. Fair or not, he could forgive her for sleeping with his best friend, but couldn't forgive his best friend for fucking his wife. Would never forgive him. Ever.

At that moment, he wanted nothing more than to dismember Father Rees with his bare hands. But that made him the perfect person to turn to. Matt smothered hatred with duty and spoke. "Has anyone from back home moved to Franklin?"

Jason furrowed his brow. "You mean recently? Um, Mrs. Kensington—"

"—is in her nineties and senile. Anyone who'd know Mon or me."

Rees looked at the ceiling, eyes wandering over the featureless off-white expanse before settling on the portrait on the wall of Jesus with a lamb. "No. Don't think so. Not much of anybody moves to Franklin these days. What's this about?"

"I need you to take in Monica for a while."

Jason choked on nothing. "Excuse me?"

Matt looked into those same steel-gray eyes that he'd dreamed of strangling the life out of countless times and tried to find his childhood friend. His mind smothered any pleasant memory with the lying, opportunistic traitor he'd wanted to kill for the better part of a decade. He expected the whispers to egg him on, but they remained silent. Maybe this hatred didn't need egging. "You heard me. I want Monica to stay in Franklin for a while, and I want you to look after her."

"Can I ask why?"

Matt ran his tongue over his teeth. "You need to know why, so you don't do something stupid. She's pregnant, and worried to death about it, and I need to go out of town for a bit. And someone's trying to kill us."

Rees froze. "Pardon?"

Matt told him everything he knew—about Dawkins, Lake Kivu, the hit squads sent after them the night before, even the bonk-guns.

"So we came here."

"Why?"

"Because they aren't going to stop trying to kill us, and anyone who knows me knows that I'd never leave my wife with you, not for one goddamned second. It wouldn't occur to Momma or her momma or Justin or anyone else to even consider it, if ICAP goes asking where we might have gone."

"I still talk to Justin sometimes—"

"Don't care. Just don't tell him she's here and don't invite him up. And if she needs to go to the hospital, she needs another name. Better, she needs another name for around town." He cut off Jason's question before he had a chance to ask it. "I hope no more than a few weeks, and we'll get out of your hair."

Jason sighed. *We have a halfway house—*

Matt slammed his hand down onto the desk, careful not to break it. "No halfway house. She needs to stay away from junkies." He ignored Rees's startled look, picked up the scotch, and set it between them. "And no booze." Bile rose in his throat as he admitted her weakness to the man who took advantage of it. "It's been a hard few years. For her. She got into some things she shouldn't have, alcohol, more than that, but she's been clean a while, and she needs to stay that way." *For her. For the baby.*

"Where am I supposed—"

Matt cut him off with an upraised hand. "Make up a story, make up a name, and find her a place local, somewhere that takes dogs. Just leave back home, White Spruce, and anyone we know out of it. And don't you dare drink in front of her. She doesn't get a drop, not even at service."

I'm so sorry—

Matt snarled. "Don't. You try to apologize, and I'm likely to get violent. We're here because you're good cover. We're here because you love her, and you're going to act out of that love and shelter her until her husband returns."

Jason said nothing for a long moment, then nodded. "Yeah. I will." Time stretched as the silence grew between them. "So, what now?"

"For me? It's better you don't know."

* * *

As Matt left the church, the whispers gibbered in murderous relief. He let their undirected, primeval hatred skitter across his mind, then gasped as they entwined with his own. He stumbled to one knee and stayed there, eyes closed, peeling away tendrils of inhuman monstrosity until only his remained. He shuddered, took a breath, and stood.

He approached the Oldsmobile on wobbly knees and found Monica dozing in the back. Ted stared at him from the driver's seat, tail a whirlwind of berserk, undirected love and loyalty. He took a deep breath, whole again, and grabbed the handle. She opened her eyes as he got in, and sat up when he closed the door.

"He wouldn't do it, would he?"

Matt didn't look at her. "He said yes. You'll be staying here a while, until I can figure out what's going on, get ICAP to back off." *Or something.*

"What if they don't?"

Then I kill everyone I have to until you're safe. "They will."

She reached forward to scratch Ted's nose and rolled her eyes. "Baby, you just killed twenty people they sent to murder us. And 'they' are a multinational organization that kills superhuman monsters all over the world with basically no jurisdictional boundaries. What could you possibly do to get them to back off?"

He closed his eyes and leaned his head against the window. "I'm not sure. But I think I need to talk to Jeff."

"Can you trust him?"

A vision swam in front of his closed eyes. *Monica, crying over a coffin draped with an American flag, Jeff behind her, face solemn for the cameras. As he turns toward the car, he raises a hand to cover a lopsided smirk.* Unsure where the vision fell between premonition and imagination, he shook it off and turned to look at her.

"I have no idea. He's never done me wrong that I know of, and he doesn't tell me everything, but he tells me he doesn't tell me everything . . . ." He picked up her hand and kissed it. "And I don't tell you everything, either. It's the nature of the beast."

"That don't answer the question, baby. Do you trust him?"

Matt ran his fingers over hers, conscious of Jason watching them from the doorway to the church. "Six months ago? Hell, yeah. Yesterday, maybe. But not today. The order might not have come from him, but there's a good enough chance it did. And even if it didn't, if he's given a choice between him and me, I don't think loyalty would tie him down too hard."

"What about your team?"

He shrugged.

"What does that mean?"

He shrugged again. "I don't know, babe. I know Akash has my back, but I'd have bet on Conor, too, right up until I had to kill him. Sakura's all business, but she's insightful and doesn't trust Jeff or Brian, and Garrett . . . . We work well together, but I don't think he likes me much."

"What if you told them the truth? Showed them the injector-guns?"

"Yeah. Maybe." He nodded, more for her benefit than his. "I think so."

"Then trust your gut. Call them."

Chapter 13

Jeff Hannes walked into the dry cleaner's and didn't seem to notice when the "Open" sign went dark. He held out his ticket and a twenty-dollar bill, the same transaction he made every Tuesday on his way home from work, and drummed his fingers on the counter as the small Laotian man stepped into the back room. Matt stepped out from behind a suit rack and snatched Jeff's Glock 9mm from the concealed-carry holster under his left armpit.

Jeff whirled in surprise, and Matt put the barrel under his chin.

"Do I need this, Jeff?"

His eyes widened, and he licked his lips. Then he smiled his smarmy, car-salesman's smile and spoke in a low almost-whisper. "Hey, buddy, we all thought you were dead! What the hell happened?" The smile didn't touch his eyes. Not for the first time, Matt wondered if "buddy" meant "I'm lying" in Jeff-speak.

"I asked you a question."

Jeff shook his head. "No, man, you don't need that. We're totally cool, you know, if you are."

Matt brushed the safety back on with his thumb and stuffed the gun in the back of his pants. "I'll hold onto it for the moment, if you don't mind." He plucked Jeff's cell phone from the breast pocket of his blue dress shirt, turned it off, and put it in his front pocket. "That, too."

Mr. Ketthavong carried in a pile of gray suits, all smiles. Jeff took them, gave a quick smile, and Matt followed him out the door with a polite wave.

Smile still plastered to his face, Jeff walked to his car, a dull silver BMW four-door from a decade past. He blipped the alarm, opened the back door, and hung the suits from the handles above the doors. He raised his eyebrows at Matt, and Matt nodded to the driver's seat.

They got in, and Matt set Jeff's pistol on the floor. Jeff started the car, checked his mirrors, and pulled out. *Where am I going?*

"Take the expressway south," Matt said, cutting off the unspoken words. "We need to talk." He made a show of unplugging Jeff's GPS and left the cord dangling.

"What the hell happened?" Jeff put on his blinker, cut over two lanes, and merged with the traffic headed south.

"That's what I was hoping you could tell me."

Jeff licked his lips. "When you didn't show Monday, we sent some folks to your house. The place looked clean, like nobody's home, but it was too clean, you know?" He glanced at Matt, and when he didn't respond, Jeff continued. "So we send in a forensics team—just covering our bases—and they find blood traces everywhere. I mean, everywhere. Kitchen, bedroom, hallway, outside. They fly me out there, and your furniture's different. New couch, new chair, new rug. It didn't look at all like that time I visited. We found a piece of shrapnel embedded in your fireplace, and it tested positive for gunpowder. With that helicopter accident in the woods behind your house, we knew something just didn't add up."

Jeff passed a tractor trailer and skipped the next exit. When he didn't continue, Matt prompted, "And?"

He threw up his hands, then grabbed the wheel. "And what? We put out an APB for you and Monica—on the down-low—and started checking with our sources. We thought maybe Dawkins's men got to you, some kind of retaliation. We've been shitting ourselves for two days."

Unconvinced, Matt waited. *So what do you say we turn the car around and—*

"We're not turning the car around, not yet."

Jeff's teeth clacked shut.

"Take the next exit."

"Where are we going?"

"Just drive." He put his hand on Jeff's shoulder to stave off the pending objection. "No, of course I don't trust you. I'd like to, but after what happened—"

"If you told me what happened—"

"I may come to trust you, but that's going to take some investigation." Matt squeezed Jeff's shoulder with just enough force to be uncomfortable, then brought his hand down to his lap. "In the meantime, just to be safe, I'm going to assume you had something to do with this. So if you screw with me I'm going to snap your neck and leave your twitching body on the side of the road. If everything pans out, we can be friends again."

Jeff sighed. "Fair enough, buddy." He took the next exit, and Matt directed him down a maze of back roads.

Matt timed it so that they pulled in to Walker's farm as full dusk settled in. Matt hoped that the circuitous route they'd taken had Jeff turned around and lost, and that the overcast darkness kept him from recognizing the place, if he knew it at all. Matt shut his door harder than he had to, and Buster's high-pitched, ululating bark answered from inside. A spotlight hit them in the face a moment later, and the screen door creaked.

Matt stared past it, his eyes compensating for the glare in ways that Jeff's couldn't. Aaron Walker's grizzled face squinted out into the darkness. He held the giant flashlight in his left hand, and a shotgun pointed at the floor in his right.

"Rowley? That you?"

"Hey, Aaron," Matt said.

"Where's my truck, you asshole?"

Jeff froze in place as his whole body tensed.

"In a minute." Matt jerked his head at Jeff. "You know this fella?"

Aaron blinded Jeff with the spotlight. "Sure do. He come round not an hour after you stole my truck, askin'—"

The whispers slithered through his skull, and Matt struck, blocking Jeff's wrist before the tiny, concealed pistol got anywhere near Matt's temple. He squeezed until the bones ground together.

Jeff cried out, and the weapon fell from his limp fingers. He dropped to his knees and grabbed for it with his left hand, and his fingers crunched as Matt stomped on them. He gasped in pain and pulled both arms to his chest, curling his legs up into a fetal position.

With an exasperated sigh, Matt plucked the pistol from the ground. "Don't be stupid, Jeff."

A shotgun cocked, and Matt looked up past the barrel and into Aaron's eyes.

"Just what in high heaven is going on here, Rowley?"

"Well, Jeff here just tried to shoot me. I'd appreciate if y'all didn't go and make the same mistake." He flipped the snub-nosed revolver over so that he held it by the barrel, and offered it grip-first to Aaron. "Hold that for me, would you?"

Walker set the spotlight on the ground, stepped forward, snatched the gun out of Matt's hand, then tipped the shotgun over his shoulder. Much of the tension drained out of him as he spat on the ground, toward but not quite at Jeff. "What's his story?"

Matt looked down at the man still writhing in pain on the ground. "Aaron Walker, meet Jeff Hannes. My boss."

Walker spat again. "I reckon you're fired."

"Reckon so. Can you get me some ice for his injuries?"

"He'll keep," Walker said. "First, what about my truck?"

Matt shook his head. "I can't tell you where I left it, not in front of him." They locked eyes. "It ain't just me they came for."

Aaron spat again. "My wallet was in the glove box. A hundred in cash inside."

"Eighty-seven." He reached down and pulled out Jeff's wallet, opened it, and pulled the bills out. "Here's two hundred and sixty. I'm good for the rest of the value assuming I live through this. Either way, take the insurance and run."

"For insurance, I got to report it stolen, which I ain't done yet on account of who stole it. Then they'll look for it, and maybe find it. I still got the sedan, and won't need to do any real hauling until

December. Reckon if I hold off on reporting a couple days they'll still believe me?"

Matt smiled. "I'd appreciate that." He looked down at Jeff, still fetal, and the smile vanished. Any plans of letting him go went out the window—ICAP didn't know about Aaron's truck, but now Jeff did. Matt wasn't about to lead them even an inch closer to Monica. "You got any rope?"

"Just real big stuff. How about bailing twine?"

Matt shook his head. "Not strong enough. Got any bailing wire?"

Aaron made a brief nod toward the barn. "Reckon I do."

* * *

Jeff jerked his head away from the smelling salt, coughing. Matt pulled it aside and stepped back from the folding chair he'd snagged out of the backwoods motel hallway. Matt had stripped Jeff to his boxers and secured his ankles to the chair legs and his arms behind his back. He'd twisted the bailing wire enough to keep Jeff from wiggling a limb free, but not so much that it would cut off his circulation. Still, it couldn't have been comfortable against the deep bruise on his wrist.

Jeff looked around the dark room with wide eyes. Matt had taken out the phone, and the nondescript bed and end-table would give him no clues. "Where am I?"

Matt snorted. "Really?"

Jeff took a few deep breaths, then met Matt's bland stare. "Look, it wasn't personal. I was just following orders—"

Matt held up a hand, squeezing his eyes shut against the urge to tear Jeff's head from his shoulders. This wasn't the whispers, just good honest rage. He opened them, now on eye level. "ICAP agents tried to kill *my wife*. You're going to tell me why, or bless your heart, they're going to take you out of this room in real small pieces."

Jeff winced against his bonds. "Do you have any painkillers?"

"I force-fed you four Advil to help the swelling, and you won't cut yourself if you don't struggle. You'll be fine, if you talk."

He spoke through gritted teeth. "Look, it wasn't me, alright? LaLonde sold you upstairs, Frahm ordered the hit, I rode along to make sure nothing happened to Monica."

Bonking him would have ensured Monica's death, but he let the obvious lie go for a moment. "Brian ordered me killed because I asked about a file?"

Jeff shrugged and winced against the pain. "I'm middle management. They don't tell me anything I don't need to know." The hint of a smirk twisted his lips.

Matt sighed. "Look, there's no reason to stall. Your clothes weren't bugged. We're hundreds of miles from your car and phone, and while you were unconscious the GPS transponder in your thigh developed a bad case of very high voltage."

Jeff's eyes widened at this last piece of information. He tried to look down, to see the burn mark.

"There ain't no cavalry coming."

For the first time, desperation crept into Jeff's eyes. He licked his lips, cleared his throat, looked around the room. He swallowed, then met Matt's gaze, smirk in full-force. "Let's get real here, Matt. What are you going to do, torture me? I know your psych profile. You're capable of violence, incredible violence, but not torture. You're in deep shit here, and I might be your only friend at ICAP. So what's this going to be?"

Matt met his gaze. Matt's psych profile literally sat in a folder in Jeff's office, and they both knew that Matt didn't have it in him to torture someone for information. Matt stood. "You got me pegged on that score, Jeff." He walked to the bedroom door. "I don't have it in me to torture a person." He knocked.

Garrett Johnson walked in, his massive frame followed by Akash and Blossom. Akash set a silver briefcase on the bed and popped the clasps.

Jeff frowned as his gaze darted from face to face. "Aw, guys, you don't want to get messed up with this. This is between Matt and—"

Matt grabbed his jaw and turned him so that they looked eye to eye. "Hey, you asked what this was going to be, so shut up and listen to the answer." Akash pulled an autoinjector out of the case and loaded in a phial of clear blue fluid. Matt took it from him and pointed it at Jeff. "This is infrared retinal enhancements. I picked it because of all the Gerstner Augmentations available to ICAP agents, it's one of the least likely to bonk you. Unless Dawkins was telling the truth, of course. That'd mean that you'd be looking at 'when,' not 'if.'" He looked at Akash. "Rastogi, would you mind? The non-broken fingers, please."

Akash untwisted the bailing wire on Jeff's right wrist, grabbed his fingers and twisted, presenting the inside of Jeff's elbow to Matt. Dark purple bruises marked where Matt had squeezed to get him to drop the gun. Matt tapped the vein with his fingers, then placed the needle against Jeff's skin.

"Wait!" Jeff's desperate eyes skittered across the needle, then locked on Matt's.

Matt hesitated. "The ICAP agents that showed up at my house were trying to bonk me on purpose, so they could put me down after I killed Mon and the Walkers and God knows who else. I showed these guys the weapons."

"I didn't order the hit! I didn't! But Frahm sent me in on the cleanup when they realized you weren't neutralized. They briefed me en route, too late to stop anything."

"Why?"

"They think Dawkins compromised you."

Blossom knelt next to him. "Who's 'they'?"

"Upper management. I got my orders through standard chain of command, through Director Frahm's office. I had nothing to do with trying to kill you."

Blossom rolled her eyes up to Matt. "First part is true. Last is a lie."

Matt raised an eyebrow. "How do you know?"

"Flash of worry on his face, too fast to see without computers. Unless you're trained. Or pumped up with Gerstner Augs."

Matt looked back at Jeff. "Okay, so why is ICAP trying to kill me?"

Jeff's smirk disappeared in a snarl. "Because Dawkins is trying to destroy us, and you're buying his lies. You've been compromised, and a rogue agent is way too dangerous to let live."

Jeff flinched as Akash's lips brushed his ear. "Which parts are lies?"

"All of them."

Blossom shook her head.

"Dammit, Tsuji," Jeff said. "I'm telling the truth!"

Matt jammed the needle into his arm, and Jeff writhed.

"Jesus, no, please don't do this." He looked at Matt with tear-filled eyes. "Please."

"Three," Matt said.

"Look, we can make a deal—"

"Two." He put his thumb on the green button on the back of the injector.

"Okay! Okay! Just take it out!"

Jeff gasped in relief as Matt pulled it out. A bead of blood formed on his skin—Jeff's eyes didn't leave it.

"Last chance, Jeff. Start talking. And if Blossom thinks you're lying, even once, you're going to be able to see heat all of a sudden."

Jeff shuddered, and then words flowed out of him in a rush. "He's right. Dawkins is right. ICAP controls the world supply of Gerstner carbon. Jade, too. They've got her chained up in a lab in D.C."

Matt exchanged confused looks with his team.

"Who's 'her'?"

Jeff's eyes flicked to Blossom, then Matt. "The source. Gerstner. She's some crazy scientist or something from Germany."

Garrett snorted. "They chained up a scientist, and she still works for them?"

Jeff's eyes widened at the needle. "I don't know. It's something like that."

Blossom stepped behind Jeff, next to Akash, and signed, *He's holding back something. But ask him about the insanity first.*

Matt shook his head. "Don't add up, Jeff. Jade's been a problem pushing ten years, and she's the only one who can make it?" Blossom's nostrils flared and she signed, *Insanity?* Matt ignored her for the moment. "What is this, Breaking Bad? It's chemistry. Like following a recipe. They could figure that out in a decade just by watching her work."

"Not a decade. A lot longer. Hitler's goons used her for their *Übermensch* program in the forties."

Garrett snorted again. "She'd have to be a hundred years old. Older."

Jeff nodded. "They found her in that bunker in Dresden, strapped to a gurney with metal banding. She was . . . old then, too."

"Bullshit," Matt said, snatching up the autoinjector.

"It's true!" Jeff's stared in horror at the needle. "I swear on my life it's true!"

Matt glanced at Blossom, who signed, "true." He knelt so that he was at eye level with Jeff, resting the injector on his knee. "And what about the rest of it?"

"Rest of what?"

Akash rolled his eyes, still bending Jeff's hand behind his back, exposing his vein.

Matt patted the autoinjector. "Why you're so afraid of this. It's just IR vision." He stroked the needle down Jeff's arm, eliciting a horrified shudder. "There is no safe dosage, is there?" He ignored Blossom's satisfied, sarcastic grin.

Jeff squeezed his eyes shut and nodded.

"You son of a bitch," Garrett said, his hands balling into fists. Matt stopped him with an upraised hand.

"So you expect us to believe that ICAP created and distributed GS technology, continues to supply the whole world with it, and spends hundreds of billions of dollars on super-soldiers to combat their own supply who they know are going to go insane?"

Jeff nodded again, his eyes still shut. "They didn't mean for it to get out, but they're not willing to stop just because it did. So you're there to curb the problem as much as possible. That's everything, I swear." He continued in the barest of whispers. "You're going to kill me, aren't you?"

The whispers danced through Matt, urging him to do it. He opened his mouth to ask "why?" when Akash cut him off. "How do we cure it?"

Jeff licked his lips. "You don't. There's no cure."

Blossom scowled. "Lying."

Jeff shrieked as the needle entered his arm, struggling against the wire that bound him to the chair. "NonononoNO—" Matt hit the plunger. The injector emptied with a hiss, and Jeff's protest changed to a mindless wail.

Garrett stepped forward and slapped him hard enough to wrench his head to the side. "Shut the fuck up." He backhanded him the other way, and Jeff stopped screaming, his face glowing red from the force of the strikes.

Matt put his fingertips on Garrett's chest and backed him up a couple of feet, glaring daggers, then turned and looked at Jeff, who hung his head. Matt lifted his chin with a finger, and he didn't protest. "You want to go nuts, Jeff? Kill your family, innocent people, until monsters like us put you down?" He gestured at the case, and Akash loaded up a dose labeled Late-Second Precognitive Therapy. Only one in ten thousand applicants cleared for augmentation, and less than five percent of them cleared for precog.

Jeff swallowed, tears springing to his eyes. "No. You can't. It's not fair."

He took the autoinjector from Akash and held it in front of Jeff's face. "You were going to bonk me on purpose, let me kill my wife, kill my neighbors, until you put me down like a rabid dog. If it's anything, it's fair." He smiled a smile he didn't feel. "But I'm not a rabid dog. I'm a man, and a better man than you. So tell us what you know, and this goes back in the case."

Jeff squeezed his eyes shut. "You're going to think I'm lying."

Matt ran his tongue over his teeth. "Try me."

"Gerstner isn't human."

Garrett interrupted him. "So she's an alien?"

Matt glared him into quiet. "Go on."

"We're not sure what she is, but she was an old woman when the bombs buried her under the rubble of Dresden. American

~ 152 ~

operatives uncovered the bunker in the late fifties, and she was still there, the only thing still alive, buried under rock for almost fifteen years, with nothing to eat, nothing to drink. They found her half-loaded into the incinerator, laughing." Matt exchanged glances with Blossom. "She claims she's a Nephilim."

Blossom raised an eyebrow. "What is nay-flim?"

Jeff closed his eyes, then opened them. "A fallen angel."

Matt glared at Jeff. "That's ridiculous."

Jeff shrugged against his bonds. "I didn't say it was true. I said it's what she claims. What we know is that she's very old, that Hitler's *Deutsche Physik* program victimized her until a bomb sealed them all in to die, that everyone in that bunker killed each other or themselves, that she was rescued by the group that eventually became ICAP, and that Gerstner Augmentations stop working when you unplug her from the machine."

Akash let go of Jeff's arm and stepped around where they could see each other. "I don't get it. Why not just unplug her?"

Garrett frowned. "Better question: How do you know all this?"

Jeff looked at each of them in turn but answered Garrett first. "Because my grandfather told me."

Blossom frowned. "And your grandfather is who?"

"One of the historians who went with Brian Frahm into the bunker."

Matt grunted at the impossibility. "Excuse me?"

Jeff sighed. "I think you know Frahm's family history. How he and I got involved with ICAP."

"Sure," Matt said.

"I don't," Blossom said.

He sighed again. "Our grandfathers served in the Special Activities Division of the CIA, just grunts. His group, under Lieutenant-Colonel Petrie, uncovered the bunker under Dresden. Before he passed, Gramps told me the truth of it." He looked past Matt, through him, quoting. "'The floors were slick with long-rotted bodies in SS uniforms. Until they breached the doors there wasn't enough oxygen for full decomposition, and almost all of them were suicides. The smell was unbelievable. They found her, this emaciated, skeletal body strapped to a gurney with spring steel, half-loaded into an incinerator, the walls everywhere stained with old blood. They helped carry her out, to winch her up the stairs to the dark sky waiting above, and the whole time she laughed a wheezing, inhuman laugh, too dry to come from living lungs.'"

His eyes focused on Matt. "Only that's not true. It was my grandfather, but wasn't Frahm's. It was Frahm."

"Bullshit," Garrett said.

Jeff's eyes flickered to Blossom and then back to Matt. "I lied, but not about that. Brian's real name is Kurt. Kurt Frahm was born on August seventeenth, nineteen-hundred-and-fourteen in Omaha, Nebraska, and uses Gerstner's power, whatever it is, to keep himself young."

Matt pulled the picture from his wallet, smoothed it out, and passed it to Garrett. "Gottschalk sent this to me a few days ago."

Garrett snatched it out of his hand, looked at it, showed it to Akash, and passed it to Blossom without comment.

"What about your grandfather?" Akash asked.

Jeff shook his head. "He didn't want in. Said it wasn't natural, that it went against God's plan. He wasn't happy when I took the job. He told me the truth to keep me away, only it didn't work. I want to be like Frahm, young forever." He raised his head in a defiant sneer. "And so does everyone else."

I don't care about this story, Blossom signed from behind him. *How do we stop it?*

Matt wanted to hear the rest, but saw her point. "Alright, say that's true. How do we stop it?"

Jeff shrugged. "Like I said, she's in the machine. Take her out and it all stops."

"And Frahm dies," Akash said. "Instantly?"

Jeff sighed. "I don't know. But it's not just Frahm. The rest of upper management, and some bankers, and CEOs, and politicians. A lot of people with a lot of money don't want to die." His eyes dropped to the floor and he muttered, "I don't want to die."

"Us," Garrett said. "What's going to happen to all of ICAP's augs?"

Jeff looked up at him, then swallowed. "I have no—"

The world went white.

Monica screamed, a cry of mournful terror, and behind it, pain.

Her pregnant belly bulged, then writhed. Her legs jerked, and she clutched at bloody sheets with feeble hands. A shadow with eyes of jade enveloped the bed in wings of smoke, and whispers gibbered homicidal praise to its glory. Her head lolled back, and she murmured, "Please, don't. Not my baby."

She gritted her teeth, panting short, desperate breaths, then gasped as her stomach ruptured in a spray of blood and amniotic fluid. Black claws tore through her abdomen. The sleek, almost-human head that emerged behind them shrieked in release, and the shadow joined it.

Matt blinked and found himself on his knees, hands clutching his head. He tasted bile, and his throat burned.

Akash knelt in front of him, concern in his eyes. "You okay, man?"

"Something's wrong with Mon." He looked at Garrett, who frowned at him. "Get what else you can out of Jeff. I'll be back." Garrett grabbed his wrist and hoisted him to his feet.

"You need backup?" Blossom asked.

The memory of shadow loomed in his vision. "Um. Maybe."

Akash grabbed his kit and followed Matt out the door. Blossom met them at the car and took shotgun.

"How do you know?" she asked.

Matt fired up the engine and hit the gas. "I don't know how I know. A . . . a vision. Something like that."

Akash flopped back in his seat. "What kind of aug causes visions?"

Matt shook his head. "Not one I've had. Precog doesn't stretch out beyond a split second, but I've had that, too." He buried the speedometer needle; if he passed a cop, he'd deal with it one way or another. "What kind of aug causes immortality? There's too much here we don't understand."

Akash cleared his throat. "You ever going to tell Jeff that was saline?"

Matt shook his head without taking his eyes from the road. "No. Maybe. I guess it depends."

"On what?" Blossom asked.

"I don't know. He'll figure it out when his eyes don't change in the next couple of days. I figure he can use the worry."

"Yeah," Akash said.

Chapter 14

The SUV screamed into St. Martin's parking lot, empty except for a lone Save-A-Lot shopping cart tipped over next to the curb. Matt popped the door before the car had come to a complete stop, jerked the parking brake, and stepped out into the morning drizzle. He caught the assault rifle as Akash tossed it to him and ran to the rectory, Akash and Blossom at his heels.

Jason opened the door on the third bang, and Matt froze, fist in the air. The priest's eyes widened at the weapon in Matt's left hand, barrel pointed at the floor. Matt cleared his throat. "Get out of the way, Jason."

"Holy shit, Matt." He put his hands on the doorframe, blocking the entrance.

Matt shouldered past him, sending him stumbling into the loveseat. "Where's Monica?"

Rees's eyes darted from Akash to Blossom back to Matt, then strayed again to their weapons as he picked himself up. "Back room. Down the hall on the left."

Matt smothered his impatience. "Show me."

Rees led him past a modest kitchen adorned with a cross on the wall, down a small hallway, to a door. He licked his lips and touched on the stock of Matt's REC7 with two fingers. "Is this necessary?" They locked eyes.

"I don't know."

He put his hand on the doorknob, nodded to Akash and Blossom, and opened the door.

The Virgin Mary stared down at the twin-sized bed from a frame on the wall, next to an inverted crucifix. The comforter held the shape of a body curled in a fetal position. Ted sat at her feet, tail thumping as he looked up at Matt. There were no wings of smoke, no demon with eyes of jade. Matt kneeled next to the bed and put his hand on Monica's shoulder. He shook her gently.

Ted hopped off the bed and wandered over to Matt, jamming his head into his thigh with a happy whine. She didn't move as Akash reached past him, lifted the cross from the wall, and handed it to Father Rees.

Ignoring their quiet, confused chatter, Matt shook her again. "Mon?"

She shuddered but didn't roll over, so he pulled back the comforter. As the fabric slithered over her body, the whispers chittered across his brain. He pushed them to the back of his mind, and caressed her bare shoulder with the back of his fingers. "Hey, baby. You okay?"

A sheen of sweat covered her skin and soaked her pink tank top. Her head shook, the barest shiver of blonde hair on the pillow. She rolled over, and Matt's heart skipped a beat.

Her teeth gritted in pain, with eyes filled with tears, she clutched her pregnant belly and the bloodstained area below. "I'm losing him." Her pale face creased with pain. She wouldn't meet his gaze.

Blossom disappeared in a breath of wind. Somewhere in the distance, Matt heard the rectory phone clear the cradle and then three button clicks.

The whispers tittered in glee. He shook them off, leaned in and kissed her forehead. "Ambulance is on the way, baby." Blossom's voice confirmed the statement as she reported a pregnant Jane Doe bleeding on the side steps of St. Martin's church.

The whispers changed, softened, oozed with dark promises. The fragile, fading life inside Monica pulsed in Matt's mind, cried out in desperate pain. A terrible certainty gripped him: his son's heart couldn't handle the strain. He wouldn't survive.

The whispers told him he could and would, if Matt shared his blood with his son, breathed life through his wife into the tiny unborn form. If he didn't, the boy would die. She would die. A cut, a suckle, and they'd both live, even thrive.

He froze in panic. These weren't incoherent whispers, these were something else. Intelligible, intelligent, seductive. *Is this it? Am I crazy? And if not, are they telling the truth?*

Matt shook off the thought, and the whispers shrieked their impotent rage. Would sharing his blood with Monica infect her, and their son, with the taint of Gerstner Augmentation, the promise of death in madness? Could it be worse than the madness and death he would bring if he stayed with them? He tumbled back from the bed and into a startled Father Rees's arms, then accepted Akash's hand up.

Blossom appeared in the doorway. "Ambulance is coming. Take her purse. She needs to be Jane Doe." She glared at Matt. "And we can't be here."

Monica reached out and grabbed his hand, and he leaned close.

"Don't leave me."

He kissed her. "I have to, babe. They can't know who you are, and they're looking for me. They'll take good care of you at the hospital, and Jason'll watch Ted." *And if I stay, I might save our son and damn you both.* Without turning he handed Rees a slip of paper. "That's a new email account. Send word as soon as you know anything."

The priest took it and said nothing.

"Matt," Akash said, putting his hand on his shoulder. "We got to go."

Monica wrapped her arms around his neck. "No, baby. I need you."

The whispers told him to tear at her throat with his teeth, to squeeze her until she ruptured and bled out, to gouge out her eyes and turn on the priest. Something darker told him to cut his own wrist and pour the blood into her throat. He kissed her, stroked her hair, told her he loved her. And then he pulled away, until only their fingertips touched, and then not even that.

She sobbed, and he touched his heart. "I'll be there, baby. Let Jason and the EMTs take care of you."

He snarled in tearful grief as he backed out of the room. He staggered and ran to the car. The ambulance screeched into the parking lot as Akash put it in gear. Matt watched in the rearview mirror as paramedics unfolded a gurney and wheeled it into the rectory. Akash took a right, and the church disappeared from view.

"There's nothing you can do, boss."

From the back seat, Matt tried not to sneer. "I know." It wasn't Akash's fault he'd brought nothing but pain to his wife and unborn child.

Blossom turned around and poked him in the forehead with two fingers. "You know it here." She poked him in the chest. "But not here." She turned around without waiting for a reply.

The car bled through the miles.

* * *

Matt had underestimated how hard things became when you needed to remain anonymous. They had cash, but in the age of smart phones there weren't many places that had computers you could just walk in and use. Even the public library wanted to see your library card. They hit a Best Western, and Matt walked into the "Business Suite" as another guy walked out—no keycard needed.

He had one message, from JRees. *Admitted. Still strong.*

He typed, *K*, clicked send. He resisted the urge to throw the monitor across the room, to smash everything just because he could. In a hopeless rage, he opened Google and typed in "Nayflim." After a few tries, he gave up on the spelling and tried "fallen angel."

Mentioned in the books of Enoch and Jubilees and a few other places, the Nephilim were the spawn of angels that had defied God to come to Earth and breed with human women. God cast these angels, called the egregoroi and led by Shemjaza or Chemyaza or various other names depending on where he looked, into the eternal darkness of Tartarus. The book of Jubilees said that the Great Flood wasn't about the sins of man, but God's way of ridding the world of the Nephilim. But in his unknowable wisdom, God let a few remain as bodiless demons, to tempt humans before Judgment Day. It didn't say anything about wings of smoke, or Hitler or *Deutsche Physik* or whacked-out vegan Manson cultists.

He started as the chair next to him scuffed against the floor. A woman in sweat pants and a halter top sat and logged in. She smiled and averted her eyes, glanced at him again, and blushed. Her slender, uncalloused fingers rested on the keys, and she eyed him askance before typing.

He closed the browser, logged out, walked outside, and got in the car.

Blossom's inscrutable look told him nothing.

"Drive," Matt said.

Akash drove.

* * *

"All I'm saying," Akash said as he pulled into the motel parking lot, "is that if any part of what Jeff said is true—"

"It's true," Blossom interrupted.

Akash frowned, and Matt shared the irritation in his reply. "He believes it's true. That doesn't mean it's true."

Blossom rolled her eyes. "Yes, okay. He believes it's true."

"Anyway," Akash said, "if any part of it is true, then we don't have a choice, eh? Whether she's a Nephilim or a demon or some weird scientific anomaly or freaking Bob Hope, we have to go in and get Gerstner, get her off the machine."

"But we don't know what that will do," Blossom said. "It could bonk every aug on the planet. What then?"

Akash shrugged.

"Shrug isn't good enough, Akash," Blossom said. "The death toll—"

Matt interrupted them. "The door's open."

"What?" Blossom said. She looked up, then disappeared. The car door slammed in her wake, and she appeared next to the motel-room door, pistol raised. She glared at them as they got out and rushed to the door. "No sound."

Matt led the way inside, and swore.

The room stank of sulfur and gunpowder. Garrett lay face up on the carpet, eyes wide, odd puncture wounds all over his skin, and a single bullet hole in his temple. Bits of blood and brains scattered over the cheap carpet. The through-and-through had exited behind his ear, and powder burns indicated a point-blank shot. Jeff's chair sat empty, the bailing wire around the legs slick with blood. Both Garrett's REC7 and his pistol were missing.

Whispers chattered, and Matt body-checked Akash out of the doorway. He grunted at the sudden pain in his shoulder, a bee sting on steroids accompanied by a weapon report. They hit the floor as another spray of bullets peppered through the walls.

Matt scrambled across the floor as bullets punched through the room, shredding the mattress, shattering the lamp.

"Ow!" Akash screamed. "Goddamn it!"

"You alright?" Matt asked as the gunfire died.

"Through and through. I'll be fine. Fuck!"

Tires shrieked. Blossom vanished out the door as he helped Akash up.

"Thanks—" Akash started, blood gushing from his thigh.

Matt bolted for the car, sparing a glance at the red Mustang fishtailing out of the parking lot. Blossom got in as he turned the key and gunned it over the curb, across the lawn, and into the path of a black van. The van skidded sideways and tilted up on two wheels, passing through the space they'd occupied a moment before. He jerked the steering wheel left, gritting his teeth against the grinding itch in his shoulder.

"What about Akash?" Blossom asked.

Matt swerved past an oncoming sedan and into the correct lane, pedal to the floor. "We'll go back for him."

The Mustang disappeared behind the trees, still hanging on to the last of their leaves. Matt rounded the corner at full throttle and eased through the drift on the oil-and-stone road. He gunned the gas across the left lane and shot back into the right just as a yellow, early-model VW Beetle rounded the next curve.

Blossom's seatbelt clicked into place. "Don't kill us."

Eyes on the road, he gave her a curt nod. "I'm more worried about Jeff."

The brake lights pumped on the Mustang, and Matt smiled in grim satisfaction. Jeff had neither the reflexes nor the training to take full advantage of the giant motor on winding, back-country roads. By Jeff's choppy driving, Matt figured the massive torque proved more a liability than a help. All the augs in the world wouldn't help them catch him if he hit the Interstate, though.

An enormous dump truck lumbered ahead of them, its hulking mass obscuring the road in front of it. Gravel spit as Jeff gunned the Mustang and swerved into the left lane, only to jerk back as an oncoming coupe blared its horn and blew past. He tried again and disappeared from view.

The truck hit the brakes and Matt gunned the SUV. It lurched forward, and Matt veered left just enough to see around. If nothing went wrong, he had enough time to make it before getting plastered by an oncoming minivan. The tires slipped as he accelerated.

"Matt." Blossom's clipped voice betrayed her nervousness.

"I know." He wasn't even sure what that meant.

The dump truck tried to give him room, but there wasn't much shoulder, and the ditch had him boxed in. Matt hugged the truck, his sideview mirror folding back and popping forward as it brushed along the irregular, rust-stained metal. Ahead of him, the minivan swerved, almost into the ditch, then overcompensated into the path of the truck.

"MATT!"

"I KNOW!"

A thousand possibilities screamed through Matt's mind, so he picked the best one and prayed. He eased past the truck, blocking out the screaming curses from the cab, cut into the right lane—and into the path of the minivan. Instinct told him to veer left; precognition told him that would get them all killed, and the whispers begged him to do it. The van jerked to its right, and Matt cut to his. Gravel crunched under his tires as they hit the shoulder, right tires almost in the ditch. The van passed with inches to spare, and the truck driver skidded to a stop behind them, already screaming into the CB, glaring at Matt through the rearview.

"You're crazy," Blossom said, knuckles white in her lap.

Matt accelerated, closing the distance to the red sports car. He locked eyes with Jeff through Jeff's rearview, noting the look of grim determination and the nervous sweat on his brow. Matt shook his head and mashed down on the gas as they rounded a curve.

Jeff stretched his left arm out the window and let a small object fall from his hands. Matt accelerated over the grenade, and flinched when it exploded behind them.

"Where the hell did he get that?" Blossom asked.

"Garrett. Which means he's got, what, two more at most?"

The second grenade spattered the driver's side with shrapnel, and Matt backed off. Jeff lobbed the third grenade high, and it tumbled into the ditch. Matt didn't even hear it go off as they roared past. He hit the gas just as they rounded the bend onto a straightaway.

The forest opened up into a valley with a small farm community at the bottom. Miles ahead, a single bridge traversed a small river—no more than an overgrown creek—just before a railroad crossing. Matt saw the train churning its way from the east, and swore.

Matt had the needle buried past ninety, and Jeff pulled away from them on the straight road. He gauged the distance to the crossing as the Mustang peaked, and Blossom voiced his thought.

"He won't make it."

Matt took his foot off the gas. Whether or not Jeff did, they had no chance of beating the train. The red lights at the crossing flashed, and the gates closed. Clouds of dust kicked up behind the red car, and Matt couldn't help admiring the beauty of the sleek machine as it did what Detroit had made to do. But it wasn't enough. *C'mon, Jeff. Just stop.*

The train blared its horn, two perfunctory blasts that said, "Here I come." Then another, long blast. Brakes squealed, but the locomotive had a hundred cars behind it and had to have been going fifty miles an hour. The best it could do now was buy Jeff a second, maybe.

Matt pounded the steering wheel and brought the SUV to rest. "Goddamn it, Jeff."

"He's dead," Blossom replied.

Matt didn't need precognition to see it coming. The train beat the Mustang to the intersection by a split second. Jeff shielded his face with his hands as he blasted through the gate, and then vanished in a shriek of metal as the Mustang hit the locomotive at a hundred-something miles an hour.

The enormous engine rocked as shredded metal blasted off of it. A single tire launched into the air, careening over the train in a high arc even as the first railcars blew past. The crumpled back end of the Mustang flipped end over end next to the train, tumbling down the embankment toward the water, spewing gasoline as it went. The front of the car had ceased to exist, and the red mist clouding the railway could have been paint or what little remained of Jeff.

Blossom muttered something in Japanese.

Matt said a prayer of thanks that the train didn't derail, did a U-Turn, and drove back the way they'd come. The dump truck driver flipped them the bird on the way past; with any luck he hadn't called the cops on the reckless drivers, and they'd be long gone before the police caught up to them.

Matt knew better than to count on it.

* * *

Akash met them at the curb, tossing a duffel bag into the back seat as he got in.

"Lost you, did he?"

"He's dead," Blossom replied. "Hit a train. Squish."

"Holy shit." He locked eyes with Matt in the rearview. "Seriously?"

Matt nodded, then took a right out of the lot. He kept it at just under the speed limit and breathed a sigh of relief when they crossed the state line into Tennessee. He'd feel better if they had a different car, just in case the trucker and the train engineer put two and two together, but stealing a vehicle would paint just as big a target on them. At least crossing state lines made it more of a bureaucratic mess.

"I don't suppose y'all have a police scanner in that bag?"

"Nope," Akash said. "Good idea, but sorry."

"How about a clean shirt? This one's got blood on it."

"No can do, but I've got an ICAP windbreaker." He passed it up to Matt, who didn't bother to put it on yet.

"Where are we going?" Blossom asked.

"I'm thinking Maryland," Matt said.

"Why?"

"'Cause Janet LaLonde lives in Maryland. And if anyone knows where they're keeping Gerstner, she will."

"Or can find out," Akash added.

"Right."

"Did you find anything else?" Blossom asked.

Akash shrugged. "Only sort of. The bailing wire was still intact, but there was a lot of blood on it."

Blossom turned in her seat to face him. "You think Jeff used blood to slip through?"

"I have a hard time believing Garrett would be that sloppy."

"Me, too," Matt said. "And what were those puncture wounds?"

"I don't know. They almost looked like someone jammed acid-dipped needles into his skin. There wasn't any sign of forced entry."

"So what happened?" Blossom asked.

In the rearview mirror, Matt watched Akash shrug.

* * *

They hit a Motel 6 outside Tina, Kentucky, to see if Father Rees had tried to contact them. Without using a credit card, they couldn't rent a room if they wanted to, but Matt could slip into the hospitality room. He had one message. It read, *Call me.* His heart jumped to his throat.

He approached the front desk, where a bearded thirty-something sat at a computer, clicking the mouse with too much enthusiasm for it to be work related. He hit the spacebar and looked up. "May I help you?"

"Y'all got a phone I could use?"

He lifted his chin toward the wall. "Courtesy phone's right there. Just enter your room number, then dial nine." He turned back to his game.

Matt cleared his throat. "I don't have a room number."

The man raised an eyebrow. "Sorry, pal. Phone's for customers. Company policy."

Matt put a ten dollar bill on the counter. "How firm's that policy?"

He smiled, exposing teeth stained yellow-gray. "Not that firm." He scooped the ten off the counter and stuffed it into his pocket. "Dial star-one-five-five-one, then nine. You have a nice night."

He grabbed the phone and dialed Father Rees's cell. He picked up halfway through the first ring.

"Hello?" His voice sounded strained, worried.

"It's me. Talk."

"Hey, I think you need to get here."

He closed his eyes. "What happened?"

"I think maybe it'd be better in person—"

"Tell. Me."

Silence, then, "I'm so sorry, Matt. She's in surgery now, they're going to have to perform a hysterectomy."

Light exploded in his head, cold and without mercy. He forced a word through a dry mouth that had forgotten how to speak. "Why?" He asked God and Father Rees at the same time. Only Rees responded.

"Uterine bleeding. She's going to bleed out if they don't do it. She . . . She didn't want them to. Fought them. Said she'd rather die. They had to sedate her to save her."

When he could breathe again, he asked, "She's going to be okay?" He didn't ask about their son. He didn't need to hear what he already knew.

"Yeah. She should be out of surgery in an hour or so. Then a couple days in the hospital and a few weeks of rehab." He paused. "And she's going to need counseling."

"She's already in therapy," Matt snapped.

"I know. But she'll need more. Grief counseling. After this, maybe couples counseling."

He couldn't reach through the phone and snap Rees's neck, so instead he said, "When's she coming out of surgery?"

"The doctors said a couple hours, then she'll sleep through the night. I'm sure that's on purpose. They're going to keep her in ICU."

Matt did the math in his head. "I can be there in three hours, give or take."

"See you then. And Matt?"

"Yeah."

"It's best you come alone. Someone saw your friends, the dark guy and the Asian woman, carrying those assault weapons. Police put out an APB, came to talk to me and everything."

"What'd you tell them?"

"I told them I haven't seen anyone but I'll keep an eye out."

"That it?"

"That's it."

"Thanks." Matt hung up, and the pitying look on the clerk's face took too much to bear. He left the motel with tears in his eyes. Before Akash could say anything, he said, "We're going back. I need to be with Mon." He could just make out Blossom's form through the blur. "Can you drive, please?"

She slid into the driver's seat, and he took shotgun.

"How fast?" she asked.

"Don't get pulled over. But fast."

* * *

Matt left Blossom and Akash in the parking garage and stalked through the hospital to the information desk. "Hi," he said to the young black man behind the counter. "Where's your ICU?"

He pointed down the hall to the left. "Follow the blue line. Who are you here to see?"

Matt walked away, using the blue line as a guide through the warren of white-tiled halls lit with sterile, lifeless fluorescents. He stepped through the doorway under the huge "Intensive Care" sign and approached the desk.

A freckled nurse with bottle-red hair too bright for middle age smiled at him. "May I help you?"

"You had a Jane Doe come in from surgery."

"And you are?"

"I'm here to see her."

She pursed her lips. "Sir, I'm going to need a name, and you're going to need to sit right there and wait." She nodded to a bench, a recycled church pew, against the wall behind him. He cut left, looking in each room as he went by. She got up and stalked after him, cross-trainers squeaking on the hard tile floor. "Sir! You have to wait on the bench!"

He found her in the fourth room and wrinkled his brow at the haggard, unconscious form under the sheet. The life leached out of her, Monica's pale face held no comfort of sleep. The nurse grabbed his arm as he stepped through the door. He turned, pried her fingers off his arm, and placed his fingertips on her sternum above her breasts. He took one step and extended his arm, propelling her backward out of the room. She flailed and stumbled into the desk. He stepped in and closed the door, then approached his wife.

He stopped in shock at the round lump of her belly, and turned to Jason as he stood from the seat in the corner.

The priest's sad smile held more joy than Matt expected. "Good news."

Matt shook his hand and sat next to the bed. He took Monica's hand in his, kissed her brow, and looked at the priest. "Tell me."

"It wasn't as bad as they'd thought, and they were able to stop the bleeding without removing her uterus. But it's going to be touch and go for a while, for both of them. They recommended termination; I fought them on it."

He closed his eyes and inhaled a haggard breath. "Thank you, Jason."

"Sure. I've been in here a long time. I'm going to get some rest. I'll leave you with her." Matt heard his footfalls echo down the hall.

He held Monica's limp hand and waited for her to wake up. A few hours' dozing in the car had refreshed his body more than it needed but left his mind raw. Given how he'd treated the nurse, it came as no surprise when the policeman appeared at the door a moment later.

Mid-twenties, tall and muscular with a black crew cut and a ragged scar across his forehead, he didn't offer his hand. "Can I ask you a couple of questions, sir?" His uniform and badge identified Officer Voss as a Simpson County Sherriff's deputy, not a Statie.

Matt nodded to Jason's chair, adjacent to the giant white monitor that kept track of Monica's vitals. "Have a seat, deputy. And close the door."

He closed the door, then sat and took out a pen and spiral-bound flip pad. "Can I see some identification?"

"No." Matt waited.

"I understand you gave the nurse a hard time."

When Voss didn't go on, Matt said, "Is that a question, officer?"

Voss clucked his tongue. "Alright, how do you know our Jane Doe?"

"She's my wife."

"What's her name?"

"Jane."

Voss grunted. "Last name?"

"Doe."

He sighed and flipped the pad closed. "Sir, I'm going to have to ask for your cooperation on —"

Matt cut him off with a raised hand. "Just . . . Just wait. She came here as a Jane Doe for a reason, and I'm not about to change that just because you've got a badge."

Voss leaned forward, his face flushed with anger. "I'm a police "

"I don't care," Matt said without raising his voice. "If you want my cooperation, you're going to have to forget your badge a minute and talk to me as a person, not a suspect." They stared each other down, and while Matt blinked, Voss broke first.

The policeman sighed again and sat back. "I could take you into custody."

Matt chuckled, then ran his knuckles down Monica's cheek. She didn't react to his touch. "No, deputy, you couldn't."

"Excuse me?" Voss said. When Matt didn't answer or even look away from Monica he asked, "Is your wife in some kind of trouble?"

"No, but I'm in it deep." He stroked her hair out of her face. "And there are people who would use her to get to me."

In his peripheral vision, Voss leaned forward. "Don't you think that sounds a little . . . paranoid?"

"The people I work for—"

"ICAP," Voss said.

Matt froze, and met his gaze. "How'd you know that?"

Voss smiled and pointed at Matt's chest. "It's on your jacket."

Matt looked down at the logo emblazoned over his heart. *Shit.* He made a snap judgment and prayed it wouldn't come back to bite him. He slipped out of the windbreaker, and watched Voss's eyes widen at the crimson stains on his shirt, and widen further at the no-longer-concealed pistol holstered under his arm.

"Sir," officer Voss said. "This is a gun-free zone."

"Yes, it is, but you're not taking my weapon." Matt stared him down, and Voss averted his gaze to Matt's shoulder.

"What the hell happened to you?"

Matt grunted. "My boss shot me."

"Why?"

"That's what I'm trying to find out. And until I do, Jane Doe has to stay a Jane Doe. In a perfect world, nobody would even report she's had visitors, aside from Father Rees and yourself, of course."

He leaned forward in his chair. "You've got good range of movement for a guy who's been shot."

Matt thought for a moment how to best handle that line of inquiry. He fished into his pocket, extracted his multitool, and opened the three-inch blade; deputy Voss's eyes tracked him the whole time, and his hand moved toward the collapsible baton on his belt. Matt held up his left hand, then brought it down on the knife, impaling his hand straight through. He hissed through gritted teeth. Bright red blood leaked down the polished metal onto the back of his hand.

Voss stumbled backward out of his chair. "Jesus!" He stared, eyes wide.

Matt pulled the knife out, wiped both it and his hand on a tissue, and held out his palm. A thinning pink line held the only trace of what had just happened. "Regenerates."

"Does . . . did that hurt?"

"Of course it hurt. My shoulder hurt when my boss shot me, too."

"What happened to your boss?"

Matt made a show of folding the knife and putting it back in his pocket. "Was I somehow unclear about the need for secrecy, here?" He grabbed Monica's hand again, and gave it a squeeze. She didn't respond. "The more you know, the less safe she is."

"The station already knows someone besides Father Rees is here to see her. That's why I came in. I can't just tell the lieutenant I didn't get any information."

Matt crossed his arms and tried to keep the irony from his voice. "If it makes your job easier I could overpower you."

Voss snorted. "Unlikely. I can bench three fifty."

Matt believed it, but rolled his eyes anyway. "Officer, last year a bonk threw a Prius at me. I threw it back." Only ten feet, and he'd pulled every muscle in his body doing it, but Voss didn't need to know that.

Voss paused and sized him up, doubt in his eyes. "Look, guy, I'd like to help you out, but you have to give me something. You're not above the law—"

"No, that's true, but right now I'm going around it, and if you get in my way it's not going to be pretty."

He moved his hand from the baton to his pistol. "Sir, I don't want this to get ug—"

Whispers interrupted him. Matt caught the REC7 Blossom tossed to him without turning toward the door. "Company," she said. "ETA one minute."

Voss's eyes widened at the assault rifle. "Holy shit. You can't—" As Blossom stepped out the door, Voss's grip tightened on his pistol. Matt grabbed his wrist before he cleared the holster, and shook his head. Voss's eyes narrowed in determination. "Sir, I'm going to have to place you under arrest."

"Sorry." Matt head-butted the deputy, hard enough to knock him out but not crush his skull. He plucked the Glock 19 from Voss's hand as the policeman collapsed, checked the safety, and tucked it into the back of his pants.

He bolted to the nurse's station, where Blossom knelt, weapon aimed out the glass automatic doors that led to the Emergency Department. Next to her, a trio of scrub-clad nurses lay face down, hands folded over their heads, eyes wide and terrified.

"What are we up against?"

"Tactical van, with a bonk. Akash's outside, behind them. Hope they don't know that."

"Jason sold me out." Matt looked down at the nurses. "Ladies, I'm going to need you to run. Out the back. Fast as you can."

They looked at each other, then bolted. The fire-door alarm went off right as a black-haired bonk in tactical body armor walked through the Intensive Care Unit door, ducking its head to fit under the eight-foot doorframe. Its lips peeled back to reveal massive, square teeth—a smile. Matt recognized Murdock Yardley but had never worked with him. A former MMA superstar, he'd joined ICAP after a career-ending concussion and had earned a reputation for brutal efficiency and a casual disregard for collateral civilian casualties. He dropped the mirrored visor on his helmet, covering his eyes, the one target vulnerable to bullets.

"We don't have the gear for this," Matt said. He dropped to the floor as weapons barked from behind Yardley, peppering the nurse's station with bullets. Frightened screams erupted from the patients' rooms.

"Take the men," Blossom said. "I got the bonk."

"MURDOCK," Matt hollered. "I HAVEN'T BONKED. YOU'RE BEING LIED TO."

Yardley's grin never wavered as he charged.

Matt rolled out and took four short bursts between Yardley's legs, shredding ankles and feet. Cries of pain joined the cries of panic from the patient suites. As the massive creature trundled forward, Blossom hit him head on. The impact sounded like a gunshot as she shattered the bullet-proof visor with her hand, and before he could grab her she slipped around him and delivered a vicious two-handed strike to the side of his knee. Her coupled fists bounced off.

Matt advanced, firing over Blossom's head to force the rest of the fire team to take cover. Yardley kneed Blossom through the wall and she disappeared in a cloud of plaster dust. Matt shot Yardley twice in the throat, and the bonk roared, a deafening bellow that drowned out the sound of gunfire from outside.

Bodies fell as Akash shot them from behind. The bonk charged, and Matt's world compressed to the immediate fight. A massive fist crushed into his shoulder, and the assault rifle spun out of his numbed fingers. He rolled with the impact, turned, and pulled the Glock out left-handed. He rammed it under Yardley's tactical vest and pulled the trigger. Matt got off three shots before Yardley wrapped him in a bear hug, pinning his arms.

Yardley squeezed and Matt groaned. Bones shifted, then cracked, and he couldn't break free. He lost feeling in his arms. The pistol clattered to the floor. Matt tried to kick but had no purchase. Red filled his vision, and he tried to breathe. Air left his lungs, but wouldn't go back in.

Huge brown eyes widened in confused surprise as Blossom shoved an oxygen canister down the back of Yardley's vest, the mask still attached. She followed it with a grenade, then dove into an adjacent room as he shook her off. He must not have realized the danger, because he grinned and squeezed again. "Goodbye, Matt," Yardley said, two octaves below human normal.

The shockwave shattered Matt's eardrums. He rebounded off of a steel medical cart, his hair on fire. He smothered it with his hands and leapt to his feet. The bonk sprang up, his back a butcher's block of shredded meat.

Yardley stepped forward with a roundhouse kick. Matt ducked it and landed two punches, his fists burning with the impact. Yardley's downward chop blasted through his block and crushed him to the floor, forearm bent thirty degrees. He rolled away from one stomp that caused the whole floor to shudder, then another and another. He hit the wall and looked up into a massive boot tread, with nowhere left to go.

Blossom appeared behind Yardley, a surgical knife in her right hand. She severed his exposed spine between the shoulder blades, then again just above the hip. Matt scrambled out of the way as Yardley dropped to his knees, then his face. Blossom tore a ropy bundle of nerves straight out of his vertebrae. She knelt, jammed Voss's Glock up through Yardley's viscera and under his solid-fused ribs, and pulled the trigger over and over. He flailed his arms and head, and blood spurted out his mouth. The weapon clicked empty after the twelfth shot.

Dripping gore, she smiled and said something. Between the wail of the fire alarm and his ruptured eardrums, Matt couldn't hear her. Akash signed to them from the ED doorway. *Let's go.*

Matt stumbled into Monica's room, where deputy Voss lay in the corner in a fetal position, clutching his head, legs twitching. It stank of urine; he'd pissed himself. Matt ignored him. His ribs and shoulder screamed in protest as he scooped his pregnant wife from the bed as gently as he could and hurried out toward the parking garage.

Yardley's eyes followed him as he carried Monica by, and the giant man's fingers twitched. Even after that punishment, the tough bastard would live . . . if this newest round of trauma didn't push him over the edge into uncontrollable psychosis. He couldn't have much time left either way.

Matt carried Monica past the assault team scattered across the hallway like broken dolls, ten men with ruined legs, bloody torsos, one with a half-missing head, all wearing ICAP emblems on their body armor. One man panted in short, frantic breaths as he pressed both hands to his gushing thigh. "Sorry," Matt said as he stepped around him. He meant it; these men were soldiers doing their jobs.

Akash had collected four bandoleers of grenades and dozens of extra magazines for the rifles, and wore one of the assault team's ear pieces. He spoke as he gave half of the ammo to Blossom, and, though muffled, Matt could understand him. "We've got two ICAP choppers and every cop in the state incoming." He looked around at the carnage, then at Matt. "Good thing we were here, eh? They thought it was just you."

"I'd be dead," Matt said without slowing down, and Akash winced at the volume. "Yardley by himself would take care of that."

A beat-up, maroon Caprice Classic shrieked past them through the garage, Father Rees in the driver's seat. Akash choked up his REC7, but didn't fire. The car disappeared around the corner.

Matt didn't waste time with him, instead running to the SUV. Matt set Monica in the back and hung her saline IV from the handle above the door, then climbed in next to her, draping her legs across his lap. He wrapped the seatbelt around her as best he could while Akash took shotgun. Blossom climbed in the driver's seat and hit the gas, the door slamming shut as she accelerated.

She put on her blinker and pulled out into the street.

Three minutes later, a police car passed them, lights on and sirens blaring. Then another, and another. Matt kept a lookout for helicopters, but aside from the two that converged on the hospital, he didn't see any.

Chapter 15

Matt leaned back on his haunches, pulled the binoculars to his face, and looked at the light green, two-story farm house. "I'd feel better if we had full kit." His breath frosted in the chilly air; he worried that Monica wouldn't handle the cold in her weakened state, but they couldn't just leave the car running. She'd taken her second bag of saline, but had had no nourishment or painkillers. *Wake up, babe.*

Blossom snorted. "We grabbed what we could."

"I know."

The well-manicured lawn and fastidious but barren flower garden contrasted with the controlled chaos of a turkey farm down the road, whose halogen lights bathed the clouds in an orange glow. Smoke streamed from the chimney, and he saw no dog house, no tie-outs. Their approach options sucked; they could come in from the road or through a massive fallow field overrun with goldenrod and brambles.

A single light popped on at five am, illuminating the upstairs bedroom. Matt watched as Janet LaLonde clambered out of bed, and almost averted his eyes when she stripped off her light green flannel pajamas. He grunted in surprise at her muscular, well-toned back. The leggy, gum-chewing IT specialist had a green—no, a *jade*—Iron Cross tattoo stretching from the base of her neck to her perfect ass, and full across her shoulder blades.

"Wouldn't have pegged her as the religious type," Akash whispered next to him.

She left the room without turning on the hallway light, and came back a moment later, still naked, toothbrush in her mouth. With her left hand she pulled a bright blue dress out of the closet, held it up to her body, then laid it out on the bed. Akash muttered "wow" as she walked out of the room, and Matt couldn't help but agree.

The bathroom light came on, and Matt let the binoculars hang at his neck. He picked up his REC7 and crept through the brush until they reached the edge of the yard, thirty feet from the house. A tractor fired up in the distance. Most of Fulton, Maryland, still slept, but not for long.

Security? Matt signed.

Blossom shook her head. *I don't see any. Maybe on the doors or windows.*

Matt looked back at the bathroom window. Fog built up on the inside glass.

Go.

They approached the house weapons-ready. Matt didn't expect resistance, but shit and the fan were too well acquainted to play it safe this time. Besides, none of them knew whether or not Janet had any field training.

On the side porch, they spread out to multiple windows. Matt closed his eyes to listen and heard only the patter of water from the shower. Opening one window, he saw no telltale lights or keypads that would indicate a security system. Her furniture, like her lawn, had an aura of severe order to it.

Clear, Akash signed, though he looked unsure.

I see nothing, Blossom replied.

Same here. Matt tried the knob. Locked. The old farmhouse doorframe had warped over time; he could see the latch mechanism through the crack. A moment's work with a knife, and the door opened with a creak.

Akash took point, leapfrogging with Blossom through the living room and up the stairs. Matt followed behind them after a quick sweep for a security pad; he found no evidence of one. Janet hummed in the shower, and he recognized the tune as he opened the bathroom door: "I'm Gonna Miss Her" by Brad Paisley.

He stepped through billowing steam, rifle pointed at the floor. The foggy glass shower doors left little to the imagination. Janet arched her back and ran her hands through her straight brown hair, water cascading over her head. A quick check revealed no firearms he could see. *Here goes nothing.*

He banged on the wall.

Janet jumped, stumbled back, and put her hand over her heart. Eyes wide, she exhaled, then inhaled. "Fuck–a-duck, you gave me a heart attack, Matt."

It wasn't the reaction he'd expected, and he hesitated.

She opened the door a crack, peered at him, then turned off the water. She reached an arm out and grabbed a faded maroon towel. She held it to her chest, obscuring just enough to be even more distracting. "He said today, but holy shit, I wasn't expecting you to bust in on my shower at the butt-crack of dawn." She raised an eyebrow and slid the door the rest of the way open with her toe. "Do you mind turning around? It ain't like I'm going to come out shooting."

Instead, Matt stepped back and Blossom took his place. He took another step back, lurking around the corner with Akash.

"Not better," Janet said. A pause, then, "Whatever. I'd be paranoid, too."

"Hurry up." Blossom's voice held no humor. "When you're done, you sit on the couch."

"Sure."

She stepped out a minute later, the maroon towel around her head, a large beige bath sheet around her midsection. She exuded a confidence that unsettled Matt, even patting Akash on the cheek on her way by. "Morning, Rastogi."

She sauntered downstairs, feet leaving tiny puddles on the steps, and sat on the couch, legs crossed.

"You were expecting us," Matt said.

She nodded. To her right, Akash stood at ease in the doorway. Blossom took up position on the stairs, eyes scanning the doors and windows.

"Cavalry on the way?"

She shook her head. "Nope."

"You know why we're here?"

"You're looking for information." She reached one-handed into a large, garish purse on the end table, and instead of pulling out a piece of paper or a gun or something that made sense, she opened a pack of Orbit, popped out a square, and put it in her mouth.

"What information are we looking for?"

Janet flashed her eyebrows and chewed her gum. "You want to know where to find Fraulein Gerstner, and Jeff didn't tell you before he pancaked himself. But I don't know where she is. It's not in the computer."

Matt exchanged looks with Akash and Blossom.

"How . . . do you know this stuff?"

She scowled, gum between her teeth. "Dawkins told me before you captured him."

"There's no way he could have known that."

She rolled her eyes. "He can if he's fucking psychic. Your precog ain't got nothing on his." She held up a finger. "Here, I'll show you."

She opened a thin drawer under the coffee table—he never would have noticed it—and removed a cheesy-looking romance novel. She flipped through, found a scrap of paper, and handed it to Matt.

Matt took it and grunted. It read, "Rowley, Rastogi, Sakura. October 29th. Your house."

Akash raised an eyebrow. "I don't get it. If he's so damned psychic, why didn't he just give us Gerstner's location?"

She sat back, re-tucking the towel to keep from flashing them again. "Look, you're already in this, yeah? You know he's telling the truth?"

Matt wasn't sure of all of it, but close enough. He nodded. So did Akash. Blossom's eyes didn't leave the windows.

"So get this: he knew either he was going to capture you or the other way around. Every scenario was worse than the last—in every one he tried to get away, he ended up dead instead—so he planned for both contingencies, arranged the best final outcome he could either way," she pointed her finger at Matt and went 'bang' with her thumb, "which was to blow up your life to the point that you either help him or get yourself killed."

Matt frowned. "So if you can't help us, what are we doing here?"

Her smile met her eyes for the first time. "He knows where they're holding Gerstner. I know where they're holding him. You're going to break him out, then you're all going to shut this whole sick thing down."

Nobody said anything for a moment.

"What's your stake in this?" Akash asked. "Why is it so important that he walks free?"

She raised her eyes just enough to meet his. Matt gasped just before she said it. "He's my brother."

* * *

Monica stirred as Matt set her on the bed in Janet's guestroom. The sparse furnishings included a full-sized bed, a small nightstand, an empty bookshelf, and a cheap floor lamp. The candy-apple-red wallpaper and faded teal throw rug accentuated the unspoken message: *whoever you are, we'll make you feel welcome, but we don't really want you here.*

He ran his hand through her hair and shushed her. "It's okay, baby. I'm here."

Her brow furrowed in confusion, and she hissed as she tried to sit up. "Where are we?"

He tried to remember if she'd ever met Janet and landed on "probably not."

"Don't sit up. There was a . . . problem at the hospital. We had to move you." As if on cue, Akash carried in a narrow wooden coat rack, from which hung another bag of saline. Her eyes widened, fluttered closed, opened again. Her head lolled to the side. "I'm so tired."

He kissed her cheek. "I know, baby. You need to rest. I got to get going—"

She dug her fingernails into his wrist. "No, no." *I lost our baby.*

He put his hand on hers and cut her off before she could voice the thought. "No, you didn't. He's okay."

Her eyes snapped open and her hands covered her belly. "What? They . . . the doctors said they had to—"

"The surgeon patched you up, Mon. Saved the baby. You're going to be okay. Both of you."

Worry drained from her face, replaced with exhaustion and joy. "Really?"

"Really. But you need to rest."

She grabbed his arm. "I will, if you stay with me."

He kissed her.

"I would if I could, babe. But what happened at the hospital, it could happen again." She furrowed her brow, and he realized she wasn't conscious for the battle. "Don't worry about it." He smoothed her bangs out of her face. "The important thing is that you rest."

Instead of responding, she rolled her eyes over to Akash. "I don't want drugs."

In reply, he knelt, rubbed the inside of her elbow with alcohol, and inserted the IV needle. "You need fluids, and we don't want you getting up if you don't have to. You need to rest, and we'll fetch you some food."

She grimaced. "I'm not hungry. I feel . . . queasy."

"That's the anesthetic," Akash said. "It'll wear off, and you need to keep up your strength. For you and the baby."

She looked back and forth between them, and when Matt nodded she closed her eyes in resignation. "Okay."

Matt turned on the drip, and Akash injected the sedative into the plastic bladder. Her sharp breaths faded to smooth, deep sleep. Akash left the room. Matt followed him out several minutes later.

Janet, dressed in jeans and a Florida-Georgia Line T-shirt, met him in the hall. "I took a personal day. They weren't real happy about it and'll probably call me in anyway if forensics figures out that Jeff took a dirt nap."

"It's not likely. No ID, stolen car, wrong state. With how much damage there was, they'll need DNA to ID him, if it's even on file."

He looked back at the guestroom, then at Janet. "Don't answer your phone, and they can't call you in."

Her smirk held no mirth. "This job don't work that way."

He didn't have enough in him to argue. "Just look after my wife."

"And you bring my brother home safe."

* * *

The address Janet had given them matched an abandoned warehouse near Anacostia Park, across the river from the US Naval Yard. She couldn't provide them with headsets, but current security codes and building schematics made an excellent consolation prize. The facility depended on ignorance for safety, the busted-out windows and gangland graffiti the perfect camouflage for an underground detention facility.

Six rooms: three large cells, a bathroom, and an office, arranged around a pentagonal common room accessible from the street via secret elevator. Matt didn't consider himself much of a conspiracy theorist, but "secret underground detention facility" fit the bill. A building of that size couldn't house more than a half-dozen guards, but given the nature of their prisoners, he'd bet they were augged.

Five security cameras lay hidden throughout the street level. There was no approach that wouldn't be seen, but Blossom moved so fast he doubted a person would notice her on camera. Matt's infrared overlay showed no obvious guards, but two homeless men lay on opposite ends of the building, and their bulky torsos were muffled in his IR vision. *Kevlar.* He hadn't known Garrett well, but already missed his tactical prowess—their simple plan should be foolproof, but doubts plagued him.

Blossom, dressed in a ratty hoodie and torn blue jeans, pushed a shopping cart past the first man. His infrared signature spread underneath him, and by the time she'd hobbled to the other side of the building, he'd cooled by more than a degree Celsius. The same happened to the second man, and then Blossom vanished inside.

Six seconds later, she appeared next to Matt. "Charges are set. Eighteen." He set his internal clock for eighteen seconds as she disappeared again. At eleven he ran, and at two he crouched behind the cinder-block outer wall.

A sharp bang shook his bones, then he rounded the corner. Akash ran from the opposite direction, and they hit the elevator shaft a bare moment after the secondary charges blew the lower doors. Blossom had emptied half her magazine by the time his feet hit the lower level. He choked up his assault rifle and scanned for targets.

What the hell? Streams of dusty sunlight illuminated the five-sided room and the enormous chalk pentagram that dominated the floor. An altar of black basalt sat dead-center, the emaciated body on it surrounded by fat, sagging candles flecked with green specks. Everything stank of burning fat and sweat and feces and blood and Jade, tinged with gunpowder. Whatever he'd expected, it wasn't this.

A hooded man stumbled back from a giant leather-bound tome, spurts of blood gushing from his chest. Another screamed and choked up a sword—a freaking claymore of all things—and dropped it when his head shattered in a spray of gunfire from Akash. Matt fired two tight bursts, turned and fired one more. Three bodies dropped to the floor, and silence reigned.

The cells held dozens of filthy, half-naked people, jammed in to standing room only. Their haggard, dead-eyed stares held no sense of hope or even interest at the unfolding events. Except for one.

Dawkins smiled at Matt from across the pentagram. "Hurry. But don't—"

Matt stepped forward, then stumbled to the side as whispers screeched through his mind. Streams of thought swirled around the pentagram, a maelstrom of hate and vicious cruelty his psyche couldn't hope to survive. He gasped, braced himself on the wall, and circled around to the first cell.

"—cross the chalk," Dawkins finished.

Matt punched in the code Janet had given them. Nothing happened, so he grabbed the iron bar and pulled. "Hurry up,"

Akash muttered from across the room. The lock bent, then popped, and the door sprang open. Blank stares in empty faces, not one of the prisoners moved to escape. He popped the next, and then approached Dawkins.

They stared at each other through the bars. Shirtless and too lean, the drug dealer had lost weight, and dark circles ringed his glassy eyes. Weeping sores dotted his cracked, bloody lips. Tattoos criss-crossed his body, each one a copy of Conor's gruesome body art, but defiled by a crucifix over the top.

Matt hesitated. "You're as strong as I am. Break out."

Dawkins reached up without averting his gaze, and grabbed the bars. He hissed in pain as his hands sizzled and smoked. He dropped to his knees to wretch between the staring, vacant men that crowded him, then let go and held his hands to his chest. He gagged, spat, then spoke. "I can no more open those bars than you can cross that pentagram. Now hurry."

Matt had too many questions to ask, so he wrenched the bars apart instead. Behind him, Akash shrieked. He whirled around, weapon raised, and gaped in horror.

The headless man drove a clawed hand up through Akash's abdomen, lifting his twitching body from the floor. Blossom fired on full auto, emptying a clip into the dead man. As blood seeped from his wounds, it congealed, hardened.

Akash coughed blood as Matt fired, riddling the corpse with bullets. Each wound sprouted a long black thorn, glistening with blood, and the air filled with the scent of burnt matches. He paused to reload, and the corpse tore Akash in half.

Blood and viscera splattered on the floor. Akash's upper body landed on the altar, his mouth gaping. The light in his eyes died, and his body went slack. From it, shadows rose. Jade eyes opened in blood-soaked nothing, and wings of smoke unfolded to banish the sun. The emaciated body under Akash crumbled and remolded, forming naked, skinless muscle for the being that rose from the carnage.

The whispers filled Matt with praise. *Brother.*

Dawkins shouldered past Matt, snapping him from his adulation. He stopped at the edge of the pentagram and sneered.

The angel—it couldn't be anything else—barked something in a language Matt didn't recognize, and Dawkins responded in what sounded like Hebrew. It roared, and the earth shuddered. Dawkins knelt and clasped his hands together, head bowed.

"Stop her," he said.

Matt scrambled around to where Blossom knelt, busy carving into her forearm with a combat knife, eyes rolled back to expose only whites, drizzling blood into a pool on the floor. He shook her, and when she didn't respond, he brought his knee up into her temple. She collapsed sideways, but her arm flashed and he stumbled back, abdomen bleeding from three deep cuts. Prone, she dipped two fingers into her blood and traced a symbol onto the floor. The blood hissed and bubbled, and the angel laughed as millions of motes of chalk rose into the air, mingled with Blossom's blood. More of it flowed from her self-inflicted wound, streaming upward into the air to join the maelstrom around the pentagram.

Matt could lose himself in that laugh, surrender to it, and die in its glory. The whispers begged him to. He needed it, more than anything. More than . . . Monica? Their unborn boy? He shook off the perverse thought and dove at Blossom.

Her knife glanced off his rib and missed his heart by inches. Ignoring the pain, he wrapped her in a bear hug. He couldn't hope to compete with her speed—she'd head-butted him twice before his arms had closed—but he outmatched her strength two-to-one and healed much faster.

She snarled in feral hatred and struggled, a writhing bag of snakes, and, while blood gushed from his shattered nose, he held on and fell atop her. He gritted his teeth as the knife ground between his ribs, and wheezed as his lung tried to reknit around the steel.

A strong arm gripped him in a headlock. Cruel black thorns pierced his neck, his back, his legs. He maintained his grip on Blossom as the thorned corpse lifted him and sank its jagged, barbed teeth into his shoulder. He jerked his head back, then forward, and each movement rewarded him with the crunch of shattered cartilage. Blossom went slack in his arms, so he let go and reached behind him.

His hands came away slick with blood and sweat. The teeth ground into his collar bone and shifted upward, toward his carotid artery. He coughed blood when the thing's clawed hand punched through his abdomen below his ribs, and struggled upward. He put his feet under him, found purchase on the floor, and heaved with his legs.

They flew backward and smashed into the wall, but it wouldn't let go. Hot blood splattered his face, and he tried to block out that it came from his own neck. He slammed back again, to no effect. Pulling the knife from his chest, he flipped the grip and thrust just above the teeth. He spun as it let go, and a roundhouse kick sent it stumbling into the pentagram. The thing shrieked as it staggered across the chalk line, and collapsed.

Next to him, Blossom struggled to her hands and knees, eyes cloudy. The headless corpse lay just inside the pentagram, steaming but with no thorns in sight—and no teeth. Matt put his hand to his neck and held the pumping artery until it closed, and pulled them away as the muscle healed over it. He sank to his knees.

The angel stood at the edge of the pentagram in a chaotic swirl of jade thought. The bodies had crumbled, dissipated, become one with it, and the tome next to the altar blazed with green light. Dawkins knelt just outside its reach, flanked by dozens of blank-eyed, slack-jawed men. Their emaciated bodies swayed with his, and their lips moved in a parody of his chant.

The pentagram contracted as the chalk lines slithered toward the altar, and the angel stepped back in a roar of fury. The spell broken, Matt stumbled forward, toes brushing the edge without crossing it, and joined the chant. He didn't know the words, but they filled him, spilled from him, and he felt their power. The whispers cowered in his mind.

Inside the circle, the swirling energies collapsed in on themselves, streaming into the angelic form. The angel's shriek filled not only Matt's ears but his mind, drowning out the whispers and dominating them, its will forging them into a barb that punctured his soul. Choking on blood he pushed forward, and the dark power coalesced as it stumbled back. Wings of smoke became stringy skin, its body fading from brilliant, metallic light into pallid flesh as it inched away from the collapsing chalk toward the basalt table.

The candles blazed, melting to reveal ten-inch blades upon which the fat had been impaled. Matt recognized the almost sweet, bacony smell from a HMMVW accident in the Big Sand, and his stomach churned at the delicious aroma of long pork. He reached forward as the pentagram shattered, his hands sizzling on the white-hot metal of the candle holders.

"NOW!" Dawkins shouted, and Matt struck.

The candles impaled the angel's temples, stabbing out the other side to slice Matt's fingers. Its hot blood mingled with his, and the whispers entangled with its shriek of unholy rage. The body crumpled, sizzled, then crumbled to dust.

Matt collapsed, and dreamed.

The sky burned a deep green. Matt sucked Jade-tinged air into his lungs, and they shuddered in protest. The plain before him crackled with energy, and a thousand million desperate souls staggered over a field of skeletons. Their emaciated bodies shuffled forward, the green tinge of bruised skin a telltale sign of advanced Jade addiction. They stumbled into an unending pit, deep and eternal, not the smallest shred of sunlight reaching its walls, and they shrieked praise to Tartarus as they fell.

A smoke-winged angel rose from the unending darkness, a shard of God's will corrupted by lust and greed. He couldn't bear to look at it; he couldn't bear to look away. It bellowed in triumph. Another followed it, and another and another, their voices joined in a majestic choir of unending dread. They streamed into the sky, and where their shadows touched men knew only despair. And still the bodies marched, falling into blackness so that the damned might rise.

His head rang, and the vision faded. It rang again, and he opened his eyes. He put out his hand, and instead of slapping him again, Dawkins hauled him to his feet. "We got to go, man."

"What the hell was that?"

Dawkins dragged Matt forward without responding, the giant tome tucked under his arm. Blossom took point as they clambered out of the ruined elevator and disappeared into the suburban landscape. They hugged the river and hiked north, keeping to the shadows as much as possible.

"Tartarus," Matt said.

Dawkins led them through an alley, ducked behind a dumpster, and only then met his gaze. "What about it?"

"I saw it. I was there, and I saw it."

"Matt," Blossom said, her voice disgusted. "You cannot believe this stuff about Nephilim."

Dawkins stopped, put one hand over the book, and closed his eyes. "I've seen enough in the past months to believe in the devil on Earth."

"Is that what we saw?"

"No," Blossom said.

"I don't think so, either," Dawkins said. He hefted the book and walked again. "But I intend to find out." It occurred to Matt that he knew where they were going, knew their plan without being told.

"So those crazy men, they're ICAP?" Blossom asked.

"Yes," Dawkins said. "As far as I can tell, ICAP is not and never has been an international government organization. It's a cult, dedicated to spreading Jade use around the whole world, to bring about some kind of apocalypse and rule the ruins."

Matt snarled. "And you helped."

Dawkins held the book to his chest and shrugged. "I didn't know."

"So you became a drug dealer just for the money?" Blossom said.

Dawkins sneered. "I don't think they knew how effective their first precognitive treatments were going to be with me. After the treatment, I saw . . . so many things. I was angry that they had condemned me to inevitable insanity, and they knew it, and I wanted to hurt them. Over the past ten years I've stolen most of their illegal cash flow, leaving them only government corruption to line their pockets. And I've worked to destroy them.

"I . . . I didn't know what Jade was, how it all tied together. Gerstner used me as a puppet, and I danced on her strings. By the time I'd teased out what I thought was the truth, Pandora's Box had blown right open, and I only saw one way out. I can't change what I've done, but maybe I can stop them and that thing they serve. That's something."

"I don't think forgiveness comes that easy."

He shrugged. "Life doesn't have a rewind button. If I'm going to hell, so be it. I don't have to take the rest of humanity with me."

Blossom rolled her eyes. "So what now?"

They arrived at the small dock, where the four-man, deep-V aluminum fishing boat sat tied to the last post with yellow nylon rope. Dawkins got in and fired up the motor. "I want to see my sister."

Chapter 16

They trolled up the Potomac at a maddening crawl, the boat winning out against the current by the barest of margins. It didn't take a half-hour for Dawkins to regain his color and musculature—something about their cells had inhibited his regenerates and, if he'd told the truth, the rest of his augs as well. If he could be believed, hundreds had died on the altar in the short time he'd been imprisoned, but today's events comprised the first and only time anything else had happened.

Matt brooded, trying to tease facts out of what he'd experienced and what Dawkins had said. Dawkins had lied to him before and now claimed that Matt never would have believed the truth if he'd told it. At least that much rang true; Matt wasn't sure he believed it now that he'd seen it. A corpse had killed Akash, and Dawkins subdued an angel with prayer. Or his mind. Or something. He looked down at his hands, red and raw from the candlesticks, even after all this time. And they *hurt*, long after they should have healed.

Angels. Matt had always considered himself kind of religious, but now that the existence of angels had slapped him across the face, he didn't know what to believe. It wasn't an aug; it had coalesced, appeared out of nothing, and subsumed dead bodies into itself. He hadn't hallucinated, or Blossom and Dawkins wouldn't have seen the same things. Blossom remained adamant that an inevitable scientific explanation would come to light, even for her own bizarre actions, which she remembered and apologized for but couldn't explain.

Proof of God filled him with doubt.

They beached at Ruppert Island and swam to shore at the Clara Barton Parkway, where Janet waited for them. Matt stood with Blossom while the siblings hugged. They piled into Janet's four-door Nissan and cruised at just over the speed limit back to Fulton. Matt allowed himself a brief doze in the back seat and woke as Janet pulled into her driveway. He flexed his hands; they hurt less, and he'd regained full mobility. Still, far too slow for a simple burn.

Matt tiptoed upstairs, where Monica slept. Still pale, she now had some color to her lips and cheeks, and her slow, steady breathing encouraged him. She didn't move when he kissed her, so he closed the door and went back downstairs.

Dawkins set the giant book on the kitchen table, and, for the first time, Matt noticed the tiny, wandering script that weaved a sinuous pattern around the cover. Dawkins ran his finger along the curving path, muttering guttural words as he went.

Blossom grunted. "You can read it?"

Dawkins didn't stop until he finished, at which point he looked up at her. "I've heard it read aloud many times, before each sacrifice. I could recite it without reading it."

"What does it say?" Matt asked at the same time Blossom said, "What language?"

He nodded to Blossom first. "It's early Aramaic, what you see on artifacts from the Achaemenid Empire."

"Fluent, are we?" Matt asked.

Dawkins's bland look said all it needed to. "You've got eidetic enhancers, too. It's not my fault if you haven't used them to their full potential."

He ignored the barb. "So what does it say?"

"It's a prayer"—he smiled as Janet set a cup of coffee in front of him and hugged him yet again—"to 'the sister' for success against the unutterable one's injustice." He underlined the last phrase with his finger as he said it.

"The unutterable one," Janet said. "So they're fighting Voldemort?"

Dawkins chuckled. "No. In ancient Judaism, most people weren't allowed to say or write the name of God, not even the Tetragrammaton, which early Christians bastardized into *Yahweh* or *Jehovah*, while the Jews usually used *Adonai*, which means 'Lord.'

Punishments ranged from death to less pleasant things." He looked at Janet and then Matt. "They're fighting God."

"Doesn't sound like a winning battle," Matt said.

"Have you watched TV lately?" Janet asked.

Dawkins opened the front cover and examined the first page, then flipped through several more thick vellum pages, handwritten and illuminated with devils and angels in faded, ancient colors that had flaked and torn where the writing had not. Rubbery fibers, maybe sinew, bound the pages to the wooden spine. The style reminded Matt of manuscripts from the middle ages like he'd seen in movies or museums. On closer inspection, the script had faded much more than the drawings, and the writing didn't look like anything he'd ever seen before. Only that wasn't quite true. The almost Arabic, almost Hebrew script matched one of Conor Flynn's tattoos.

"More Aramaic?" Matt asked.

"Phoenician," Dawkins said without looking up. "Easy mistake. Aramaic uses the Phoenician alphabet, and they share some vocabulary, but the grammar's different." He ran his fingers over the page. "The letters were carved into the leather—let's hope it's calf—with a stylus, then filled with some kind of sticky powder, probably charcoal mixed with resin or pitch. Call this a couple millennia or so BC. I have no idea what they used to glue the paper to the parchment, but judging by the style of the art, that came maybe thirteen hundred AD."

"What's it say?" Janet asked.

Dawkins looked down to the manuscript and Matt turned so that Janet couldn't see his hands. He signed to Blossom: *Track his eyes. Make sure he's reading and not making stuff up.*

He just caught her curt nod.

Dawkins sighed. "It's an excerpt from the Book of Enoch. Sort of. 'In defiance of YHW'—that'd be God, folks—'the seraph Semjaza led two hundred angels from paradise to Mount Hermon, where in their lust these egregoroi, the watchers, lay with human women and sired abominations, the Nephilim. Jealous that the egregoroi would take form and thus steal from Him His most precious creation, YHW cast them into the pit of eternal darkness, called Tartarus. By the time their angelic fathers had been cast down, the Nephilim had spread throughout the world, fearsome giants who sought to twist and corrupt His creation into kingdoms of their own.'"

He turned the page, revealing an illumination of what could only be Noah's Ark, complete with a pair of unicorns. The image had once been in color, but had faded and flaked away so much that it almost looked black-and-white. "'In His unjust, petty rage at these poor children, YHW brought forth great waters to destroy what He couldn't control, drowning the Nephilim and their human mothers alike, and countless other innocents. But the Nephilim were crafty, and many hid in the dark corners of the world, to emerge again as spirits and take their place as the rulers of man.'"

Matt interrupted him when he reached the bottom of the page. "That's not what I read. The Book of Jubilees says that God allowed a fraction of a fraction of the Nephilim to remain as incorporeal spirits, to lead man astray before the Final Judgment."

Dawkins shrugged. "I said, 'sort of.'" He turned the page. The faded illumination depicted a bunch of swirling curlicues which could have been clouds or smoke. "Huh," Dawkins said. "This is Hebrew, and it's a lot newer, maybe fourth or fifth century." Dawkins's voice dropped. "'Like their fathers the egregoroi, the Nephilim grew jealous of what was not theirs. In their quest for dominion of man, the surviving Nephilim conspired to destroy one another. Of sixty times two hundred, only one stayed true, only one stayed righteous, only one loved and sought to free her fathers.

"'Join us, righteous men, and serve the daughter of shadow, the triumphant sister, the dark mother, she who dares defy HaShem'—that means 'the Name,' so that's God again—'and free her holy fathers from the unending darkness. Join us, righteous men, and drink of the true blood, not of everlasting life but everlasting youth. Join us, righteous men, to free the angelic fathers and rule with them the all . . . .'" He licked his lips and sat back in frustration. "I'm not sure how to translate this next phrase. It's something like 'eternal lands taken by the mighty.' I don't know what it means. Earth, maybe?"

Matt shrugged. Janet sipped at her coffee. Blossom scowled out the window.

He turned the page, scanned it, then flipped through the next several. The pages looked newer, crisper, the text darker and more pronounced as he flipped through. "These are interesting. Each page shows a victory of this Nephilim over another. According to this cult, she's responsible for the destruction of everyone from Osiris and the pharaohs to the Cabal of Thirteen in ancient Babylon, the Medici dynasty, even Tezcatlipoca in the New World."

He stopped a third of his way through the book, on a page written in German with no embellishment but two symbols in black and white: Matt recognized the first as the double-lightning bolt of the Nazi SS, but not the second, a diamond with an SD in it. Blossom stepped around him to read it.

"It's a patient dossier for Edith Gerstner. Born 30 April 1879 in a Munich hospital, was arrested for violation of Jewish quarantine in 1942 and sent to the *Vernichtungslager*—Death Camp—at Sobibor. It says she went with seventy-two other women into the petrol exhaust shower, and after all had succumbed to diesel fumes, she walked out, unharmed but docile.

"Healthy for her age, she agreed to every treatment and test and even cooperated in designing experiments to test the limits of her body. She made no attempt to escape with the others on 14 October 1943. You see here," she pointed at a box Matt couldn't read, "it's an order of transfer to the *Sicherheitsdienst Reichsbunkersystem* at Dresden on 15 October 1943, signed by Phillip Lenard himself. They closed Sobibor just after."

She turned the page and frowned. "This is something different."

The next page, and the rest after it, had more similarity to the first few pages than to those that came later. Dawkins frowned in frustration at the faded, almost invisible runes.

Matt frowned with him. "Is that 'Uruk Proto-Cuneiform'?"

Dawkins raised an eyebrow. "How did you know that?"

"It looks like the tattoo from Flynn's body. And yours, for that matter. Care to explain them?"

Dawkins looked up from the book and out the window. "I don't have an explanation. I don't. I had a compulsion to create them, something I couldn't resist, but with a lot of meditation I avoided using other people's blood, though I really wanted to." His smile held not the slightest trace of warmth. "The whispers didn't like that much, and oh how they shrieked when, after each, Janet would deface them with crosses."

"Are you a Christian?" Matt asked.

Dawkins shrugged. "I don't know what I am, but I know power when I feel it." He tapped the book. "Like this. You can almost feel it hum."

Matt touched the vellum. The parchment felt like parchment, the grooves cut to make the runes felt like cut grooves. "I don't feel anything."

Dawkins looked back down at the book.

"What's it say?" Matt asked.

Dawkins chuckled. "I have no idea."

"How do we find out?"

Blossom rolled her eyes. "This is a waste of time. So now we believe that this old woman is a child of angels? That she is an ancient killer of gods?"

Dawkins chuckled again, a tired rasp devoid of joy. "I don't care what you believe, Sakura Isuji. If it makes you feel better, there is no God, and when you were breaking me out those guys brought that body back to life through alien parthenogenesis or voodoo or unchecked stem-cell research or global fucking warming. I don't care where you believe she came from or what she is, but unlike that thing back there, Gerstner has fed and grown for thousands of years, and she is a thousand times more powerful."

Blossom grunted and looked out the window. "But removing her from this machine will stop the augs."

"Yes," Dawkins said.

"You're certain."

"Yes."

She glared at him. "And this will stop the madness? This will keep the survivors sane?"

He opened his mouth, closed it, then opened it again. "I think so."

She scowled. "I want to believe you."

"I'm telling the truth."

She shot an annoyed glance at Matt before turning back to Dawkins. "I believe that you believe you. I am less sure that what you believe is true."

Matt tapped the book and repeated his question. "So how do we find out?"

Dawkins looked at his sister.

Janet leaned back in her chair. "Don't look at me, D. I can't read that shit." Matt wondered if Dawkins had a first name. She wheeled over to her laptop and pulled up a browser. After a few minutes she clucked her tongue. "But something doesn't add up. The Uruk culture dates to 4000 BC, and they wrote on clay. Parchment scrolls, writing on rawhide, didn't exist for another fifteen hundred years. That we know of."

"Fair enough," Dawkins said. "Can you access the linguistics files they pulled up during Conor Flynn's autopsy? If you get us those files, we might be able to piece together what this says."

Matt raised an eyebrow. "You expect us to learn a language in an afternoon?"

He shook his head. "Not really. Grammar takes a lot longer than that, but we can learn the vocabulary and at least get a sense of what this says. Uruk is grammatically similar to Phoenician, Aramaic, and Hebrew, so I can help with that if you can help translate on a word for word basis."

Instead of replying, Matt looked at Janet. "So can you get them?"

She stopped mid-chew, gum trapped between her incisors, then sucked it back into her mouth. "Yeah, but not from here. I'll have to go to work."

"They won't get suspicious?" Matt asked.

She bobbed her head back and forth. "Um, I can't access the files without it getting flagged, and my own access doesn't send the flag to me. I'd need to generate a request from someone, and when they follow up it won't check out."

"Careful, sis," Dawkins said.

She held up a hand. "Maybe you don't get it. This ain't about careful. I don't do this right, it'll burn me. They've got their heads so far up their asses that it'll take them a week or three to get around to vetting the document request, but when they do, if it gets back to me, I'm done."

"I don't think it'll take near that long," Matt said. "When I poked around the servers, Jeff called me before I'd finished, asking me what I was up to. I guarantee he wasn't watching for me, so they must have some kind of spy program working in the background."

Janet walked over to her brother and rested a hand on his shoulder. "So how do we play this?"

Dawkins closed his eyes as she rubbed his temples. His face twitched, then his whole body shuddered. Blossom opened her mouth to speak and Janet stopped her with an upraised finger that returned to his temples as soon as Blossom had closed her mouth. After a few minutes, his eyes snapped open.

Janet stepped back. "Consequences?"

He cleared his throat. "We burn Tufts. He requests the file, then goes dark. It's the only way we get it without killing an asset."

Matt raised an eyebrow. "Avery Tufts is one of yours?" The fifty-something former Scotland Yard bureaucrat had the looks and personality of a herring. Matt knew nothing about him except that his name appeared on a lot of reports and that none of his coworkers paid him much attention.

Dawkins's smile didn't reach his eyes. "As far as Tufts knows, he's working for the CIA. Still a traitor, of course, but at least it's not Islamists."

Matt wanted to ask how many agents Dawkins had in ICAP, but knew he wouldn't get an answer. Instead he said, "So that's the plan?"

"Yes," Dawkins said. "He'll request the file along with a bunch of others, we'll intercept, and he'll retire in Aruba on a comfortable government payday to a Swiss bank account, blissfully unaware that he's living off of drug money." He smiled at Janet. "But first we need to get you to work."

He used a prepaid cell phone to report his red mustang stolen from the Hill Country Motel and Pool Spa, and gave Jeff's description to the policeman on the line. In that time, she'd rubbed under her eyes enough to create vicious bags, scrubbed off all her makeup, and completed a quick workout that gave her a flushed, sweaty glow. "Do I look sick enough?" she asked as he hung up.

"Sis, you look like absolute shit."

She'd thrown on a George Mason University sweatshirt and sweatpants, slipped on a pair of pink crocs, and left her purse by the door. Twenty minutes later Janet's phone rang. She let the phone ring a half-dozen times before picking it up with a groggy, "Hello?" She let out a deep sigh, muttered an okay, and hung up.

She kissed Dawkins on the cheek. "Back soon."

"I know."

She disappeared out the door.

An hour later, Dawkins pulled up the file. Forty thousand lines of text had been scanned from photographs of clay tablets, analyzed, and converted into an incomplete and all-too-short dictionary. Most of the words pertained to professions and money, construction, and religion. Matt found that to his surprise, Dawkins's trick of using the eidetic enhancers made learning the vocabulary a trivial exercise, and while it took a lot of time, they could for the most part read the parchment.

"It's an instruction manual," Matt said for Blossom's benefit. They read a while longer, and with each new revelation his dread grew. "It talks about the angelic fathers of the Nephilim, in the present tense. Names them and the women with whom they had children, and the order in which God cast them into the darkness."

"Instructions for what?" Blossom asked.

"Mass human sacrifice of possessed men," Matt said.

"How to free them," Dawkins added. "She's setting the egregoroi free to enslave mankind and take their vengeance on God's creation."

Blossom exhaled, an abrupt blast of air brimming with annoyance.

"Amazing," Matt said. "This mentions camps for killing—death camps—and bronze birds that kill from the sky. Look here," he said, running his finger under a sentence. "'Twin suns will destroy the, um, something, cities in the land of dawn.' It's talking about World War Two."

She froze. "I thought this part was thousands of years old."

"It is," Matt said.

"Then it's forgery."

"It isn't," Dawkins said. "The book is real, and the writing is that old."

"Impossible."

Matt brushed aside her skepticism and turned back to the book. At some point Janet returned, and Dawkins briefed her on what they'd learned so far. Matt read a sentence, re-read it, then read it again. He pushed the book over to Dawkins. "Does this say what I think it says?"

Dawkins bent down. "In the ninth age, the jade slaves will give themselves in pleasure to the Servant, and as her multitude of voices enslave and consume them, the ladder will descend into the dark pit." Matt grunted in agreement, and Dawkins continued, silently. At last he sat back.

"Holy shit. The whispers. We're not going crazy. She's possessing us." He looked up at Janet. "She's going to kill every aug, every Jade user on the planet. We're the possessed men whose souls she'll use to free her fathers from the pit."

"When?" Blossom asked. Matt wondered if she'd started to believe.

They read further, then Matt said, "The first just before the sun 'inverts as the wise men see,' and then it looks like one a season until the last, their leader, is freed. 'When Semjaza returns from his exile, the rule of man will turn to unending slavery for the glory of the Watchers under the jade sky.' The Bible says there were two hundred egregoroi who followed Semjaza, so if we know what that last line means—"

Janet cut him off. "The sun's magnetic field reverses every eleven years, but we've only had the technology to detect it for a couple of decades. Would that fit the bill?"

"I think it would," Dawkins said. "Hard to be sure, though."

Matt raised an eyebrow. "So if that's right, we've got, what, twenty or thirty years before Semjaza and the apocalypse, give or take?"

"No," Blossom said. "Only a couple years before we go crazy."

"We've got to think long-term," Dawkins said.

Blossom slammed her hand down on the table. "We don't have long-term. We have years. Months. That's it."

Janet plucked the gum from her mouth. "I've got another fifty, give or take. Barring any accidents." She popped the gum back into her mouth and gnawed it back down.

Matt ignored Janet to agree with Blossom. "I'd rather not become a casualty. Still," he put his hand atop Blossom's, "this is bigger than us. Even if we don't live through—"

She yanked her hand away and stormed to the window, where she stared out at a tractor trundling toward the turkey farm down the road.

"Just hold on," Dawkins muttered. He closed his eyes and his face went slack.

Matt turned back to the book while Dawkins twitched and jittered, Janet rubbing his temples. The whispers tittered as he read of their true nature, the infusion of the last surviving Nephilim into his spirit. They laughed as he read of the golden ladder, his soul but a rung for the egregoroi to climb to escape their divine punishment. He shook it off and slammed the book shut, then waited for Dawkins.

Minutes went by, then Dawkins stopped jerking, his breathing calmed, and he opened his eyes. He hugged his sister, then turned to Matt. "You're not going to like this."

Matt held up his hands. "Hit me." Blossom appeared at his side, frowning.

"Well," Dawkins said, "our best chance of success is to recruit more people to our cause, undermine ICAP's true masters wherever we can, and build a resistance movement that survives us. I can't see what I can't live, so I don't know if it will work, but everything premature I see leads to disaster."

"Unacceptable," Blossom said. "I won't go mad if I can stop it. I won't."

"You don't have a choice—"

She cut Dawkins off. "There is always—"

"WE CAN'T WIN." Dawkins sat back, took a deep breath, and continued. "Yes, you can choose to do something else, but if you do, you're going to die and solve nothing. We go in ourselves, Gerstner destroys us, and we're looking at an apocalypse. A real, honest end of the world apocalypse."

"You say this madness, it possesses us, like a demon?"

Matt answered for him. "Yeah. That's what the book says."

Blossom turned her gaze on him, eyes ablaze. "So when we go mad, it's not just our body that dies. We die forever or go to hell or whatever?"

Matt shrugged. "It looks that way."

"Then we have nothing to lose. Damned either way, yes?"

"But everyone else—" he tried.

"I don't care about everyone else," she snarled, then fell to the floor Indian-style, her arms wrapped around her head. "We need to do this," she mumbled. "I won't let my daughter fall to madness."

"Look," Matt said. "I don't know what she has to do with this, but—"

Blossom disappeared.

He blinked and looked at Dawkins. "Where did she go?"

He shrugged. "I didn't look into this."

A door slammed above them. Matt's heart went cold, and he bolted for the stairs. He met Blossom halfway up, her defiant eyes full of tears. "You give me no option."

He tried to grab her wrist, but she twisted away. He tried again and she hit him, an open-palm strike to the sternum that knocked him backward. He fell, arms pinwheeling as his feet left the stairs. His head rang as it hit the floor at the bottom of the landing, but his hand struck out to grab her ankle as she flashed by.

She fell to the floor and kicked at him, but he dragged himself over her and wrapped her in his arms. Her struggles weakened to human level, and then to that of a scared kitten. She sobbed against his chest, and from the floor he looked up at Dawkins and Janet, unsure of what to do.

"Please check on my wife," he said.

Janet padded past them as Blossom's tears soaked his shirt. A few minutes later she came down stairs and set an autoinjector on the floor. He read the number on the cartridge and recognized second-generation regenerates. His arms tensed as he squeezed Blossom tighter than a comforting hug.

"What did you do?"

Her tear-filled eyes held only anger. "We go now. No waiting."

He crushed her arms to her side and squeezed the breath out of her. "What. Did. You. Do?"

She slammed her forehead into his face. Stars exploded in his head as his nose broke, and she used the advantage to slip from his grip. Dawkins dove for her, but not before Janet cried out and slapped her neck.

The three of them went down in a heap next to Matt. While Janet scrambled out of the way, they pinned Blossom to the floor. She screamed and cried and thrashed, but her speed couldn't compete with their strength. After a while—minutes or hours, Matt had no idea through the stream of anguished wailing—she calmed, sniffled a few moments, and lay still.

"Can we let you up?" Dawkins asked.

She gave a curt nod. "I'm done."

They let go, and as they got to their feet Matt asked her again, "What did you do?"

She raised her chin, as defiant a gesture as he'd ever seen out of her. "Now you're like me. Desperate. Two months ago, my daughter, the doctor says she has glioblastoma multiforme—brain cancer. Inoperable, very fast. Three months to live, maybe less. I smuggled out regenerates to save her, but now she's going to go mad unless we stop this." She turned to Dawkins. "These aren't angels or devils. Still, you say they can be stopped, so we're going to stop them. Or your sister"—she turned to Matt—"and your wife and child, will pay the same price as my daughter."

Black rage consumed Matt. He stood, and Dawkins forced him back down with a hand on his shoulder. "No, Matt. Vengeance here solves nothing." He looked at Janet, his face a blank mask, then back to Matt. "We have to try."

*   *   *

Monica lay on the couch, weak but less peaked, and nursed a cup of tea. She smiled a sad smile when she saw him and winced as she stood, but Matt hugged her anyway. "You shouldn't be up." Going by his own experience, she'd feel both giddy and miserable for a day, then never feel ill again.

She squeezed and didn't let up. "I feel a bit better. When I woke up you weren't here."

He held her and didn't apologize; he couldn't be sorry for what had to be done. She swayed on her feet, and giggled, and used his embrace to keep on her feet. He let her down, hand behind her head and the small of her back, and kissed her eyelids to close them. He waited with her until her breathing settled to the deep flow of sleep, then turned his attention to his companions. Janet sat on the loveseat, legs crossed, and Dawkins sat on the couch across from her, a pair of long knives in his lap.

Dawkins tightened his grip on the knives. "Once we're done with Gerstner, you figure out what you have to do, and I'll figure out what I have to do. Meantime, Sakura's an asset, and we use her." He looked everywhere but at Janet, and Matt forced himself to quash the twinge of sympathy in his heart. Whatever else he might be—brother, crusader—Dawkins held his place in history as the most prolific drug dealer in history, with all the murder and treachery that entailed.

"Okay, let's talk to her."

They entered the kitchen and sat on either side of Blossom, who fiddled with her fingernails and didn't look up. Dawkins had left the knives in the other room; Matt presumed he didn't trust himself yet.

"All right," Matt said, "we do this." He looked from Blossom to Dawkins. "So where are they keeping her?"

"Where do you think?" Dawkins asked. Matt's hopes slid as he continued. "Frahm's house."

Matt grunted. "There goes Plan A." Blossom raised an eyebrow, so he added, "Air-fuel bomb."

"Why is this not an option?" she asked.

"Frahm lives in a residential neighborhood. He may be willing to slaughter innocents, but I'm not."

Dawkins shrugged. "This is war. Everyone dies if we lose, so why not do it the most efficient way?"

Matt snarled. "You don't get to dictate the terms of my help. I'm in this because I have to be, because you forced me to be, because she forced me to be." He thrust his chin at Blossom. "But I'm not about to cause another Lake Kivu." The international community had labeled it a natural disaster and gave no credence to Congolese claims of international terrorism. He still couldn't be sure whether Dawkins or ICAP had detonated the island, and he no longer cared. They were all monsters in their own way, and he refused to join the callous slaughter.

"Okay," Dawkins said. "Then what's the plan?"

Matt frowned. "We need more information. Can Janet access the blueprints?"

With a glare at Blossom, Dawkins replied, his words clipped. "Janet isn't able to do anything right now. It'll be days before she's recovered from the augmentation." Matt remembered his regenerates treatment and the odd combination of euphoria, extreme nausea, and headaches that had accompanied it. The side effects hit people differently, and augmentation had laid Janet out with debilitating migraines. "Regardless, Frahm's house isn't ICAP property. There'd be no reason for them to have that information."

"Someone had to have built it. There has to be records."

"Incomplete. They don't show anything below the basement."

"How do you know she's there?"

Dawkins squirmed a little. "Because we're going to go inside, so I can see it."

"Do we come out?" Blossom asked, sneering.

He ran a hand through his hair. "I don't know. My ability to see stops at the door." He looked at Janet, queasy on the floor. "I don't think I survive. I don't know if you do."

"How did you end up so precognitive?" Matt asked.

He shrugged again. "You want some irony with that question? Brian Frahm. He hand-selected eight of us to beta test the first precognition augmentation. We were like test pilots during the Cold War, willing to risk our lives for that next great tactical edge. I'm the only person who didn't bonk out within four days. And then it showed me what ICAP really was."

"So Gerstner allows you to see how to defeat Gerstner?" The question made Matt's head hurt.

Dawkins shrugged. "Don't ask me how it works. I don't know that there are rules to magic."

Blossom clucked her tongue and changed the subject. "What resources do we have?"

Dawkins smiled in a manner that promised murder if he could deliver it. "Anything you want, Sakura: AKs, helicopters, boats, explosives. In a couple days I could assemble a small army of mercenaries, including some really augged-out monsters a hair's breadth from bonking out, but anything I do, Frahm will catch wind of it. He knows I'm out, he knows I'm going to try something, and it would be a mistake to assume he doesn't have moles in my organization."

"Do we need an army?" Matt asked.

"I don't think so. Satellite recon shows that Frahm's house doesn't get a lot of traffic. Sometimes he gets late-night boats with their lights off that never reach the house, so there has to be at least one outside entrance—"

"Wait." Matt raised a hand. "Frahm doesn't live on the river."

"Oh," Dawkins said. "Not his home in D.C. I'm talking about his home in La Madrague."

"Where is that?" Blossom asked. Her face betrayed not the slightest emotion.

"Giens Peninsula, Southern France."

Matt logged into the guest account on Janet's computer, pulled up Google Earth and typed in, "Giens Peninsula."

"Show us."

Brian's home was the quintessential European villa on the water: trees screened it from the street and a picturesque half-wall surrounded the small property. With no yard to speak of, the two-story retreat ended in a rocky bluff that led down to a private dock. Someone had uploaded a picture of a brilliant purple tree growing under Frahm's balcony, giving them a perfect view of the ocean side. Invisible from above, a small cavern led through the bedrock into the darkness.

"All right," Matt said. "It's a big house, but not that big. What's it like underground? Raccoon City?"

"Could be," Dawkins said. "The bedrock could support something that large, though history suggests that there haven't been any ridiculously big construction projects going back as far as World War Two. My guess—and this is a guess—is no more than ten thousand square feet, and probably a lot less than that."

Blossom glared at the picture. "No army, but what about a small group? Are there a few people you trust with this?"

"With this?" Dawkins snarled. "No. There's a reason I had to be forced into this." He ran a hand across the back of the couch. "I could make something up that they'd believe. A revenge hit on a rival drug lord, or something. But Frahm might still find out."

Matt looked out the window. "If we can use your money, I have a better idea."

Dawkins caught his eye. "How much do you need?"

"Let me find out."

Chapter 17

Matt and Blossom got off the plane into a blast of heat. The causeway had to be a hundred degrees and stank of straw and body odor and burnt cumin. The mass of humanity didn't help the heat. Or the noise. Or the smell. The oppressive humidity made for a pleasant change when they stepped outside.

Blossom handed a fistful of pesos to a vendor, picked up an apple, took a bite, and spoke with her mouth full. "I'm not sorry. You'd have done the same."

"Don't," Matt said. "If there's even a chance of saving Monica, I have to take it, but don't mistake that for trust or friendship. You could have told us."

"Dawkins would not go along to save my daughter."

"I would have."

She closed her eyes, nodded once, then opened them. "You really think taking some old woman off a machine will cure addiction? There's no such thing as magic."

Matt grunted at her continued denial of the fantastical truth. "I don't know. Two days ago I didn't believe in angels on Earth, despite what happened in New Mexico. I didn't believe a headless man could chew through my neck. I didn't believe—"

The car pulled up, a lime green 1970s Cadillac with diplomatic plates. They stood on the sidewalk as the driver frisked them. His eyes popped when he opened Matt's briefcase, but he covered his surprise with a polite cough. Blossom responded once he'd gotten back in the driver's seat.

"You believe Dawkins is psychic? Can see the future?"

He exhaled. "Yeah. That I believe all day long. I've done it myself, once or twice. Not like him, but way farther out than a split second. And I've seen too much not to believe that. He knows too much."

"And you think Gerstner is the key to stopping all this, that we won't go mad."

"I . . . maybe. I don't think the people who wrote the book knew about the machine, but if we destroy her or disrupt her somehow, I think maybe."

"You think."

He threw up his hands. "Maybe taking out Gerstner will make us all crazy. Maybe we'll all die. I have no idea. But it's a chance, and even if it doesn't work for us, even if we're all screwed, even if Mo—" He stopped, closed his eyes, swallowed a lump in his throat, and continued through the near-overwhelming desire to tear Blossom limb from limb. "Even if all that's true, if we can stop the flow of Gerstner carbon, the Jade trade will dry up, and nobody else'll get augs . . . that'd be worth doing. That'd be worth dying for." He opened his eyes and stared into hers. "The world won't need folks like us anymore."

She finished her apple in four quick bites and tossed the core into the trash bin, twenty feet away. "Okay. I don't know about angels, but I felt that thing in my brain, and I don't ever want to feel that again. If Gerstner is like that, we have to kill her. And Frahm, for using her. What happens next, happens."

Matt let silence voice his agreement, choked down his seething anger, and opened the door.

Blossom rounded the car and spoke over the top. "And Matt? There's no such thing as angels. That thing was a bonk. A weird bonk, a powerful bonk, but a bonk. Sounds like Gerstner is, too— maybe the first bonk ever, maybe the source of Gerstner augmentation, maybe even thousands of years old, but she is, or was, human. Don't screw up your head with this wishy-wash stuff. We need to be smart if we're going to save our families. Not give in to hocus pocus."

"Okay."

She gave him one last, long look before getting in. *Yeah, I don't believe me, either.*

* * *

Matt couldn't fight the *déjà vu* as they hurtled down the one-lane mountain path, between towering oaks and even taller pines. This time Blossom drove, and as they rounded the bend toward the secluded mansion, there wasn't a uniformed soldier in sight. Instead, on the veranda, Onofre and Hernando Garza stood flanked by four bonks, nine-foot monsters in full tactical body armor, one of which held a steel hammer that had to weigh two hundred pounds.

The Garza brothers wore cargo shorts and Hawaiian shirts, Onofre's blue, Hernando's green. Hernando, clean shaven with graying brown hair cut in a severe flat-top, spat as they got out of the car, the bright red saliva spattering the whitewashed stairs. Onofre sidestepped it on the way down.

He stepped forward and offered his hand, first to Blossom, then to Matt. Hernando just stared with flat, lifeless eyes. Matt grabbed the suitcase out of the back and followed the Garza brothers up the stairs, between the bonks.

Onofre gestured to the enormous guards. "You will forgive me if I don't keep our previous deal on security."

"Not a problem," Matt said. "Again I apologize for . . . before."

They entered the house, which showed no sign of the damage caused when Matt and Conor had torn it, and each other, to pieces. Even the furniture had been repaired or replaced with identical pieces. As they sat, a small man in a dark brown suit took a seat behind Hernando. He leaned forward and muttered Spanish into Hernando's ear as Onofre continued.

"There is no need to apologize for things that are not your fault. You saved me and my daughter from your companion, and for that I am grateful."

"And . . . the woman? Your maid?"

Onofre shrugged. "She lives, though she left my employ to return to her village."

"I'm glad she survived."

Blossom ignored them all, her eyes on the bonks at the door.

"As are we all." Onofre offered them coffee, which they accepted. The black brew carried a hint of cinnamon and dark chocolate. "Again you have come to me for business, and this time you have even less to offer that I might want. Why are you here?"

Matt set the briefcase on the table and opened it. Twenty million euros, in neat stacks bound with rubber bands, filled it to capacity. "Dawkins escaped ICAP custody last week. They've pulled me off the case, said I'm too close to it, taking it too personally. I know where he's hiding, and I want him."

Hernando barked something in Spanish. The man in the suit spoke, his accent more Mississippi than Mexico. "Where did a government operative get this kind of money?"

Matt ignored him and kept his eyes on Onofre. "Do you want it or not?"

"That depends on what it's for."

"The guys by the door would be a good start, plus a few more like them. Dawkins is holed up in Europe, in a house with a bunch of bonks. I need muscle to deal with them while I stick a knife in his eye. And gunships."

"And if I do this, ICAP backs off of my expansion in the American south."

Matt shook his head. "I can't control that. I'm not here on ICAP's authority. This is a cash-only deal, though we both know what kind of opportunities Dawkins's death will create for you."

Onofre nodded toward the suitcase. "How much?"

"Twenty million."

Hernando barked out a laugh and said something the suit didn't translate.

Onofre shook his head. "Thirty-five."

Matt chuckled. "It's all I've got. This is a take-it-or-leave-it deal."

Silenced stretched for too long. Blossom didn't even twitch, a sure sign of imminent violence, if needed.

Onofre stuck out his hand. Matt shook it.

"Done."

* * *

Dawkins leaned over the tome on Janet's coffee table, head resting on both fists.

Matt traced his hand around an illumination depicting three slaves chained before a giant, antlered king in golden robes. "We should destroy this thing."

Dawkins closed it with deliberate care. "We should, but I'm going to offer to sell it to Frahm for a billion dollars."

"Excuse me?"

"I figure he knows I'm out by now, knows the book is missing, and he's going to want it back. I'm an opportunistic bastard, so I'm going to set up a deal to sell it. In, say, Brussels. In eight days."

"Why would you do that?"

"So he'll be focused on the Brussels meeting in eight days instead of worrying about a hit on Gerstner in three. Even if he doesn't totally buy it, thinks it's a trap or something, it'll be a distraction. Remember, most of ICAP isn't in on the secret, and the UN sure as hell isn't, so it's not like he's got an army at his beck and call. That's why they tried to bonk you instead of killing you outright."

"Are you sure?"

"Yes."

"Certain?"

Dawkins put his head in his hands and spoke through is palms. "If we arrange the meet for eight days in Belgium and hit his Riviera house in three, it will minimize resistance. That I promise you."

"So we meet Garza's goons tomorrow, run surveillance Monday, and go in hot on Tuesday. That's the plan?"

Dawkins nodded. "That's the plan."

Chapter 18

The six scarred, muscled men that boarded the forward helicopter would have been intimidating even if they hadn't been nine feet tall. Their leader, a blue-eyed monstrosity who called himself Goro, carried a Dillon Aero M134D-T. The titanium minigun with six rotating barrels had been designed for a helicopter mount. It topped out at three feet long, and the exoskeleton around the bonk's torso that helped him wield it made him look even bigger. That his lower jaw had been replaced with serrated metal didn't help him in the charm department, but it matched up with the body modifications of the others: dorsal blades, steel plates riveted to bone, razor-sharp steel teeth.

Garza had vouched not only for their reliability but also for their tactical acumen. Matt had a hard time buying it. These men—not true men anymore—knew they courted insanity and didn't care. Such short-sighted, for-the-moment self-destruction left Matt cold. He didn't understand that mentality. Even before they bonked, bonks weren't the slightest bit sane.

The mercenaries took off thirty seconds before Matt's group did, thundering over the Mediterranean in a blast of salty prop wash. With only Blossom, Dawkins, and Matt in the passenger compartment, the second chopper had plenty of room despite their equipment. Matt had a bandoleer of grenades, two kilos of C4, a kilo of det cord, an AA-12 with a backup drum of directional explosive rounds, and in his pocket, Monica's cross and an autoinjector loaded with level-six musculoskeletal enhancements.

His gut clenched with more than the typical pre-action nerves, and his mind boiled with uncertainty.

They streamed across the black water under the light of a quarter moon, flying by eye less than twenty feet above the waves. The resort town dotted the hills with lights, but at three in the morning there were no crowds, and the cities of the Riviera offered little enough illumination. Recon had confirmed that Brian Frahm had gone to bed at midnight. There were no visible guards.

Matt suppressed the urge to kill Blossom. Enemy or not, they stood a better chance with her, and her motivation burned no weaker than theirs. She and Dawkins had argued over whether or not they had the right location; Brian's presence didn't guarantee Gerstner's. She didn't trust his precognition, and if they attacked the wrong place they'd tip their hand. In the end, she agreed to follow his lead, but her already taciturn personality had turned black.

On cue, nine seconds to touchdown, light blossomed under the stabilizers on the first helicopter. A pair of missiles fell, then streaked forward in a burst of blue and yellow flame, a second pair firing just behind them. They broke the sound barrier just before impact. As the explosions washed the hidden cavern in orange, the helicopters banked to avoid the updraft, and slowed.

The bonks didn't rappel—they leapt. Twenty feet in the air at thirty miles an hour made for an easy jump for the massive men, who rolled on impact and came up running. They fanned out to the sides as the rear chopper rocked, firing missiles of its own. Flame shot out of the tunnel, and they followed the backdraft in, relieving Matt's first worry: the tunnel hadn't collapsed, and the missiles had breached the giant steel door inside.

He watched their progress on his heads-up display, six tiny screens on the right side of his vision, one for each of Garza's bonks. Goro led the charge, his screen a continuous burst of light as the minigun shredded the survivors behind the door. A rocket-propelled grenade streaked out of the tunnel into the water, erupting in a harmless splash of salt and foam.

Matt's chopper hovered next to the second-floor balcony. He took three short steps and leapt. As his foot hit the iron rail he fired a burst into the plate-glass door. He flew through it in a spray of glass, HUD visor tracking for targets. Blossom blurred past him into the next room.

A brunette touched with gray pulled the blanket up around her neck and screamed. Matt pointed at her. "Don't move." Dawkins landed next to Matt and pulled the trigger on his AK-47. Tufts of feathers blasted into the air. The woman twitched and fell silent.

"Fuck!" Matt said, turning on Dawkins, ready to pounce.

In response Dawkins stepped to the bed, shoved an arm under the mattress, and pulled out an H&K assault rifle. "No one gets behind us."

An explosion boomed below them, and the house shuddered. One of the bonk's display had gone dark, and two more struggled in mortal combat against bonks every bit as massive. Something crashed in the next room. A man cried out. Matt stepped around the corner, weapon raised, and lowered it as he took in the scene.

Next to the upturned couch, Blossom held Brian by the hair. She had his body twisted in a cruel parody of boxers-clad Twister, back arched, one hand on the ground to take pressure off of his head. He clutched his right hand to his chest, three fingers bent at odd angles. A machine pistol lay at his feet.

Behind Matt, Dawkins spoke. "Where is she?"

"Fuck you," Brian said through a grimace of pain.

Dawkins approached, an autoinjector in his hand. "No need for theatrics. You tell us where she is, and I don't make you psychic."

A ragged, raw sound erupted from Brian's throat; a laugh. "If you succeed, that won't mean a thing."

Blossom and Matt exchanged glances. Brian's throwaway answer filled Matt with hope he hadn't felt in forever.

Below them, Goro had run out of ammo and used his minigun as a club, crushing men and bonks into oblivion with the titanium barrels. His squad held their own, and on their cameras Matt saw even the helmetless one still stood, battered and bloody and holding a blood-soaked axe. Another rocket streaked from the darkness.

Dawkins sighed, put away the injector, and drew a knife, smiling as the house shuddered again.

"Okay, theatrics then, you coward. You might not age, but you won't regenerate either. To keep you from stalling, every couple of seconds, if we're not making progress, you're going to have one less body part to enjoy in your immortality. I'll start small."

Brian's eyes didn't leave the knife. "Okay." He snuffled as tears sprang to his eyes. "If you promise you won't hurt me. . . ." He swallowed. "I'll . . . I'll show you the machine."

Dawkins nodded at Blossom, who pulled Brian to his feet and let him go. To his credit, he didn't try for the gun.

"Where?" Dawkins said. "And remember, each lie costs you something permanent."

"Basement."

Weapons fire from below accompanied them down the stairs, through a massive kitchen, to a plain white door. Two more HUDs had gone down, but at least one of Garza's bonks kept his feet—their resilience overshadowed that of their equipment. An explosion rocked the building.

"What are we up against?" Matt asked.

Brian shrugged. "There were two dozen augs inside when I went to bed, eight of them bonks." He opened the door. "None of them know this way, though."

Blossom took point down the mortar-and-stone steps, into the darkness. Matt followed, surprised at the thermocline; goose bumps rose on his arms, his breath frosted the air. Despite the cold, everything else seemed normal.

A water heater stood in the corner next to a dingy desalination system. A mop sink, a sump pump, and shelves cluttered with tools dominated the far wall. Brian nodded to a cast-iron wood-burning furnace. "Behind there. Through the wall."

Matt inspected the mortar and stone. It looked solid to his eyes. "How do we get through?"

"Brute force," Brian said.

Matt turned to look at him, eyebrow raised. "Seriously?"

Dawkins grabbed Brian's broken pinky finger, wrenched it to the side, and severed it with a smooth upward stroke of the knife.

Brian screamed and stumbled back, sweat breaking out on his forehead. "Please! No! It's that or fight your way through down there." Another blast from below punctuated his statement, and mortar dust rained from the walls. Dawkins shoved him to the ground and wiped the knife on the front of Brian's shirt.

"Better wrap your hand. It'd be a real shame if you bled out."

"You idiot," Brian sneered. "There are shaped charges on the far side in case I ever needed to get out in a hurry. I never dreamed having to get in that way."

Matt pulled out the det cord, and Dawkins grabbed his hand. "Save it. It's only a brick wall." While Blossom took a sledge hammer and shattered bricks, Matt grabbed a crowbar from a shelf to pry them out.

Goro's HUD vanished in a flash of white, then went to static. An inhuman roar echoed through the walls. Someone screamed, a high-pitched, desperate wail of hopeless agony.

"I think they made him mad," Dawkins said.

Brian sulked, his right hand oozing red around his left palm. "You said you wouldn't hurt me."

"I apologize for my overreaction," Dawkins deadpanned, as Matt revealed a steel wall behind the brick. "But that's the exact opposite of what I said. Now shut up unless I ask you question." He tossed Brian a handkerchief from a pocket. Brian picked it up from the floor, wiped his eyes, and pressed it to his bleeding stump.

After a few more minutes they'd cleared out what looked like a naval bulkhead, smooth steel panels connected with quarter-sized rivets. Matt looked back at the tool shelf for a suitable cutter, and Blossom punched the sledge through the wall in one fluid motion. The metal shrieked as she pulled it back. Stale fluorescent light spilled through the hole, along with the scent of nitroglycerine, gunpowder, and underneath them, the stink of blood and shit and death.

Gunfire echoed through the hole, and another roar that Matt recognized as Goro's. The last working HUD lay on the floor, unmoving, giving him a view of the carnage. Goro slammed a bonk into the ceiling, then, with the help of his exoskeleton, tore him in half. He turned, his face a bloody streak over an exposed skull, and laughed. Something flashed by on the camera, and Goro's head fell from his shoulders and rolled out of sight. The headless giant just stood there, held up by the exoskeleton, as the fight moved deeper into the basement and out of sight.

Blossom punched another hole near the first, then tore the hammer downward. The wooden handle shattered and the steel head fell to the floor inside. She reached through to her shoulder, picked it up, and used her hands to bash it through the thin strip of metal connecting the holes. Bloody lines where the steel had shredded her arm faded to pink as she worked.

Matt joined her with the crowbar, creating a mad pointillism of ruined steel before tearing through it with brute force. Once they'd done sufficient damage, they tore the metal door back and tossed it to the floor, the shriek and clatter deafening in the confined space.

"For the love of God, Montressor," Dawkins said behind them. "Where to?"

Brian's voice held a touch of petulance. "At the end of the hall. Go all the way down."

Matt grunted and stepped into the tiny corridor. The whispers tittered in anticipation. The claustrophobic, smoky hall led down to a spiral staircase that had to be a hundred years old, the wrought iron steps swaying with every footfall. The sounds of battle grew louder as he descended. Maybe halfway down—he'd counted forty-six steps—he encountered a bulkhead door like they used in World War II-era subs, twisted and mangled on the floor. Through the dark opening came screams of pain and panic, gunfire, and explosions. The iron stench of blood and shit emanated from within. He readied his weapon and crouched next to the entry.

Brian stopped next to him, opened his mouth, looked at Dawkins, and closed it. Then he tried again. "Keep going. She's all the way down."

Matt ducked past the entryway and ran down the rest of the stairs. He reached the bottom and jogged down a long hallway that had to put them under the water. He pushed through the steel door, Blossom at his heels, and blinked in surprise.

A dozen naked bulbs hung from the ceiling, bathing the gigantic, whirring, clockwork monstrosity in a tepid glow. Giant brass cogs whirled, steel gears spun, and pumps forced black fluid through stained stone channels. Glass tubes crackled with lightning, and a warren of hoses snaked into and out of an enormous steel platform.

Atop it, an emaciated cadaver lay surrounded by arcane machinery, the tubes protruding from her body leading to brass canisters emblazoned with swastikas and eagles. Shriveled breasts drooped on exposed ribs too thin to belong to a living being, but they rose and fell with the rhythm of breath. Someone had carved a crude glyph on her forehead, an old bloody scab wrought by crude hands: the Ul. Withered lips couldn't cover the skeletal remains of blackened, rotten teeth. Spiked iron manacles pierced the body's wrists, ankles, and head, holding her arms outstretched and her ankles crossed in a barbaric parody of Christ.

Beneath the platform, throbbing, jade-colored tentacles pushed through cracks in the concrete like the roots of an ancient, gnarled tree. Energy pulsed along these roots, flowing from the table into the ground. Matt kneeled and pulled the C4 from his satchel. Two kilos in a confined space would make a hell of a mess, but he pulled out the det cord just in case.

"Hostiles," Dawkins said. A sulfuric stench filled the air.

Matt raised his head just in time to dive out of the way of a tendril of thorny smoke. His head rang with the realization that the whispers hadn't warned him. He choked up his AA-12 and fired. The microexplosive projectile tore a chunk off of the humanoid mass of green-gray haze even as twisted black thorns sprang from its solidifying body. Gunpowder joined the stink of sulfur.

He fired again as it closed, and it stumbled sideways. Two more rushed him. He cracked one in the head with the butt of the gun, snap kicked the other in the torso. He grunted in surprise as his foot sank in and the ribs became a mouth with gnashing, barbed teeth. He placed the barrel against the thing's chest a foot above his ankle and pulled the trigger. Bone shredded and meat exploded. As it staggered back, he yanked his boot free in a gooey string of mucus-like fluid. Bits of shrapnel and sticky blood steamed on the torn leather, but his foot didn't hurt.

He grunted in pain as his first assailant wrapped his right arm with ropy, tentacle-like appendages, its thorns stabbing into his muscle. He lost his balance on his slippery left foot and fell, the creature collapsing on top of him. Blood filled his vision as barbed teeth raked across his face. He snarled and jammed his fingers into its single, vacant eye. It shifted, giving him enough leverage to throw with his legs, and he slammed it into the wall.

Blossom decapitated it on her way by and stabbed the second assailant a dozen times before Matt had a chance to recover. Despite her speed and regenerates, her shredded Kevlar vest hung in tatters over blood-slicked skin. He sidestepped a punch from another thorn-thing, wrapped his arm around its neck, and twisted. He felt the crunch even as thorns stabbed his arms and chest, then grunted in surprise as it dissipated in a sulfurous fog.

Blossom held her own against two more, and Dawkins fought three. Brian sobbed on his knees, trying to push slimy coils of intestine back through a tear in his abdomen. Matt pulled a grenade from his bandoleer, pulled the pin, and tossed it toward the table.

A smoky form materialized, grabbed the grenade with thorny tentacles full of teeth, and burst as it went off. He threw two more. Each was swallowed by demonic forms without damaging the machine. Dawkins screamed, a guttural, choking yell that cut off in a gurgle. Matt whirled.

His throat a gaping ruin, Dawkins still fought. Blood streamed from severed arteries even as he punched a combat knife straight through the creature that had ravaged his neck. The wound grew teeth and closed on his arm, shredding muscle and bone. The knife fell to the ground. His forearm followed.

Matt fired three rounds from his shotgun. All three creatures exploded in wisps of vapor. Dawkins fell to the floor, the blood gushing from his neck and arm slowing, but maybe not fast enough. Matt turned around to help Blossom, just in time to see another creature vanish as she cut out its heart.

"We can't keep this up," she gasped.

As eight more shapes emerged from the darkness. The whispers chuckled in dark anticipation.

Matt swore. With no time to reload, he grabbed the injector in his pocket, jammed the needle into his thigh.

I'm sorry, Monica. I love you.

He pulled the trigger, flooding his system with eldritch augmentation. He gasped as power like he'd never felt consumed him.

His arms bulged as the first two reached him. He screamed as muscle layered over muscle, as bones stretched and thickened. He grabbed them and slammed his fists together, pulping their heads in a spray of blood and mist. Three more followed, but he rushed forward and knocked them aside even as they wrapped him with thorny tendrils. He screamed as agony wracked his body, not from the attack but from the walls of inhuman strength that twisted through him. The whispers screamed with him as layer upon layer of muscle wrapped thickening bones. He gloried in the slaughter.

He tore at them with his bare hands, rending flesh and snapping bone with every grasp. Tentacles wrapped him; he flexed and shredded them. Thorns pierced his skin, and he laughed at their insignificance. More came—he didn't know how many—and as they advanced he destroyed them. His fists crushed bone through the floor, blasted rib cages apart, shattered heads. He grabbed two forms and slammed them together. They disintegrated. He stepped forward into a cloud of sulfuric, bloody mist, and snarled at the lack of opponents.

He roared in challenge and whirled to find more, but a woman's cry silenced him. He froze in shock and looked down at Blossom as she screamed his name again. Part of him wondered how she'd gotten so small, become a tiny thing half his size. Another part wanted to crush her, squeeze the jelly out of her, slam her into the wall until she burst.

He closed his eyes against the madness and, shuddering, took a knee next to Dawkins's bloody form. The psychotic rage within him quieted but didn't disappear. He took a few more breaths, steadied himself, then got to work.

He pulled a tangle of blasting caps from his pocket with thick, clumsy fingers. Monica's necklace fell to the floor, bent and twisted. He picked up the cross and entwined the chain in his fingers so he wouldn't lose it. He pressed two blasting caps into the C4 and another into the det cord.

A worried glance at Dawkins told Matt he might live. He'd lost an enormous amount of blood, but the gush had dwindled to a trickle, and flesh knitted under new skin. He groped on the floor for his forearm, lifted it, and held it to the stump at his elbow. The screaming voices in Matt's head wanted to kill him anyway. He reached out—

"Matt," Blossom said. She'd reloaded his AA-12 and tossed it to him. He caught it, turned his gaze to follow hers. Six more demons—they had to be demons—materialized around the bed. He sprang to his feet and hoped there weren't many more of the things, even as he grinned in anticipation of the slaughter. If Gerstner couldn't manifest more than a few at a time, they could keep this up for a while.

But not forever.

Gerstner sat up. The shriveled corpse's dry, cracked skin sloughed off, taking the tubes and tentacles with it. The manacles that held it in place fell through its flesh as the withered meat and bone faded to black smoke. Wings of ash and fire unfolded over the machine. The angelic being rose to her feet on a pulsing column of writhing jade light.

Matt shot the column on full auto. The tiny grenades punched into it and disappeared. If they exploded, he couldn't tell. He dropped to the C4 and—

STOP.

The whispers screamed it with one voice, her voice, and Matt stopped. Blossom had frozen in place next to him, her eyes wide with panic. The sound of Dawkins's first gasping breath broke off mid-stream. The root-like tendrils of jade shifted; instead of flowing from her, they pulsed upward from the ground, filling Gerstner's shadow with blinding brilliance, at once a great beauty and a skeletal monster. Silence reigned, except for Brian's mewling, blubbering cries.

KNEEL.

Matt fell to one knee. He clenched his fists but could do nothing more. Blossom kneeled on his right. On his left Dawkins let go of his ruined neck to bow his head in homage. The demons dropped prostrate and groveled without sound.

She stepped from the table, skeletal feet cracking as she approached the crumpled form of Brian Frahm. The jade column writhed around her, at once part of her and something other. She crouched next to Brian, put a clawed finger under his chin, and lifted him. He clambered to his feet, tearful eyes locked on hers, his face an expression of pure adoration. His intestines slithered to the floor in a ropy mass as he let them go.

His voice carried the tiniest hint of breath. "I am yours."

She leaned in and kissed him with lips that weren't there, and he sighed as his body turned to ash. His human form crumbled, but instead of falling to the ground it swirled around her, joined with the majestic glory of her wings. His shriek joined the whispers as they gibbered their love for their mistress, who grew more beautiful with every step.

Matt struggled. In his mind he screamed and raged and cried out, but his massive, rippling body did nothing. He heard something then, a tiny murmur. Dawkins's lips moved, a bare whisper escaping them. Matt recognized the chant that he had used on the egregoroi. He tried to pick out the words, to repeat them even if he couldn't understand them, but his lips did not move.

Gerstner turned and glided over to kneel before Dawkins.

She smiled, lush lips superimposed over a starving skull. Dawkins shuddered as she ran her hand through his hair. The whispers spoke along with her, a single voice consuming Matt's mind and blocking out all else, all his wants and fears subsumed to her power.

"Ah, my Israel, my Jacob." Matt couldn't comprehend the beauty of her voice. "You've brought so many to my fold, would you now play Judas?"

Dawkins's chant grew louder, his voice stronger and more confident, and her anger crackled through her form in wisps of jade lightning. Dawkins sneered, continued his chant, and moved to rise in defiance of her will.

NO.

Her voice reverberated through Matt.

YOUR SINS BETRAY YOU.

She knelt and grabbed Dawkins's head with both hands. He grew louder still, his face stiffening with resolve even as his neck knitted together, but he dropped back to the floor. She silenced his soul with a kiss.

As Dawkins's body crumbled to dust and swirled into her being, Matt prayed. He squeezed Monica's battered cross in his hands and, though he didn't have the words or even the faith, he prayed for the strength to protect her from this demon, not the strength of his inhuman body, but something more.

Gerstner cooed in pleasure and glided to Blossom, brushed her cheek with the back of her fingers. "Would you be my Lydia, and follow my fathers to their deserved glory?"

As Blossom nodded with eyes raised in rapture, Matt's fist squeezed the necklace. A tiny tendril of jade broke from the column that surrounded Gerstner, slithered across the floor and touched his hand. It turned silky white as love poured from it. He felt Monica first, then Akash and Garrett and old police buddies he hadn't seen in a decade, then a torrent he couldn't hope to stop.

The dam broke. Gerstner's victims, countless thousands of souls damned to serve her, junkies and slaves, kings and emperors, human sacrifices and high priests, filled him with divine glory. The jade column surged into him white hot, not with fury but with the triumphant joy of salvation. In that maelstrom he felt the tiny, gasping light of his son entwined with Monica's faded spark.

He couldn't hold on to this power, could never survive it. But for everything he couldn't do for her, everything he couldn't provide for his son, he could at least do this. He picked up the C4 and stood.

Gerstner stumbled back from Blossom, away from him, her lack of grace a stark contrast to her prior confidence. He held out the cross and stepped toward her. It blazed a pure, white light, a tangible epiphany that illuminated the black skeleton within her stolen, ephemeral flesh. White wisps slithered from it to wrap her in gossamer threads. Where they touched the jade tendrils, they burned. The whispers shrieked and snapped, a brittle sundering that sent shudders through the angelic glory before him.

Behind him, Blossom moaned. He didn't know if she could hear him, but he said, "Sakura, run."

"I'm not leaving—"

RUN! The world reverberated with his command.

He took another step, bathing the thorn demons next to the altar in white light. They writhed, turned to shadow, and vanished.

Laughing, Gerstner backed into the table. She shimmered in the light, a woman terrible in her beauty, a black withered skeleton who drank it in. Her bright green eyes blazed into his soul. Her voice rang in his mind, her dark whispers a susurrus drowning in the sonorous clamor of those who had broken free.

"Do you think you can do what the Father could not? What his Son could not? I am Bathsheba, Jezebel, Lilith, Nyx, and you cannot destroy me. Your sad faith holds no power over me."

The jade column blackened, shriveled, devoured the light. The cocoon withered, and Matt stumbled. Blood ran down his ruined face. More gushed from his back, his chest, his leg. He burned in agony as strength leached from his withering muscles, as brittle bones splintered under too much mass. He groaned under the weight of his wounds. The world grew dull. Gone were the infrared and ultraviolet signatures, gone the superhuman strength, the speed. And yet his soul rejoiced as the yoke of the whispers left him.

Gerstner laughed again, cruel malevolence given voice. "All that you are, you owe to me. I own your body, I own your soul. You will serve me."

Matt blinked. He knew the truth.

White tendrils snaked upward, entwined Gerstner's wings of ash, solidified the smoke and bound them to the machine. Silk strands flowed down her throat, into her nostrils, and where they touched the illusion of beauty and power crumbled into dusty, skeletal reality.

"I'm a husband. I am a father. I am a servant, but not yours." He reached out with weak, trembling hands and draped Monica's cross over Gerstner's head. She screamed, a piteous wail devoid of hope for salvation. Matt smiled and shoved the C4 into her unwilling hands even as she gasped out a stream of spiteful gibberish.

"God allowed you to remain after the flood, to tempt but not to take form. You've violated His command so you could take men's souls against their will. But you can't have them. You can't have mine. And you sure as hell can't have hers."

He jammed his thumb down on the trigger. Gerstner screamed, and her rage obliterated him.

Chapter 19

Matt's eyes fluttered open on a world of agony.

Bright light. Too bright, too brilliant. He closed them. He hurt too much to sob, and he couldn't speak. A shadow loomed over him, so he tried again. He couldn't make out the face, but the curly brown hair that surrounded it seemed familiar. The world floated in a lovely warm soup. He giggled, then coughed in agony, which faded to a dull ache.

"Shhh," the figure whispered. A cool hand stroked his head. "It's okay. You'll be home soon, I promise."

He closed his eyes and drifted. *I am yours.* He shuddered as the thought wracked through him.

* * *

He came to again, and a black nurse smiled at him with unnaturally white teeth. "Hey there, Mr. Rowley. How you feeling?" She set down her clipboard and put one hand on his.

Everything hurt, more than he'd ever imagined anything could hurt, but he didn't care. He took a deep breath but it ended up shallow, cut off by a stab of pain. "Hard to breathe. My skin feels . . . tight."

She gave him a matter-of-fact nod. "That's the bandages. You looked like a fried chicken when they brought you in. Was pretty cut up with some nasty burns besides."

"Were." He smiled.

She grinned a very pretty grin and waggled a finger at him. "Don't you sass me, Mr. Rowley, or I'll swap that morphine with water. Or something worse." She left the room muttering.

He hazed out, and when he came to, Monica sat next to him, hands on her bulging belly, short, platinum blonde hair showing dark roots, her face a pale white tinged with green. His eyes widened. "Shit, Mo, you need to be lying down." His words slurred around a thick tongue.

She squeezed his hand. "I know, but I need to be here more. They brought me a cot for when I should sleep, which they seem to think is all the time."

"Where am I?"

"Saint John's. ICAP had you flown home as soon as you were stable enough."

"How long have I been out?"

"Eighteen days."

He tried to move and grunted. "I hurt."

She smiled. "I imagine, silly. You're like our first car. Remember that thing? Got a dozen broken bones, bruised lungs, some patched arteries, and I hate to say it, you won't be winning any beauty pageants any time soon." Her voice dropped to a whisper. "But you're alive, baby. And you're home."

She almost hugged him, a leaning touch that seared against his bandaged skin. He tried to hug her back and got as far as wiggled fingers before he gave up. "I love you."

"I love you, too. Now rest."

She stood to leave, but he stopped her with a question.

"Sakura?"

"She's fine. She's the reason they found you underneath all that rock."

"Can I talk to her?"

She kissed him through the bandage on his forehead. "You rest, baby. They been debriefing her the better part of the week, and they're fixing to do the same to you now you're conscious. Some real important people died, and they're all 'nothing's working' this and 'stuff ain't happening right' that. They tell me you're to blame, and some big time folks ain't too happy about it."

He squeezed her hand. "I am."

He closed his eyes to a silence where nothing whispered, and added one more word to the thought.

I am yours.

He smiled, and slept.

* * *

He hobbled up next to Blossom. He let go of his walker to put his arm around her shoulders as they wheeled her daughter into the operations suite. He knew better than to reassure her: without regenerates, Kazuko's cancer had returned, though it had been knocked back to what might be operable levels. Maybe.

She patted his hand, like the rest of him still covered by bandages. "Thank you for coming."

"Yeah."

"And I'm very sorry for what I did. But—"

"No, Isuji, don't. Some things you don't get to apologize for."

She said nothing for a while. "Thank you."

They stood there, not quite blocking traffic through the hospital. "When will they know?"

"They're going to start chemo either way."

"And then?"

"A month. Maybe two. There will be tests and tests. But my Kazuko, she's very strong. She will fight."

"I'm sure she will."

Chapter 20

Matt limped up the steps of St. Martin's with the help of his cane, a minor indignity compared to his now-discarded walker. The doctors, expecting a year of physical therapy before he'd be able to get by with just a cane, shared their amazement that he could walk at all. Matt had never been happier to prove people wrong. Even so, the crisp early March morning didn't help his shattered, arthritic joints. He stepped into the church and braced himself for the shriek of whispers he hadn't heard in twenty-one weeks. They didn't come.

He hobbled down the aisle, sat in a pew, and tried to ignore the stares and gasps, especially from small children. Even without skin grafts his scars had shown remarkable pliability, but the pink mass of scar tissue that passed for his face couldn't be fun to look at.

He sat through the service, the chanting and bells and robes and songs, neither kneeling nor standing nor going up for the bread and wine. The words washed over him, and the looks he got when he didn't respond weren't any worse than the looks he got just being there. When it finished, he waited for the precession to go by: cross, incense, giant Bible, other guy, another other guy, two altar boys, priest. He followed them out, hobbling at full speed to the wide-eyed entertainment and bemusement of the masses.

They stopped outside, the altar boy and rectors breaking to the left, Father Rees stopping to say goodbye as people exited the church. Rees took his hand when he offered it, and Matt admired how well he hid his distaste.

"Good morning, sir," the priest said. "Thank you for coming today."

Matt laughed, a haggard, unpleasant sound from a raw throat. He squeezed harder when Rees tried to pull his hand away, and despite his injuries and lack of augs, Matt remained the stronger man.

He enjoyed the pain in Jason's eyes, and smiled. "Don't you know me, Father?"

The shock of recognition jolted Rees's whole body. "Rowley. I didn't recognize you." His face tightened into a guarded, threatened mask. He tried to step back and Matt didn't let him. "I'm going to have to ask you to leave or I'm calling the cops."

Matt's smile widened. "You did that once already, only it wasn't the cops. You won't survive a second time, so let's cut the threats."

All premise, all kindness, all Christian charity dropped from his face. "What do you want?"

Matt let go, pulled out his wallet, and produced a photo. Monica sat with their son, Adam, against a cloth backdrop. Three weeks old, you couldn't escape the family resemblance: he had Monica's cheeks and nose, and Matt's eyes. "This is my son, Adam."

Jason cleared his throat. "He's beautiful."

"I almost didn't live to meet him."

Matt punched him in the stomach, and Rees folded, gasping. They knelt together, and Matt ignored the wide eyes of the parishioners who'd stopped to stare. Somebody said something about calling the police, and Jason waved them down.

Standing on the steps of an alien church in a town not his own, Matt leaned in close and whispered the only things he knew for certain were true. "You set me up. You forced me to kill good men who were just doing their job. They died for your vengeance, and there is no forgiveness for it. So God help me, if I ever see you again, or if she ever sees you again, or our boy sees you even once, I'm going to kill you and leave your body to rot in a ditch."

Jason nodded once, gasped, and Matt helped him to his feet.

"You have a nice life, padre." Matt hobbled down the steps on his cane, got into the car, and drove south.

* * *

Matt walked up the stairs to his home with the help of the railing and cursed the creaky third step that he still hadn't fixed. It went back on the list, higher this time. He opened the door to the smell of honey and a diaper that needed changing. Monica met him halfway to the kitchen, a honey cake in one hand, Adam in the other.

He mussed Adam's hair, kissed his wife, and stole the honey cake. She opened her mouth in an "O" of indignant shock as he shoved it whole into his mouth and chewed.

"You, good sir, have no manners."

He chewed a bit more, swallowed, and grinned. "I've been told that before. Good thing I'm so pretty."

She grabbed him with her free hand, pulled him in for a long kiss, then hugged him tight. "Ain't neither of us are perfect, but you're all mine."

"Yeah," Matt said. "I'm yours."

* * *

Two weeks later, just before seven am, his phone rang. He rolled out of Monica's embrace, held it up, and squinted at the screen. The caller ID read, "Sakura, Isuji."

He hit "talk" before the second ring could wake the baby. "Hello?" He shuffled to the bathroom, and a jolt of pain in his left knee told him that leaving his cane by the bedside might have been a mistake.

"Sergeant Rowley, ICAP has intelligence you may be interested in."

Matt licked his lips. "I thought ICAP was defunct." Their future funding had been rolled into pensions for former augs, since two-thirds of the upper management had died on the same day, augs had stopped working, and Jade no longer held any narcotic or addictive properties.

"Government agencies never go away." As she talked he looked at himself in the mirror. His hair had started to grow back, his scars were fading, and new muscle rippled under his robe. "I thought being an American you would understand this. Do you want to hear or not?" He flexed, and his chest bulged, lean and massive despite a lack of exercise. Maybe even bigger than when he'd gone to bed.

He hid his worry behind a chuckle. "Sure, Blossom. What's the news?"

"A creature has been spotted outside Damascus, nine feet tall with wings of silver feathers. It claims to be a god and has enslaved several villages so far. Calls itself Arakiel."

"Wow." He couldn't think of a more coherent reply. Arakiel, the second fallen angel mentioned in the Book of Enoch.

"Cults to it have sprung up in Baghdad, Jerusalem, Cairo, Al Qassim, Riyadh, Ma'an. There are twenty-seven aggregate reports so far."

"Shit, Blossom, what are we supposed to do about it?"

Until that moment, he never knew a shrug could be audible. "I don't know. But we're the worldwide experts on egregoroi now, and you're ordered to report to work at oh-nine-hundred. As a consultant."

"What if I don't want the job?"

"They've been authorized to detain you until you cooperate. See you in two hours."

He opened his mouth to protest the timeline, then heard the throaty chop of an Apache AH-64's rotors approach over the treeline. "Okay, I'll see you then."

He hung up the phone and limped back to the bed. Monica raised an eyebrow but said nothing.

He kissed her cheek. "Hey, baby. I got to go to work."

The End

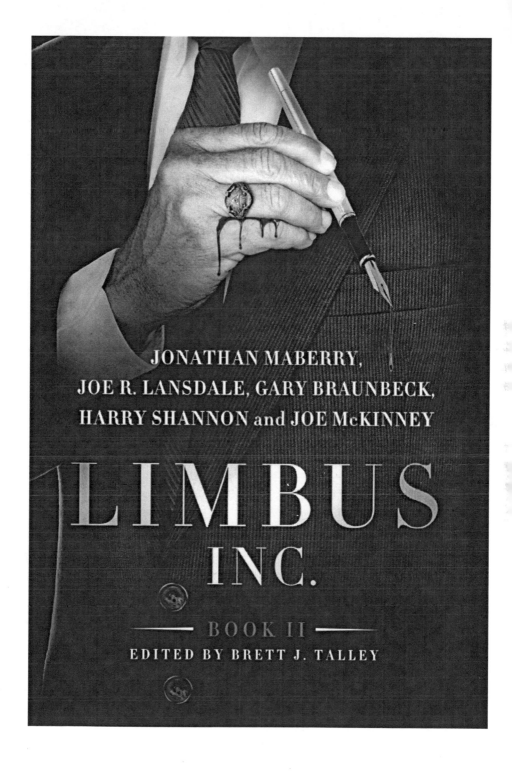

JONATHAN MABERRY,
JOE R. LANSDALE, GARY BRAUNBECK,
HARRY SHANNON and JOE McKINNEY

LIMBUS
INC.

—— BOOK II ——

EDITED BY BRETT J. TALLEY

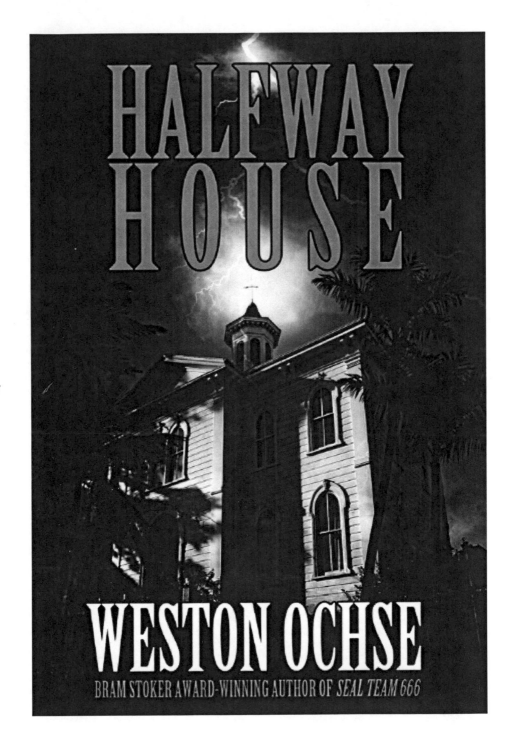

HALFWAY HOUSE

WESTON OCHSE

BRAM STOKER AWARD-WINNING AUTHOR OF *SEAL TEAM 666*

CPSIA information can be obtained at www.ICGtesting.com
Printed in the USA
BVOW05s2033140514

353333BV00001B/45/P